**He bega**

MW01226860

and, before she had a chance to protest, lifted her under her arms as if she'd been a rag doll and shifted her toward the narrow bunk bed in the corner.

By now she had lost any sense of modesty. Her teeth chattered, while her body ached and cried out for warmth. Kane stripped away her remaining clothing and, holding her close like a child, he maneuvered a soft flannel shirt over her arms and began to button the front.

"Aw, to hell with it," he muttered as he wrapped the material around her, tucking it under her arms, and deposited her in the bed, pulling up the quilt around her. She lay quivering, knees up to her chin, a ball of freezing cold. Every inch of her skin felt lacerated with the stones and icy pellets of hail that had pummeled her.

A moment later she felt the bed shift and suddenly his body was next to her, forcing her legs down, pulling her close to be enveloped in his arms. For a brief moment she protested and then gave up when the blessed relief of warmth crept through her skin and into her bloodstream.

He held her for a long time. The steady beat of his heart next to her cheek lulled her so that she dozed, woke up and dozed again.

### Reviews for *Señora of the Superstitions*

"A lost gold mine, dishonest relatives, and a man with a closed heart all present challenges to a young woman determined to solve the mystery of her father's disappearance. Only Señora, the resident ghost, seems willing to help. Fans of Paranya who have come to expect believable characters, exotic locations, and surprise endings from her will find their expectations met in SEÑORA OF THE SUPERSTITIONS. She's created a story filled with suspense, adventure and, ultimately, romance."

*~Cassandra Barnes, author of Jenny's Legacy, and of Acts of Love*

"What a story! A repressed young woman visits a ranch in the forbidding, mysterious Superstition Mountains in answer to her father's letter, only to be told he is dead. In spite of ghosts, poisonous creatures, a predatory mountain lion, and a dark, brooding man, she discovers the courage to face it all and possibly find the love of her life in the bargain. Good job, Paranya!"

*~Ramona Forrest, author of romance, suspense and westerns*

### Other titles by Pinkie Paranya

Pinkie's Early American historical, *Raven Woman*, won Silver in *ForeWord Magazine*'s Book of the Year Award (which had over 950 entries).

Her most recent releases with The Wild Rose Press include SECRETS OF SEBASTIAN BEAUMONT, TASMANIAN RAINBOW, and THE SAGA OF SOURDOUGH RED.

*to Gene*

# Señora
# of the
# Superstitions

*enjoy the mystery*

by

# Pinkie Paranya

*Pinkie Paranya*

**Señora of the Superstitions**

COPYRIGHT © 2009 by Pinkie Paranya

Cover Art by *Nicola Martinez*

The Wild Rose Press
PO Box 706
Adams Basin, NY 14410-0706
Visit us at www.thewildrosepress.com

Publishing History
First Vintage Rose Edition, 2010
Print ISBN 1-60154-608-4

Published in the United States of America

## Dedication

To my classmates of Glendale Union High School,
when I was known as Florence "Pinkie" Peterson.

Also to Teddy Landrum,
an old flame and my first book hero,
as well as Oneta Oxford, whom I've admired
for so many years and lost track of.

I especially want to mention Ramona Forrest,
a superb writer and dear friend for such a long time.

Chapter 1

The house crouched, brooding and silent, like a giant beast of stone and mortar. Waiting for her—expecting her to come.

"Aren't you at least going to the door with me?" Jowanna McFarland turned to the strange old man who had brought her out to the desert and now hurried back toward his truck.

"No, ma'am. Got to get back." His large Adam's apple bobbed in his skinny neck, a sheen of sweat beading his weathered face.

*Where is my father? Why didn't he meet me?*

Panic rising at her uneasy thoughts, she picked up one of her suitcases and reached for the other. It was hard to believe she stood at the foot of the Superstition Mountains in Arizona. She sensed that nothing much had changed in this desert land from its beginning to this year of 1948.

The letter clutched in her hand was hard to read through the tears she fought back, but she'd memorized it. The long white envelope was addressed to Jason McFarland, her brother, dead for the past ten years. The signature was that of her father, who had abandoned his family eighteen years ago. It wasn't only the bare words that had dragged her out of her comfortable urban niche and brought her to this strange destination.

And it wasn't only to confront him with the pain his leaving had caused the family, nor was it the mention in his letter of a gold mine he'd been searching for and finally found. What drew her was the raw urgency behind the words he had written. He was in trouble and needed Jason—or someone—to help him.

"Can't you at least wait until I find out if anyone's here? I might want to go back with you." She hated the sound of pleading in her voice. She'd never had to beg for anything in her life.

"Uh-uh," the old man muttered, the quavering voice coming from somewhere inside his beard. "They don't cotton to company here. Besides, there's the Señora. I ain't a-gonna get tangled up with a ghost."

*"A what?"* She fought to keep the edge of hysteria from her voice. That crazy old coot—Charlie, he said his name was. He'd so many bad things to say about the Superstitions, why would anyone stay here? Rattlesnakes, scorpions, spiders as big as a man's hand, flash floods and caves filled with poison gas, puma lairs, dropoffs into bottomless mine shafts and—as if that wasn't enough—here he was babbling about a ghost. She looked off into the distance at the towering mountain that looked sinister and menacing even from far away. She would have felt that way even if Charlie hadn't gone on about its dangers.

"The Señora of the Superstitions. Everyone knows about her. I ain't saying no more about it."

Hoping she wasn't as neurotic as her mother, Jowanna admitted to having fears of everything outside her realm of existence, and old Charlie had named most of them in the short ride from town.

But he hadn't mentioned a resident ghost before. What else wasn't he telling her?

Maybe she should have told him whom she had come out to see, but her father's letter had warned Jason not to trust anyone.

Disembarking from the train in Phoenix, she had felt a sudden thrill as she stepped off the platform not into a bank of dirty New York City snow but into the brilliant warm desert sunlight. At the ticket office they told her which bus to catch to Albandigos, the jumping floor; their intricate weaves and patterns came through even though muted by layers of dust. The ceiling was high and vaulted, with massive beams of dark wood. Books filled many shelves, and some lay haphazardly on a coffee table made of petrified wood.

It was a comfortable home, except for the air of neglect and the spooky atmosphere of shadows and silence.

The pervading desert dust clogged her nostrils, and she sneezed. She was about to turn away, but as she held the lantern high for one last glance, the blood froze in her veins at what she saw.

Footprints on the dusty floor, leading to the steps and upstairs.

Her fingers trembled on the lamp and she clutched it tighter, knuckles white. Every inch of her body sensed danger as the skin at the nape of her neck crinkled and goosebumps raised the hair on her arms.

She fought the urge to run away. Where would she go? It was dark outside by now. Somewhere in the distance a coyote howled a mournful cry in answer to the sudden darkness. Another echoed the sound. She put a foot on the bottom stair and thought of walking up that long, dark passageway, each corner holding an unknown menace.

"Hello?" She made her voice carry up the stairs even though she shouted through dry, cracked lips. If she didn't continue her search, she would never be able to stay in this house until her father came.

She began to realize what a pampered, sheltered life she had led. For the first time in her twenty-eight years she was completely alone, on her own. No demanding, meticulous mother to supervise her actions. No excuses to fall back on if she failed. Well, since her mother often accused her of willful stubbornness, she'd use that to combat her paralyzing fears.

Staring at the offending footprints only caused her

fertile imagination to magnify the threat, but she couldn't skitter away like a frightened mouse. Hadn't she called out twice with no answer? There wasn't anyone here—unless you wanted to count the ghostly Señora of the Superstitions.

Jowanna fought the panic; her heart fluttered in her throat.

She started up the stairs with grim determination. Shadows danced on the ceilings and the walls from the lamp held in her trembling hands. On the second landing a loose board under her feet screeched. The sudden noise in the silent house caused her to tilt backward in fright. She grabbed hold of the railing, steadying her wobbly legs, her fingers clutched around the lamp until they ached.

"Coward!" she admonished herself out loud, needing to hear a voice. "There's no such things as ghosts." The footprints weren't made by a ghost, a thought that offered little comfort. They were oddly shaped—made by someone wearing boots? That would seem natural out here, she conceded.

At the top of one landing was a small dormer window at right angles to the continuing stairs. She shoved and pulled, but thick paint at the base had locked it in place.

Brushing aside some of the dust on the panes, she saw where the roof extended out and then sloped downward until the ground appeared, as close as fifteen or twenty feet away. A large cage nestled in a corner near a gable. For pigeons, she guessed.

She continued up the stairs, thankful the narrow passageway offered no opportunity for dark corners.

The first door down the long hall pushed open easily.

Wasn't anything locked around here? It didn't seem normal. Back home in New York you locked your apartment door if you went down to check with the doorman for mail.

The room contained an old-fashioned brass bed with a blanket thrown over the mattress. On the floor against the wall, a fancy silver-inlaid saddle lay on its side, looking out of place. A few items of masculine clothing lay across a chair. Nothing in here was dusty. Someone had been here, and not too long ago.

Back in the hallway, she closed that door behind her and moved on to the next room, where clothes hung neatly in the closet, and the bed had been made with precise, tight corners. Only the large easel and spatters of dried oil paint on a sheet beneath marred the neatness. This room, too, was nearly dust-free.

A hard object under the bed almost tripped her when her foot kicked into it. Kneeling down, she pulled out a large portrait in oils. The woman pictured was breathtakingly lovely, with wide blue eyes, long blonde hair and delicate features. Something in the way it was painted bespoke a loving care, even if it was unsigned. Who had painted it, and why was it hidden beneath the bed?

She shoved it back under and turned away, suddenly feeling like an intruder.

With that door shut behind her, the lamplight flickered against the walls on the stair landing, and she licked her dry lips and checked the level of its oil. How long would it last? She didn't want to be caught up here in the dark. Pushing open the third door, she walked to the dresser and almost dropped the lamp.

Her own face stared back at her with gray eyes big and solemn, hair in long black braids. Jason stood next to her, tall and straight, with her father in the middle.

She felt the familiar pain of loss. It had become mixed with anger but had never quite left her. First their father had gone without a word and then—such a waste—the tragedy of Jason drowning in a boating accident.

So many years ago, now, that a stranger passing by had taken the photo of the three of them at a birthday party in the park. The last party while her father was there with them.

Trembling, she held the lamp with both hands. The room was dusty, as if no one had been here in a while. It had to be her father's room. She touched the clothes draped across the bed and picked up a shirt, holding it to her cheek, trying to inhale some essence of him, but the dust choked her.

She felt so alone. Yet the impression of someone being close by was so strong she looked around, raising the lamp above her head to search out the corners.

Was her father near? They'd always had a close understanding of each other, before he left, the one action of his that she could not comprehend. Couldn't he have come back to see them during the long years? Why hadn't he told them goodbye? She needed to confront him with her sorrow for Jason's death, her pain at being left alone over the long years without either of them as a buffer against her rigid, tyrannical mother and grandfather.

Why had he sent for Jason now, after all these years? Why had his letter sounded so urgent, so desperate, as if he had no other choice? He was in trouble, some kind of danger threatened him, or he never would have contacted them.

Unable to bear her thoughts any longer, she stepped out of the room and, as the door closed behind her, Jowanna felt the tiny hairs on the back of her neck rising. The end of the hall was shrouded in shadows, but something called her to go to it.

She stared up at the narrowed, twisting stairway, the ceiling low. In two-storied houses, especially the older ones, there was usually an additional attic space. This must be the gables she'd seen from outside. In an effort to stop the shaking, she clamped her left hand over the right as the light shone down on more footprints on the dusty hardwood landing, footprints that pointed upward.

What should she do? Go downstairs and cower in fear all night, waiting for her father? She couldn't go without sleep forever. She had come here for answers; how else to get them than to seek them out?

Coming out here alone, looking for a father she believed didn't love her—it was all so out of character for her, and well she knew it, but her behavior had started events which had become like a ball of snow rolling down the hill. She couldn't stop herself any more than she could stop whatever happened to her.

She started up the small set of stairs. As they became steeper and narrower, she leaned, holding the lamp down low, and perceived the footprints in front of her were sideways now, the steps were so narrow. The prints ceased abruptly at the end of the stairway in front of a closed door to the attic. Jowanna reached out to turn the knob.

It didn't budge. How odd. The only locked door in the entire house.

Pushing her cheek against the paneled wood, she heard nothing. When she started to turn away, a faint trace of perfume sifted from underneath the doorway.

Her hand wobbled, and she clutched the lamp tighter, fearing to drop it. Did the perfume and the eerie feeling of not being alone come from the Señora?

Did ghosts wear perfume?

With the light scent teasing her nostrils, she turned and ran down the stairs as fast as she could, feeling eyes boring into her back with every step.

Back in the living room, Jowanna brushed off a leather recliner and sat gingerly on the edge, trying to decide what to do. She didn't see many choices. There was no way to leave this place. Her father had asked for her, or for Jason, anyway, so he would surely be close by and would turn up sooner or later. She looked up at the shadowy staircase and shivered, deciding at that moment to sleep in the barn with the horse that had whinnied when she first arrived.

At least an animal was alive and non-threatening. She hated herself for fearing a ghost that a crazy old man had rambled on about, but the perfume smell still lingered, and she knew that wasn't her imagination.

Clutching the kerosene lamp and a blanket from one of the couches, she pushed open the front door and hurried out to the barn. The sky was full of stars, and the moon shone down, casting an eerie, silvery light over all the cactus and trees nearby, turning them into stealthy, twisted characters that seemed to move along with every step she took.

She set down the blanket and lamp and faced the big double doors. When she tugged on them, they didn't budge. Were the doors locked from inside? She looked back toward the house. Oh, no, she wasn't going to retreat, now that she'd gone this far to get out of that scary place. She jerked hard on the side with a handle. It flew open, knocking her down to the packed earth, jarring the wind out of her.

Once inside with the big double doors pushed shut behind, a wash of relief flooded over her, leaving her weak with a cold sweat. She straightened her shoulders and some of the tiredness left as realization of what she had done came to her.

Jowanna McFarland had marched up the terrifying dark stairs alone and faced down a handful of her most debilitating fears. Then she had gone outside in the midst of coyotes howling and tortured silhouettes dotting the landscape. And nothing had happened to her. Yet.

She looked at the two horses, munching hay from an automatic hay feeder above their heads. Slowly she walked toward them, but the bigger horse shied away, snorting, eyes rolling. A white ring encircled each of his eyes; the top of his nostrils were colored the same off-white as his back. Multi-sized spots, some dark, some light, spread like a graceful blanket of white over his back and rump. The rest of his coat was pale red.

When he limped away, she saw a cloth wrapped loosely around his leg.

The little black horse put her head over the low stall, seeming to summon her touch. One phobia Jowanna didn't own was toward horses. She remembered some good times riding in Central Park with Jason and her father. She leaned against the horse's neck, grateful for contact with another living being.

Finding a pile of straw and a horse blanket to lie on, she hesitated only briefly before blowing out the lamp. Her first instinct was to leave it burning, before she thought of it accidentally tipping over and starting a fire in the dry hay on the stable floor.

Darkness pulled in around her, but listening to the horses chewing and snorting made her feel comforted, no longer alone.

Coyotes yipped and howled in the distance. An odd whooshing noise, possibly a large owl, swooped close to the barn, followed by the shrill scream of its prey. Certain she would not be able to close her eyes one minute, she nestled down into her straw bed and slept without waking through the night.

Once, during the early morning hours, she dreamed of a figure standing in the open door of the barn, the moonlight silhouetting a large outline of someone watching her sleep. It hadn't scared her enough to wake her up.

In the morning, the contented chewing of the horses finally woke her. The stable door yawned wide, and the bright sunlight poured in. How did the horses get oats? The bins had been empty the night before. And she distinctly remembered closing that door before she blew out the lamp.

Standing to brush down her blouse and skirt, Jowanna tried to pull out some of the straw entangled in her hair.

Perhaps her father had returned.

When she started for the house, the daylight assured her there was a sensible explanation for footprints in an empty house, for a locked storeroom door. The pervasive odor of perfume at the top of the stairs could also be explained easily enough. Everything seemed logical in the bright sunlight.

Cool, damp air engulfed her when she opened the front door. Outside, the heat built in visible waves in the air.

She stepped past the entryway into the front room, but the house seemed to offer no sense of threat in the daylight. Moving closer to the stairs, she bent close to examine the footprints of the night before. The dust on the stairs was scuffed and scattered as if someone had walked over the top of the first set of prints. How odd. She'd tried to avoid stepping directly on the footprints, for some reason, when she walked up the stairs.

The smell of bacon assailed her. Her father had come in! Would she recognize him after all these years? Would he be disappointed she wasn't Jason?

Jowanna swallowed hard before entering the kitchen, preparing for the first angry words she wanted to get out of the way.

The ruggedly good-looking man, long legs encased in tight jeans as he stood there and stirred the contents of a cast iron skillet on the old woodstove, was definitely not her father. His stare was bold, and he assessed her frankly. She couldn't have missed his observation and the approval in his eyes.

Chapter 2

"Who are you?" Both of them spoke at once, and Jowanna laughed nervously. Except for a flicker of surprise, the big man didn't change expressions.

She sensed the electricity suddenly in the room but didn't back away from a confrontation as she normally would have. "I'm Jowanna McFarland. My father sent for me."

"The hell you say!" The man rocked back on the heels of his boots, the hard planes of his face a blend of surprise and annoyance while he continued to stare at her.

She glared back at him but refrained from expressing her indignation out loud at his blunt response. "I believe your bacon's burning." She smiled, striving for cool nonchalance.

"Damn!" He turned away, back to the stove, and swiped at the increasing smoke rising from the cast iron skillet.

Now that she'd had a chance to examine him while he wasn't looking, she thought that beyond his chilly greeting he was quite something to look at. His skin was weathered a warm, butternut brown from the sun, and his hair was the same color except for the sunstreaks running through the thickest part on top. He had the wide shoulders of a quarterback with the narrow hips and long, slightly bowed legs of a born horseman. She guessed he must be in his thirties.

"Finished?" He'd set down the frying pan and stood watching her, his head cocked to the side, an eyebrow lifted.

She felt her face redden. He'd caught her staring.

How absurd.

Before she could answer, he said, "I looked in on you sleeping in the stables last night. I didn't want to startle you, so I left without waking you. Since you seemed to make yourself at home, why not stay in the house?"

He pulled up a chair and motioned for her to sit. She didn't like his bossiness but decided it would be childish to protest. "I didn't stay here because I saw some boot prints going up the stairs. They could have belonged to my father, but I wasn't sure and—I admit, this house is spooky at night."

He sat down across from her and tilted back in the chair to regard her. His expression showed a touch of admiration, something she'd never been used to. But his eyes remained cool and untrusting, and the set of his jaw showed stubbornness.

"You're mistaken. No one could have made boot prints in the dust going upstairs. I would have noticed them. I didn't get here until after you left for the stables. The first thing when I get back is to check on the horses. Steven isn't good that way." His voice was firm, challenging her.

Of course she'd seen boot prints. She should just go point them out to him right now. Although maybe they wouldn't show up in daylight as much as under soft lamplight, so she let it pass.

"What's this about your father?" he asked. His voice gentled only a trifle. He continued to look at her with a steady, considering gaze that stirred her senses, made her uneasy.

"I said I was here because my father sent us a letter to come. Where is he?"

The stranger stood, arms crossed in front of his chest. His eyes were the color of coffee, with a shot of cream. It took her a moment to realize they were staring at each other as the tension between them built.

Briefly, the anger left his face, replaced by remorse. "Hard to believe, that Mac would send for his family without telling anyone."

"Aren't you going to tell me who you are? Do I have to try and guess?"

The grim look changed for an instant. The corners of his eyes crinkled with the lopsided grin that splashed across his face. His lips were long and sensuous, his teeth shockingly white against his tanned skin.

She had risen from the chair and stood holding to the back of it.

Again he motioned for her to sit, plainly accustomed to giving directions. She ignored the suggestion, preferring not to have him loom above her, which he did anyway.

"I'm Kane Landry. Your father's brother-in-law and partner."

"My father wrote of a stepson and a brother-in-law, although he never mentioned a partner." So much for the 'crusty old cowboy' notion. When Kane didn't offer to speak, she continued. "I don't understand this. My father left us eighteen years ago, never came back, and now I find out he's married?"

"Was married. My sister died from appendicitis eight years ago. She had a son, and Mac adopted him."

Jowanna felt as if her head was swimming off her shoulders with all this new information.

"Mac?"

Kane nodded. "Your father."

No one she knew had ever called him Mac.

"Where is he? Why isn't he here to meet me? I sent a telegram."

Kane shook his head, the sun streak of hair fell over his forehead in a long sweep. He raked it back with a large tanned hand. His air of self-assurance had diminished, replaced by an uncertainty that made her even more edgy.

"I didn't see any telegram. I haven't been to town in a while, and Steven's not back from Tucson yet. It could have gone to Albandigos, but they don't deliver out here."

"Something's wrong, isn't it?" She sensed a note of hesitancy in his deep voice. "Where's my father?"

He cleared his throat, his air of self-assurance suddenly gone. "I reckon I can't say this any more merciful. Your father's dead. I'm sorry to be so blunt." He looked away, as if sensing her need of privacy.

"Dead?" Her voice quivered in shocked disbelief. "But his letter...I...just received it." She stopped short. "No, I guess that's not true. My mother hid the letter, and I accidentally came across it in the desk drawer. Then it took me a while to decide to come out here, in place of my brother, and some time passed before I convinced my mother the West wasn't wild any longer and I was going to go no matter what."

"I don't know why he wrote to you. Most of all I don't understand why you came here. I don't like visitors."

She was still trying to assimilate the news of her father's death. To come all this way—to bridge the gap of eighteen years. To come so close to talking to him, touching him, asking the questions she needed answered. Only to find he was dead.

She looked up at Kane, her eyes filled with unshed tears.

"Ahh, I'm...I'm sorry to be the one to have to tell you about your father." He shifted his weight, looking very uncomfortable.

It was still too much to understand. First she had a father, then she didn't, then she did again, now she didn't. What monstrous force was toying with her life?

"You haven't explained why you're here," he said, his voice gentle but still hostile. "Your family never wrote to Mac over the years. He grieved for you and your brother." Kane's accusation interrupted her thoughts.

She stared at him, her mouth dropped open with astonishment. "*I* didn't write to my father? Of course I didn't write. I was only ten when he left. My mother told us he didn't want to be bothered with a family anymore. Why didn't he write to us?"

"You're saying you never received all those letters Mac wrote? Someone sure as hell did. None of the letters were returned, as far as I know."

"I never saw any letters."

"He showed me what he'd received once. Only a clipping from the paper saying your mother had divorced him. Years ago, before the war. No letter, no return address, just the clipping from the paper."

If Kane told the truth, then her mother had hidden or destroyed the letters as fast as her father had sent them—until they finally stopped coming.

Her years of pent-up anger were slowly disintegrating along with new vistas opening up regarding her mother and grandfather. She hoped her father had had a good life here. "How did my father die?"

Kane avoided the question. He pointed out the kitchen window that framed the mountain range like a giant portrait. "We met out there, in the Superstitions. We worked separate claims and decided to combine our efforts. It's not safe, moving around alone up there."

"Will you tell me what happened to my father?"

He stood up to pace the room, which suddenly seemed smaller because of his size filling it. "We're partners, but most times we go our own ways. We always met at least once a week at the cabin to check on each other. He didn't show up when he supposed to, so I went looking and found him...well, not exactly *him*, but remnants of his clothing, and his gunbelt and gun." Kane paused for a long moment, as if to gather his words together. He stopped behind the chair where she sat and touched her shoulder so briefly she wondered if his hand actually brushed her or if she imagined it.

"Go on."

"I found these things in an arroyo. Just below a ledge. He could have taken a bad fall off the ledge." He broke off uncertainly. "His pistol was cocked, with one bullet left. El Diablo must have gotten him. Only thing I don't understand is why he didn't use that last bullet on the puma."

The picture she was forming in her mind grew more ominous by the moment. "Puma?"

"The mountain lion we call El Diablo. He's been hanging around here since before I bought the place." He banged his fist on the table. "We've been after that sorry devil for years. Mac shot the female a few years ago. That stopped him for a while, and we thought he'd gone away, but he's back at us again—even meaner. Almost like he's carrying on a vendetta. Mac must have shot him...before.... We found blood and tracked it part way up to the caves. Mac knew it would come back for him. He might have saved the remaining shot for himself but never got to use it."

"Oh, my Lord! Do you mean my father lay out there alone and alive? Waiting to be devoured by some dreadful animal, and he would have shot himself, instead?" She heard her voice rising with beginning hysteria but could do nothing to stop it.

"Hold on, don't get hysterical on me." Kane walked back to her side, moving with swift grace for a man of his size. He reached out to touch her arm, his hand hard and his grip tight. She felt a zing of something strange run through her body, and she tried to still the trembling. He must have felt it, because he let his hand drop to his side.

"I'm okay." She was glad to be sitting down.

"It's bound to be a shock. I don't know any easier

way to tell you." He poured her out a cup of coffee and pushed it slowly toward her from across the table. "Mac was a good man. Wish you and he could have connected. You were so close to seeing him again after all these years."

She shook her head. "It's so awful. I don't know what to say." Nothing in her experience had ever prepared her for what she had just heard.

"Best thing you can do is rest up, and I'll take you back to Albandigos for the bus. You can catch a train from Phoenix."

"No. I'm not leaving yet." Jowanna didn't feel as bereft as she might have, since she had mourned her father when he first disappeared from her life so many years ago. Now there was only an empty feeling inside, coupled with the strange sensation that Kane wasn't telling her everything. Something was wrong here. What was going on?

"Did you say no?" Kane's brows crashed together in a glare that might have had her scurrying for cover, had she been thinking straight. "I don't like strangers poking around the place. That's why I live out here. To be alone. Had more than enough of togetherness for those few years with the Army, during the war."

"My father wanted me—wanted someone here to talk to. He wanted it enough to try once more to break the long years of silence." She took a sip of the coffee and felt it go down, warming all the way.

Kane groaned and sank down in a chair, stretching out his Levi-clad legs, an expression of stunned disbelief spread across his rugged features. "Do you have the letter with you? I'd like to know what he said, exactly."

Why the sudden hint of caution edging his voice? She decided not to show him the letter. It contained too many things that needed explaining.

"It was a request, a demand, that Jason come here to his ranch immediately," she hedged.

"*His* ranch? That's unbelievable." He struck the table with the side of his hand. "The Superstition Ranch never belonged to Mac. It's mine. He held a mortgage on it, I'll grant you that. It was me who insisted we get papers signed, all legal-like."

"Why?"

"I had to go to Boston to search out a claim, and I needed some money. But the claim didn't pan out. We haven't dug enough out of that mine to make expenses."

That wasn't the way the letter read. "Then whose name is on the title to the ranch?" She stood to look out the window.

He came up close behind her. She felt the warmth of his breath on the top of her hair, felt the heat emanating from his body behind her.

"His and mine, but that's not important. He didn't want this ranch."

"Well, he wanted me, or someone, here."

"You'd best be getting back to New York, before you get in some kind of trouble. I reckon Old Charlie filled you in on all the godawful things that could happen, especially to a city lady."

Was that a threat?

"My father mentioned someone called Delia. She disappeared, or maybe died. That seemed to worry him."

Kane was sitting again, straddling the chair backward. He looked at her, his face closed. She couldn't read his eyes.

"Leave it alone. Delia's got nothing to do with what we're talking about."

"I want to know who Delia is, and why my father would be upset about her."

"She was my wife," Kane said shortly. "She took off, and good riddance. I'm not talking about it."

He looked away again, but not before she caught the haunted look in his eyes.

She shivered and rubbed her arms to get rid of the goosebumps. "Is my father buried on the ranch property? Surely they must have brought his remains back from the mountains."

"Mac wanted...he wanted something else done with his remains when he died."

"But..."

Kane waved his hand in a gesture that stilled her next question. "Not now. I'll get to that. You shouldn't stay here."

"I can't leave yet."

"Won't your family worry about you?" His calm voice, the low timbre of it, was at odds with what she thought might be a calculating look in his eyes. He stood and walked past her to the stove.

Jowanna watched his wide-shouldered, rangy body move with easy grace from the stove to the table and back to stand close to her again. How strong would a person have to be to shove an older man off a ledge or hit him with a prospector's shovel? She tried to push away the unwelcome speculation.

Kane reached out a hand, and she had all she could do not to sidestep away. He gently pulled some hay from her hair.

"Don't flinch from me; I won't hurt you."

"No, I don't suppose you would."

"Your hair's like Mirla's."

"Mirla?"

"The little mare. 'Mirla' means 'blackbird' in Spanish."

"That's pretty."

He touched her shoulder, lightly, just to turn her around to face him, looking down at her with a curious mixture of arrogance and admiration. The sharp planes of his cheekbones contrasted with the thick dark lashes fringing his eyes. He bent his head down and she felt drawn to him but fought against it. He was trying to scare her into leaving by his attention, probably guessing that she was not comfortable with a man in close range.

She stepped away to distance herself from the current of emotion between them. His head jerked up, and he moved back to the stove to pour coffee in the thick ceramic cups.

He motioned toward the chair. "Your family—won't they come to find you if you don't leave now?"

Why was the answer to that question so important that he had to ask it twice?

After she spoke the truth she wondered if that was a mistake. "No. My grandfather's dead. There's only my mother and Bernice, who takes care of her. They've never left the city in their lives. I told them I'd write to them when I arrived."

"City people don't get along in the desert, as a rule. Delia hated it."

"Then why was she here?"

"Long story."

"I told my mother I'd be gone at least a month." Should she have kept that information to herself? Maybe it was foolhardy to let this man know she wasn't expected home for some time.

Not expecting her back for a month could give someone a lot of leeway. Kane still hadn't explained his missing wife. If she'd only gone as far as Phoenix to take out an annulment, she could be anywhere or nowhere. What if she'd returned to lay claim to the mine and then disappeared? Like her father. Delia's disappearance had made her father very uneasy, if Jowanna had interpreted the letter right.

Kane poured the coffee, and the strong fragrance enveloped the room. His eyes, unguarded for a moment, looked troubled beyond what they had been talking about.

She decided to move away from the subject of her father for a while, since she wasn't getting the necessary answers.

"I like your house, although it's kind of spooky. Especially at night. Who would expect anything like this out in the desert?"

He grinned. "It needs work. Someday when—someday I'm going to put in a generator, underground so it won't disturb the silence. That would give us lights and hot water."

"On the bus coming out from Phoenix there didn't seem to be many people in houses scattered about the desert. I expected more of a population."

"The only ones who settle out this way are those who like to be left alone. The fellow who built this place—he was rich but eccentric. Didn't want neighbors—or company." His voice was firm, as if he held his annoyance in check. His dark brown eyes reflected implacable determination.

She swallowed hard, lifted her chin, and boldly met his gaze. "I'm not leaving until I get some answers and see my father's grave. I'll sleep in the barn, if it's no trouble to you. And furthermore, I'm not afraid of your damn ghost."

His brows drew together in an angry frown. "Where'd you hear that crazy rumor?"

No wonder poor Delia wanted to get away. He was impossible. "Charlie said you had a ghost. A ghost who lives at Superstition Ranch."

A muscle quivered in his jaw. "That rumor's cost me plenty. It's all silly nonsense."

"If you don't want strangers out here, it could work to your advantage to scare people off with the ghost story."

He looked at her enigmatically, his dark eyes saying nothing. She could see where worry had begun to trace lines into the tautness of his face.

"Not everyone would give the superstitious notion of a resident ghost any credence," he reminded her.

"Maybe not. But most ranch hands are normally

unsophisticated, wouldn't you say? They'd be apt to believe the story, or at least prefer not to get involved."

"It may work that way. I can't get any help on the ranch. No one wants to live out here, and it's a long drive from town each day."

"That old man seemed to take the legend seriously."

"He runs off at the mouth a lot, but that's the yarn they like to tell in town. When I bought the place, it had been empty for God knows how long. No one would have anything to do with it because of that crazy ghost story."

"Charlie called her the Señora of the Superstitions, but he wouldn't go into details."

"That's the old coot's way of setting you up. He delights in scaring folks. I've got him to thank for people leaving us alone, I reckon."

"Do you believe in the legend?"

He shrugged. "No. But Steven, my nephew, does. I'm not big on phantoms. Since he was a kid, Steven claims to have seen her. A week or so ago he came up with this crazy idea of painting her."

"I'd lock my front door, if I were you. I pushed it open last night and walked right in," Jowanna said.

He scratched the edge of his booted toe on the tile as if wishing it had been desert sand. "You can't lock a door on a ghost, can you? Anyways, it's custom out on the desert to never lock a door. *She* always left the door open for her husband, or so the legend goes."

Did that mean he believed in the ghost and didn't want to admit it? Jowanna wasn't sure. She swallowed hard around a dry throat, not liking the thought of a resident ghost. The old house looked as if it could hold a flock of them.

His dark brows winged downward as he looked at her. "I forbid Steven to talk about her." Kane's voice held a note of finality that said the subject was closed and he didn't want to hear about it again.

She wanted to keep him talking. At first she'd taken him for a man of few words, a taciturn cowboy type, but the more they talked the more he seemed, if not happy about it, relieved to talk to someone. She sensed he had a hard time expressing his feelings.

He made her think of a passage in a book she'd just read. *A strong, quiet man is like a shade-giving tree in a thirsty land.* It seemed to fit Kane.

He dished up his eggs from where they were keeping warm on the back of the stove and sat down again, pouring a thick, tomatoey-looking substance from a jar onto his eggs. When he saw her questioning look, he lost some of his earlier antagonism.

"Salsa." He explained. "If you try some, go easy. An Arizonan uses it on everything, including ice cream."

She laughed. "No, thanks. I'm not a breakfast eater, but I'll go for a piece of bread and jelly."

He snorted. "It figures."

She let that pass. "Hmm. Good bread. Who makes homemade bread anymore?"

He looked embarrassed. "It's sourdough. My sis taught me how. It's a helluva good therapy when something goes wrong."

She thought of those powerful hands patiently kneading dough and somehow the image was comforting.

When he finished, he tilted back in his chair at an alarming angle and regarded her through lashes touched with gold on the tips. Like his hair.

"I'd take you back to Albandigos this morning, but I usually wait for Steven. Sort of like to know he made the trip okay. We can go as soon as he gets back."

Tears filled her eyes, and she leaned forward, letting her hair fall forward to hide them, but not before he saw.

He reached across the table to touch her shoulder, clumsily, smoothing back the long dark hair from her

27

cheek with surprisingly gentle hands. His expression seemed to reflect her pain, as if to help absorb some of it for her.

Jowanna straightened her shoulders and looked into his eyes. "How many times must I say I'm not going anywhere yet?"

His look of compassion disappeared and for a long moment the silence deepened between them.

"I suppose you could use your father's room. Got to warn you, nothing's much changed in his room since...well, since...."

She decided it was time to change the subject, lighten up. "How did you get here? I didn't hear a vehicle."

"Steven and I both have pickups. We park outside the gate sometimes. You might have noticed we don't have a driveway. Gives us time to see visitors approaching."

Why didn't they want visitors? So many questions still unanswered.

"There's something else I'd like to know." She didn't know where her sudden bravery came from, looking at him waiting, a dark eyebrow raised.

"It's about Delia. Don't you have any idea where your wife went?"

"Why? Did Mac say something in his letter about her?" His face suddenly went grim—closed tight against her.

"Only a line or two. He mentioned she left—abruptly."

"I don't know where she went, and don't give a damn. It didn't take me long to figure out she hated it here. She married me to hold on to her grandfather's mine. The one I went to Boston to check out. That's where I met her."

That was hard to follow.

Who in their right mind would marry a stranger and come all this way to share in a mine?

the time I hauled him home over that bumpy road, he was really ticked. Soon's I stuck him in these stables, the rascal started kicking and stomping and turned everything within reach to kindling. Believe me, it was a shambles and the name fit."

"Will his leg be okay?"

"Yeah, just a tendon pull. He'll be good as new in a few days. But to make sure, I'll have to leave him behind when I go tomorrow. He hates that. I can use the burros."

"Are these two all your horses?"

"We have a remuda of mustangs with our brand on them running around out there in the foothills. I bring one in when I need an extra. Mirla came from that bunch."

"Steven's horse?"

Kane laughed. "Hardly. Steven will ride if he has to, but he doesn't like horses much."

She figured Mirla had belonged to Delia, his missing wife. Why did he need to be so secretive about it?

"Aren't you afraid Mirla and your horse will mate? Ruin your idea of a pure strain?"

"Damn right. I keep a close watch."

"But they'd be good together. I'll bet the foal would be beautiful."

"That's plain dumb. You don't mix a registered horse with a mustang, no matter how..." He threw up his hands. "It never works."

Kane had broken off speaking and turned away, but she caught the pain in his eyes. He'd been talking about more than horses. Perhaps it was about his and Delia's relationship. Did he consider himself a mustang and her a thoroughbred?

"You ride?" he asked.

She nodded. "Some. My mother sent me to a girl's school in upstate New York. I forged the permission slip for lessons and then rode for the four years I was there. My father used to take us out to Central Park to ride." Riding horses was the last thing she remembered about him.

That was the hardest to bear, this love-hate feeling she'd held toward her father for so long.

"Don't ever try to touch Shambles. He doesn't even let Steven come near."

She flipped her hair back from her shoulder in a gesture of annoyance. Nothing worse than a smug know-it-all. "I assure you, I'm not afraid. Once at school the girls taunted me to ride this horse that no one else would. He brushed me off twice against the fence and threw me out of the saddle a couple more times, but I rode him."

Those thoughts brought back very unhappy memories. Memories of long, lonely days and nights away from home, which made her miss even the cool comfort of her mother and their endless arguments. Because she was shy and reserved, the girls called her Miss Priss.

Until she rode the horse. It was the only completely fearless thing she had ever done in her life, except for coming out here to find her father.

Kane ignored her bravado as if she hadn't spoken.

"Gotta have a horse on the desert. That road out there isn't open to traffic. We used to ride horses into Albandigos, but now Steven's got his vehicle and I keep the old truck."

"Charlie made it out here," she reminded him.

"I'm surprised. That old keg of nuts and bolts he drives isn't long for this earth, but it'll probably outlast him."

"We did sort of bounce around," she agreed. "Most times I was more vertical than horizontal, for sure."

He laughed, a deep, pleasant sound.

"You must have made a good impression, for him to bring you out. He's really hooked on avoiding this place."

34

It was a spare compliment, but it warmed her.

"If you're determined to stay a few days, you shouldn't stay alone here without some way out. I'll leave the keys to the truck when I go."

Great. She didn't drive, but she didn't want to tell him that. What use was a car in Manhattan? No one in her family except for the Senator had ever owned a car

"Apache Joe might scare you. He's sort of a self-appointed shaman/medicine man, a little loony, if you ask me. Comes wandering through occasionally and helps himself to supplies. Never takes much and most times brings replacements. We've missed some tinned food and figure it's him."

"I'm not afraid to stay alone," she said, knowing she spoke with more defiance than courage.

He looked at her, his mouth easing to a slow grin. His teeth looked white and square and strong against the tan of his face, and his grin said he knew she lied.

As far as a wandering Indian, he was surely making that up. It probably didn't even take a ghost story to discourage strangers. Not many people would be anxious to come down that long, dusty, bumpy trail.

Jowanna was still thinking about the noises upstairs. Just as she started to mention it, she changed her mind, not wanting to chance ridicule. He hadn't much patience with talk about the ghost. Had the sounds been her imagination? She didn't want him mocking her tenderfoot status any more than he had already.

"Did you bring anything with you besides those duds you're wearing?" Kane's voice penetrated her thoughts.

"Of course," she said in her primmest manner.

"You're the whitest little person I've ever laid eyes on. Not even a freckle to your name. Don't you get outside?"

Five feet four inches was not exactly little. Not when both Bernice and her mother were even shorter.

She stood tall, straightening her backbone. Maybe to someone like him, way over six feet, she might seem short, she conceded.

"No. Hardly ever get outdoors. I'm actually a vampire and this is the first time I've been out in daylight in centuries. Watch your neck when you fall asleep at night."

His mouth twitched at the corners, but he didn't seem put off by her heavy-handed sarcasm.

"Well, Miss Vampire, you should be right at home with the Señora, then."

The ghost again, and this time he mentioned it himself. Did he think she was a child, so easily frightened?

"Anything in your suitcases resembling a pair of Levis, or a long-sleeved shirt to hide those lily-white arms from the sun and the brush? You should stay indoors. Without boots you'd barely keep one jump ahead of the rattlers."

He *was* trying to scare her. Wasn't he? She drew in a deep breath for calm, which had always helped in dealing with her mother. Before she had time to bristle a retort, Kane spoke again.

"Steven's only about four or five inches taller than you, and he's skinny. You can borrow something from his closet until you leave. He won't mind."

The big oaf. Who did he think he was bossing around?

"Wouldn't it be easier to borrow something from Delia's closet?" She fished, wanting to find out if Kane's wife took her clothing when she left. That would be a clue to whether there had been foul play or not.

Kane's gaze raked her from top to bottom and settled on the top of her head.

"She was—is—a lot taller than you, and more—" He put his hands up to his chest and made a round gesture, grinning mischievously.

Jowanna blushed. *Touché.* He'd paid her back for asking too many questions.

"Delia's things are up in the storeroom, locked away."

At least knowing that her clothes were in the storeroom cleared up part of the mystery of the locked door, yet it left something unanswered. Because Delia's possessions were reputed to be inside, that didn't seem a valid reason for it to be the only locked door in the house.

"I don't like to leave you, but Steven will be here by the time I head up the mountain tomorrow, early. I can't wait for him any longer. You'll be okay if you stay put. Just don't poke around too much."

"I seldom 'poke around' as you put it. But is there some reason I shouldn't?" She ignored his frown. "I'm not worried about your resident ghost."

"Hell, the old house creaks and groans on its own. I'm not talking about the ghost, which is pure nonsense. I'm talking about cholla cactus and rattlesnakes and other things the desert can toss at you if you aren't aware."

No way was she going for his bait, tempting as it was just now. She had come here to see her father and, damn it, his grave would have to do, and she wasn't leaving without saying goodbye.

"I'm not afraid of noises," she lied. "I'm curious, though. Is it so important to find this gold or whatever it is you search for? Why did my father need to find it so badly?"

He studied her, as if to try and get behind her surface to what she really thought.

She looked away, not wanting to let him in.

"At first, I reckon Mac searched because he liked the quest. It was like a complicated puzzle to him, a puzzle he had to solve. Maybe it kept away some of his memories. Then when we—ah—when we came close to finding something once, he developed a real objective.

37

He figured to take the money and go back to hire a bunch of lawyers to clear his name. Poor sod, he never got that far."

How terrible that her father didn't know his son and daughter never gave up thinking he'd return to them.

"And you?" She persisted, needing to change the subject that hurt like a sore barely scabbed over.

"At first I looked for gold because of the quest, too. I bought the ranch and property with some money I won riding the rodeo circuit one year. It didn't take much, since no one else wanted the place."

"You rode in rodeos?"

He nodded. "For a while, to get a grubstake. You ever been to one? The 200-watt grin he turned on her said he knew she hadn't.

This time she had him.

"Only at Madison Square Garden a few times." She tried not to gloat at his surprised look.

"That must have been something to see. Every cowboy dreams of going there."

"It was special," she agreed. At the time, sitting next to her mother and Bernice, the rodeo didn't seem to have much point, but it was quite a spectacle.

"How come you're not still in the rodeo?".

He laughed, a short bark of a laugh that turned in on himself. "Didn't take me long to see rodeo entertainers seldom retire gracefully from their work. Most of them wind up with broken backs, steel rods in their knees—broken noses and rearranged faces are the least of it. Hell, I got scars you wouldn't want to know about."

His nose had a slight bump in the middle, which gave a ruggedness to his even, clear-cut features that he probably hadn't been born with.

"I came out here to live fulltime when my sis and Steven needed someplace to go."

"Did you start mining then?" She flushed,

embarrassed by the question. Her mother would have been shocked at her lack of finesse, but she really wanted to know.

"A man can make a couple of dollars in prospecting if he's willing to work at it. I like being outdoors, making my own hours, being my own boss. There's no bigger thrill than to find your first nugget in the gold pan or see a wall of quartz mixed with that shiny yellow stuff."

"Have you ever seen that?"

His eyes looked shadowed for a moment, unreadable. "We don't ask questions out here. Not about a man's claim."

"Sorry. I didn't know."

"'Course you didn't. Now that Mac's gone, the prospecting doesn't look so inviting. I got used to having company up there. After I met Mac and he came here to live, we were kind of like a family, even after my sister died, until Delia..."

"You want to get out of mining now?"

"It's no longer a boyish adventure to pursue. I need to start my horse ranch. Steven wants to go back East—do some more studying."

Her thoughts moved back to the mine he shared with her father, but he had warned her to stay away from that subject. She was still suspect in his eyes, an interloper possibly out for what she could get. Delia's defection had probably cost him a lot in lost faith.

He didn't trust her any more than she trusted him.

"Come on back to the house. We'll find something for you to wear."

She followed behind his long strides. He didn't wait for her to catch up. Cretin. No man she had ever met would be so inconsiderate.

When he brought a handful of clothing from upstairs, she grabbed them up and went into the little storeroom off the kitchen where she had washed up

Pinkie Paranya

and brushed her teeth earlier. Angry at his bossy attitude, she threw on the clothes and stepped back out again, prepared for his laughter at her strange attire.

What she wasn't prepared for was the unmistakable look of approval in his eyes, which he quickly hid by turning away, toward the window.

She looked in the mirror on the bathroom door. *Hmm, not bad.* Her mother would have had a fit. Some New Yorkers affected jeans, cowboy hats and boots, but none of her acquaintances did.

The faded jeans were big on her, and she'd rolled up the hem several times. If Steven was small compared to Kane, he was apparently still bigger than her. The vivid plaid shirt reflected color to her face and, with the thick dark hair streaming over her shoulders, she liked the young woman grinning back at her.

"You look delicate—like you'd break in someone's hands, but I'd lay odds there's cactus thorns under that softness," Kane commented.

Jowanna thought about his words. No man had ever spoken to her like that before. Most of her would-be suitors were men she'd met through her mother's friends. They knew all about her circumstances and were impressed with either her background or the trappings that went with it.

They walked toward the front room.

"I could tidy up a bit, to pay for my room and board." She gestured toward the living area.

"Not necessary. Does the dust bother you?"

"It brings out my allergies."

"How'd I know you'd have allergies?"

His smug grin made her defensive.

"No big deal. It runs in our family."

"That's right. Mac could start sneezing and be in tears before he stopped. By the way, there's some wildflowers out by the stables. My sis always had a

40

bouquet of flowers over the mantel. They never bothered Mac, not much smell to them."

Did Delia have flowers? "Speaking of smells..."

She was going to tell him about the fragrance she'd smelled upstairs, but surely he would have noticed. Why tell him? It would just make her look nervous and skittish.

He reached to take her hands in his, turning the palms up. Both fit fully inside his one hand. When he rubbed his big thumb over her skin, it did strange things to her midsection.

She felt a warmth seep upward and jerked her hands away to stand back. If he was coming on to her, as some way of striking back at Delia or assuaging his wounded ego, she didn't need any part of it.

"Hmm. You wouldn't want to get calluses on those delicate little hands."

"I've certainly tidied up a room before."

He laughed, that low, throaty sound that brought a smile to her lips in spite of not wanting to. "I don't think so. You're not the wildflower type, you're a hothouse orchid—same as...."

"Go on, same as who?" She knew he was going to say Delia and waited to hear the words. It might open communication between them and provide her with some much-needed answers.

He turned away and she blurted out her thoughts. "Does it hurt to say her name?"

Why did she need to know that?

"Hurt?" He spun around to look down into her upturned face. She thought he wasn't going to answer for a long moment.

"No, it doesn't hurt—not anymore. When love's gone, it's gone. I'll never be a sucker like that again."

She recognized surprise in his voice and knew he had confronted his pain and conquered it—admitting it probably for the first time.

An unexpected exhilaration coursed through her

as she thought of what this surrendering must have cost him. But was he so hardened by the experience that he would never take another chance?

Why should she care?

She dared not allow her guard down, not for one second. Something didn't feel right. She caught a glimpse of the powerful energy within him, and it made her nervous. Jowanna was torn between wanting him gone so she could explore and wanting him to stay so the house wouldn't close in around her.

"Soon as Steven comes, he'll take you back into town. I expect you to go then." He stood up, his expression closed, as if regretting his brief openness.

She stood to face him, keeping a distance between them as she remembered the odd feeling when he held her hand briefly.

"I'll leave when I find out why my father wanted me here." And why he had to be buried a certain place. She wanted to see his grave, it was the only way she had of telling him goodbye.

Kane's frown was formidable. She held her ground.

"In the first place, he didn't want *you* here. In the second place, he's gone. What does it matter? You don't belong here. We don't want strangers."

"Why not? I'd think you'd welcome company with open arms, the quiet is—it's disheartening."

"It isn't. The quiet grows on you, energizes you, if you let it."

"But being all alone, that's pathetic."

"Not necessarily. Maybe it's your life that's pathetic."

"What do you mean?"

Kane took her hand again and held it up for inspection. "You're not wearing a wedding ring. Your only brother died. You spent your childhood at a rich girl's school, away from home. Your father abandoned you. Now you probably live with a very controlling

42

mother in some fancy place in New York, judging from the address Mac used and the way she kept those letters from you when you were young."

"My, my, a detective. How interesting. What else do you presume to know about me?" She jerked her hand away, uncomfortable with the warmth spreading through her midsection again from the feel of his strong, hard hands.

He shrugged. "You should know there are all degrees of loneliness. Most of it comes from inside."

His words hit too close to home when she thought of her barren life. She changed the subject abruptly.

"I want to hear more about my father. Was there an investigation? I have to see his grave." So many unanswered questions.

Kane made a noise deep his throat, a short harsh sound that grated against her taut nerves. "The sheriff was here, if that's what you mean. He gave us permission to bury Mac's clothing and what was left where he asked."

"You said you found that strange. To bury clothes?"

"Of course," he admitted. "Mac and I were friends, as well as partners. We trusted each other. I don't know why he left that note in his bureau drawer, insisting on the exact spot to be buried."

"I'd like to see the note."

"Sure. How about showing me the letter he sent you?"

She didn't want that. The suggestion of desperation, the urgency, came through the message loud and clear, along with the warning not to trust anyone. What if that turned out to be something this man shouldn't know? He claimed her father and he were friends, that they trusted each other. What about this inheritance he spoke of in his letter? Kane had denied its existence.

It didn't look as if this man wanted to share

anything with anyone.

That could prove very, very dangerous. With her father dead and the mine and ranch to himself, his dreams had a closer reality.

Kane's dark brows descended and his eyes flashed with a temper she could see he struggled to control. "Stay as long as you like. But don't expect us to babysit you."

Before she could lash out a retort, he turned away, staring into the cold fireplace.

Should she leave? It would be so easy to catch a ride back with Steven when he came.

*Find the grave. You must find the grave.* The soft voice whispered into her ear, stirring the hair around her cheek so that she jumped back, rubbing the skin to take away the creepy feeling. Was this place driving her balmy? Now she was hearing voices.

Jowanna opened a book lying on the end table near the couch, struggling for normalcy. An old leatherbound copy of poetry.

"Are you reading this?"

He looked puzzled. "Why no, I thought you were."

Edgar Allen Poe's works, the fright-writer, her grandfather had called him, forbidding his books in the house.

She wasn't ready to face her mother. It could never be the same between them after this. If there was an inheritance that only her father knew about and wanted her to have, it could mean independence for her. Even though she wasn't welcome here, she couldn't go home without answers. Unfortunately, it was not the first time in her life she didn't belong anywhere—not anywhere at all.

Chapter 4

When Jowanna awoke the next morning, the house was strangely quiet and she knew Kane had left. How comfortably she had slept last night, in her father's room, with no odd noises except the usual creaks and groans of the old house. Knowing Kane slept in the room next to hers had given her a curious sense of security, and his going left an emptiness behind, a void hard to understand.

Once during the night she had crept out of bed and sidled to the door to peer out into the hallway. Kane's door was open, and she left hers open, too.

After making coffee on the old woodstove as Kane had shown her how to do, she took her cup and walked outside, restless and not knowing why. He'd warned her not to get too far from the house, but that was nonsense; he was trying to scare her.

Jowanna stepped carefully, watching for creatures, stopping once in a while to look at small flowers hugging the desert floor, skirting away from a wicked-looking cholla cactus. Would those huge hairy spiders Old Charlie had mentioned leap out at her from holes in the ground?

So many new things to worry about. Again she wondered why her father had preferred this alien place to civilization in a big city. But then, he wasn't able to go back, was he?

The air felt crisp and cool. The smell of the desert was a blend of earth, rocks and brush growing low to the ground like salt and pepper sprinkled on scrambled eggs.

As she walked toward an arroyo, she caught a

movement down inside the gully. She stopped, her heart in her throat, ready to turn and run back inside the house at the first sign of any sort of animal.

"Hi. That you, stepsister?" A disembodied voice rolled up over the rocks and settled around her feet.

The voice had to belong to Steven. Relief coursed through her body, easing away the adrenalin that had been pumping when she started to run away.

"What are you doing down there? I can't see you." She wasn't moving a step forward until he answered.

"Painting, of course. No wind down here. Come on, pull up a rock and sit."

She slipped and slid down the short embankment into the dry wash.

There stood Steven, a man somewhere near her own age, holding a paintbrush and waving at her. He wore his Stetson the same way Kane did, tilted down in a rakish manner so that a great portion of his face was in shadow. Nevertheless, she sensed his handsomeness, the dark, slender grace of him.

"Good Lord!" He dropped his paintbrush on the ground and hastily reached to retrieve it, wiping the bristles carefully on rags tucked in the pocket of his jeans. The astonished look on his face stopped her in her tracks.

"What's the matter? Is something following me?"

She turned to look behind her, scrambling the rest of the way down into the wash in a hurry.

"No, it's nothing like that. Do you believe in reincarnation?"

"N—no, I don't suppose so. I never gave it much thought."

Sweeping off his hat, he smiled disarmingly. "You're Jowanna. My old uncle told me about you. I'm Steven."

His 'old uncle' couldn't have been more than ten years older than the nephew, but Steven looked like a baby in comparison to the rough-hewn strength that emanated from Kane Landry.

Steven wore a white shirt with jeans fitting skintight down to the polished boots on his narrow feet. "Odd name, Jowanna. Sounds Indian."

She shook her head. "Nothing so exotic. My grandfather's name was Joseph and my grandmother's Wanda. Mother combined the names in their honor."

"Anyone call you Jo?"

She smiled. "Never."

He grinned back. "Good. That's what I'll call you, then. You should wear a hat out here. By the way, my clothes never looked better, even if you did have to cinch your belt tight and roll up the cuffs." He seemed to have recovered from whatever had surprised him when he saw her.

He laughed, a pleasant sound, showing straight white teeth. Everything about Steven was pleasant, but the good humor was missing in his eyes. He had pale blue eyes that somehow didn't go with the wide smile he bestowed upon her. His eyes were withdrawn, secretive.

She wanted to like him, but instinct told her she might not. She sensed a remoteness, a false congeniality in spite of his amiable facade.

He motioned toward a large rock. "Take a load off."

Jowanna noticed the seat he offered was behind his canvas and easel so she couldn't see what he painted. She started to sit and leaped aside, with a loud scream.

In an instant he was at her side. "What's the...oh, it's a harmless chuckawalla. A lizard. The only ones you need to watch out for are the Gila monsters, and they're rare, even in this godforsaken corner of the universe." He shooed the twelve-inch lizard aside so she could sit.

He'd no sooner done that when a blur of feathers leaped forward, chasing the lizard behind a rock. With

transported a mule train of tile from Mexico—that and the adobe is what makes it so cool."

"Well, so what happened? Did she come here to stay with him, then?" She couldn't abide slow storytellers.

"You bet. He brought her out here, and as the story goes, they were very much in love. But one day he went off to his mine and never came back."

"You mean disappeared? Forever?"

Steven nodded. "The Superstitions gobbled him up, the way those mountains have many a man. Maybe someone killed him for his gold, if he had any. Left alone, over the years she waited, never giving up hope until the day she died. According to the legend, she roams the house and the nearby desert, always searching for him."

"But how did she live out here alone after he didn't come back?" Jowanna shivered, rubbing her hands on her arms to take away the chill.

Steven smiled. "You're big on logic, aren't you? Reckon the story spread far and wide and prospectors left grub on the porch and in the barn for her. No doubt some offered to take her to the city. But she always refused, waiting for her husband to come back to her."

"I just hope I never see her. I want nothing whatsoever to do with a ghost—friendly or not." Was that the strange presence she'd felt in the house last night? If she were to believe in ghosts, it could have been her father, come back to protect her.

Protect her from what?

"Do you believe it—the legend?" She asked again.

"To a certain extent, yes, I guess I do," he admitted.

She wanted to ask him about the portrait of Delia under his bed, now that she knew it was his room. But that would be admitting that she had been snooping around, and she didn't feel comfortable with that. It would probably be only natural to want to paint a beautiful woman, a member of the family, no less. No mystery there.

"This is a strange place to paint," she offered, uneasy with the silence that engulfed them.

"I like it here. One of the few places on the desert I do like. The word strange fits this place, though. Old Superstition is about the scariest place you'd ever want to visit, and I don't advise you staying long. Not that I want to sound inhospitable. I'm sure my uncle has already made that point. The whole area is rough and wild and dangerous."

"Dangerous?"

"Lord, yes, anything can happen up in those mountains. Last official count, more than sixty-eight people have died inside there." He pointed up toward the shadowy peaks in the distance. "That body count doesn't even include the Apaches and Spaniards. No one will ever know how many of them bit the dust there since the 1800s."

"How did they die?"

He shrugged, scowling at the painting as he dabbed more color on. "Falls from ledges, thirst and exposure in 125-degree heat, animals, Indians, other miners culling out competition, suicide—you name it. In the early days, Apaches lived all through here."

"Who'd want to stay here, then?"

"You got me." His short laugh was edged with bitterness. "It's tamed down considerable. Homesteaders like us get to keep the ranch and grazing areas, and Kane has the right to continue mining."

"Then it's mostly safe now?" She didn't like the way the conversation was going.

"Well, there's your father; that had to have been a terrible accident if there ever was one. Main thing is, don't ever wander about in the washes if it even looks like rain," he warned.

"I don't understand."

"Kane should have explained that to you, but he probably figured you wouldn't go outside much anyway. These dry washes fill up with tons of rushing water when it rains. Nowhere else for it all to go. Keep clear of anything like an arroyo when you see dark clouds."

She looked at him skeptically. Another joke played on the unsuspecting tenderfoot? She pretended to consider his advice. "Thanks. I'll remember that, if it ever rains here."

"Oh, it does. Comes swooping in when you least expect it. A desert storm's something to watch. We get most of them in the summer, but once in awhile we have a stormy winter."

The wash they sat in looked as if it hadn't seen a drop of water in years.

"May I see what you're doing?" she asked, not liking to be made a fool of in such a cavalier way.

"Later, maybe. This is special, I've been working on it for a long time."

Then why was he staring so hard between her and the canvas now?

"I've never shown this to anyone yet. Are you getting any enjoyment from staying here?"

"Not so much," she admitted. "The old house is spooky. I saw a funny bug scuttle across the kitchen floor this morning."

"Ah, probably only a scorpion. You don't like creepy-crawlies? Not unusual for a city person. Delia didn't, either."

Finally, maybe some answers. "Will you tell me about her? Kane wouldn't say much."

"I'm not surprised. Speaking her name is *verboten* around here. She is—was a beauty. Delicate, like a glass figurine you could see right through."

Jowanna felt a zing of envy. Not from Steven's words, curiously enough, but from thinking about

52

Kane's loving her so much. She pushed the unwelcome emotion away.

"Why would she leave without telling anyone goodbye?"

"Kane never understood her. He shouldn't have expected her to settle in out here in this disgusting emptiness."

She flinched at the venom in his voice.

"Isn't this your home? You sound as if you hate it." She found herself contrarily refusing him sympathy for the same negative feelings she'd had only moments before.

"This place is cursed. First the Señora, then my mother. A simple case of appendicitis, with Mac and Kane off chasing gold somewhere. I watched her die—not a damn thing I could do, and nowhere to go for help."

Jowanna swallowed past the lump in her throat, glad he had turned back to his painting, away from her. "I'm sorry. That had to be awful for a young boy."

"She loved it here, though. Like Kane does. I never could understand that. It must be the Cherokee blood flowing through their veins. Great-grandmother was full-blooded."

That explained those high cheekbones, the hard planes of Kane's face she found so fascinating and so formidable.

"She and Kane and Mac, they all loved it here. It's killed two of them already, and now Delia's gone. You're damn right I hate it!"

She looked down at the sand and burrowed her toe in the moving, sliding earth, embarrassed by his savage outburst.

"Come. Have a look. You'll be the first to see it."

Jowanna walked forward and stood next to him. She gasped, her eyes widened with shock. "That's me! How could you know?"

"It's not you, it's the Señora. It jolted the hell out

of me when I saw you standing there. You *are* the Señora of the Superstitions, no doubt about it."

Jowanna stared at the canvas, studying the picture. She might have been looking into the mirror. The sorrowful expression deep in the smoky gray eyes, the downcurve of the small, firm mouth and the few lines of care etched in the face of the woman facing her shocked her speechless. The hair was hers, only done up in a thick braid that twined around her head, with slight silver streaks running through it.

"That's amazing. Spooky. It's me thirty years from now."

He nodded. "You're right. It's enough that I've seen the ghost, but to have her reincarnated in you..."

"Nonsense. Stop it! I don't believe in that stuff. What do you mean, you've seen her?" She dragged her gaze away from the portrait to face him. He was only a few inches taller than her, wiry and thin, a little boy's look. He didn't resemble his uncle in any way.

"It's obvious I saw her, dear Jo. How else could I paint her?"

"I don't want to hear that."

"Whatever you say." His voice was placating.

"You've painted her with such deep suffering in her face."

"No one knows how it ended for her. Legend says she may have taken her own life."

"Oh, how awful. It must have been such a long, lonely wait for her. I can understand that she'd want to finish it."

"I don't blame her, either," Steven said. "If she killed herself, that would have been against the sanctity of her religion and could be why she can't rest in peace."

"I don't believe in ghosts or curses, but even if I did, she looks gentle and kind." Jowanna looked at the portrait again. How did he capture the torture in her eyes? It was uncanny.

"Grief does strange things to people. I'm sure it could cause a soul to outlive a body. We don't know that it wouldn't. I think she wants us all to leave this place."

Jowanna looked down at Steven's boots on her feet. They were a little big, but she wore two pairs of socks. The prosaic thought made her feel a little more normal about the conversation they'd just had.

"I don't know your uncle, I've only just met him, but I doubt he'd ever leave here. He seems to love it beyond anything."

"Yeah. 'Beyond anything,' those are the key words. No one has a right to care that much. Not about a place."

"Don't you suppose Delia might have left a note behind and it got lost?"

His mood swung around again to a more cheerful one. "I wish we knew where and how Delia is; we'd all feel better about it. Maybe Kane would get back some of his old good nature again. He's been a bear since she left. I expect it does something to a man's ego to have his wife run off without a goodbye."

That would explain the hard lines around Kane's mouth, the look of vulnerability in his eyes.

She could see Steven wanted to work on the picture some more, so she went back to her seat on the rock.

"I've got to see my father's grave," she said.

"That's going to be tough. Only Kane knows exactly the place, since he made the grave. After the sheriff had checked everything out, Kane headed up the mountain on Shambles with your father's belongings tied in a bundle."

Jowanna saw the word picture he painted and swallowed around a tight throat.

"I didn't go with him. I don't like the mountains—they scare the hell out of me. Weaver's Needle is up there...waiting." He shivered.

55

"Kane mentioned Weaver's Needle. What is it?"

"A shaft of rock sticking straight up into the air like a gigantic Jehovah's pointing finger. It's said Jacob Waltz hid a fortune in gold near there. The Lost Dutchman's Mine."

"Kane didn't mention that."

"Why would he want the responsibility of you traipsing off into the hills and something happening to you? He's got two strikes against him now, since he was the last person to see both Delia and Mac alive. The sheriff's a small-town hick, and so far Kane's got him buffaloed. My uncle's good at that. He has a certain arrogance that gets him what he wants."

"You sound jealous." She hadn't meant to say that. It wasn't any of her concern.

His eyes narrowed and his mouth became a straight line, and he clenched the brush in his hand so hard it broke in two.

"I'm *not* jealous of him. What an absurd thing to say. He treats me like a kid brother, that's all. I get tired of that." Steven's attempt at lightness made it seem a pitiful caricature of the real thing, and she knew she had struck a serious nerve. "Surely Kane wasn't blamed for my father's death. He took his own life because of the puma...didn't he?"

Steven shrugged. "Maybe. There wasn't any way to tell. But I don't see him doing that. He'd save the last bullet for El Diablo. I'd bet on it."

That had occurred to her, too. "Then what...?"

"Who can say? All I know is, if something else happens out here to anyone, it'll look bad for Kane."

That sounded so ominous. As if something was bound to happen to her. She'd made up her mind that Kane was not a threat to her, but now...Thinking about Steven's words gave her pause. But there was something about Steven she didn't trust when she first looked into his eyes, and that hadn't changed during their conversation. He too was hiding a secret.

"Looks like he'd be glad for me to leave. The only way that's going to happen is if I see my father's gravesite."

"Tell you what. I know where he keeps the map. I'll copy it for you, but I can't help more than that. I came in for a couple of days to pick up some paintings. I'm due at a showing in Tucson day after tomorrow. Why not let me take you back to Albandigos when I leave? Or you can catch a bus from Tucson."

She ignored his invitation. "Can I find my father's grave with the map?"

He laughed, a short bark of a sound that showed little humor. "Oh, you can bet on it. Mac was good at drawing maps, and he wanted to be sure we all knew where he wanted his final resting place to be, for some bizarre reason. But that's the easy part."

"What do you mean?"

"Only one way in, by horse. You ready for that?"

"It can't be far." She turned to shield her eyes from the sun, pointing toward the mountain. "Kane said it was up there, in the foothills, not too far from their mine."

"Don't let the distance mislead you. It's a long day's ride. I'd strongly suggest you wait for him. He's bound to relent and take you, when he sees you're not giving up."

She doubted that very much, remembering the strong stubborn look in Kane's eyes.

"Why do you have to see his grave? Kane said Mac wrote an urgent letter to you, or rather, to your brother. I don't get it. Anything he had to say, he could have said to his partner. He and my uncle were close."

Why didn't he ask to see the letter, as Kane had? "I have to say goodbye. Is that so hard to understand? He mentioned something else in his letter." She decided to trust Steven, even though she wasn't sure about Kane.

"Okay, I'm listening."

"He mentioned a legacy—an inheritance."

Steven slapped his Stetson against a thigh in a gesture of sudden mirth.

His emotions were mercurial. So changeable. One moment he was up, the next down. It made her uneasy.

"Sure, there's a mine. In fact, two of them. That's no secret. They've been at it for years, him and Mac. Going to do all kinds of wondrous things with the gold from that silly mine. Fix up the ranch, put in an underground generator for lights, send me to Chicago to the Art Institute where I've been wanting to go for ages."

He sounded so irritated she wanted to stop him from talking.

"Kane wants to turn the Old Superstition into a working ranch, raising prize Appaloosa stock for horse shows. He wants it so bad he can taste it. Do you imagine for one minute that if there was any gold to be had in that damn mine we wouldn't be using it ourselves?"

His amiable manner had turned sullen and angry. She didn't know what to say or do next.

His eyes flickered from her to the portrait, and his mouth relaxed in a self-conscious grin. "Sorry. I didn't mean to spout off like some wild man. It's just that we—I've been waiting so long for something to happen here. I've lived my whole life waiting for the gold from that mine."

"I'd no idea."

"Of course you wouldn't. You struck a nerve, is all."

"What did you mean, there are two mines?"

"One is the old one of Delia's grandfather. Kane and Mac wanted that one, too, for some stupid reason. There's nothing there, it's played out. Or so Kane and Mac claimed."

"They wouldn't lie about it."

"I guess not. Delia thought her grandfather's mine was worth something. I think that's why she married Kane."

"What a terrible thing, if it's true. Did he suspect that?"

Steven shrugged, his eyes hooded so she couldn't read them. "Who knows, about Kane."

"That makes it all the more odd that my father seemed to feel threatened. Why would he mention an inheritance if he knew you and Kane felt that way?"

Steven shrugged. "Can't say. Mac was a loner, especially after my mother died. Kept his thoughts to himself. Even though he and Kane were partners, none of us saw much of each other. We seldom landed at the ranch house together. That's probably what made Delia leave."

"Could my father have found something on his own? Something he didn't want to share?" She couldn't quite bring herself to tell him the entire contents of the letter, of the strange message about something blowing up in his face. It might have been an innocent expression he used. An innate caution made her hold back.

"Mac? No, Mac wouldn't have kept anything like that from us. Why would he? He was the most honest man I've ever known. If Kane is like a big brother to me, Mac was more like an uncle. He'd never hold back on us."

Steven sounded too sincere, as if he needed to convince himself. He began to gather up his oils.

Jowanna stood up. "Don't let me chase you away. I'll go back to the house."

"No, no, dear girl. I've lost the light; it doesn't stay long. But thanks to looking at you, I think the work's finished. Let's heat up a couple of bowls of Kane's formidable chili, and then I've got to be off."

She helped him fold the easel and they walked toward the house.

good run. I'm sure Kane warned you about Shambles."

She nodded. "We're kind of getting acquainted, though. I don't think he's as mean as everyone seems to think he is. He let me unwrap the bandage to look at his leg."

Steven's eyes widened in surprise. "Don't trust him. He's born and bred for the rodeo—got a mean streak in him."

"I'd like your honest opinion. Should I wait and ask Kane, or take a chance and go alone?"

Steven shrugged. "Truth? I doubt Kane will change his mind and take you out there. He's never been comfortable with women, and now that Delia pulled out on him..." He was telling her to go ahead. That was plain enough. "Say, you're getting good with this old wood burner. Delia never got the hang of cooking on it. She couldn't even boil water for coffee."

"It's not that difficult, once Kane showed me how." She had begun to enjoy pitting her skill against the sometimes reluctant fire.

They ate the spicy chili in companionable silence for a while.

When they finished, Steven told her goodbye, and she sat on the front veranda watching him leave. It was very quiet afterward, and she went back inside to read one of Kane's books.

She dozed in the big, overstuffed chair and, upon waking, discovered it was dark outside. When she opened the front door to look up at the stars, each one appeared so individually bright and huge it seemed she might reach up to grab it.

Suddenly a terrifying scream ripped apart the black quiet of the night. She slammed the door shut and leaned against it, waiting for the spasm of weakness to pass from her legs, for her heart to stop pounding.

*El Diablo.* Kane had warned her that the cry of a puma sounded like a woman's shriek of agony, but nothing could have prepared her for that cry. Was the stable door shut? What if the big cat decided to attack the horses? She trembled, ashamed of her cowardice. There was no way on earth she could ever go out that door tonight.

Jowanna found her way into the kitchen and lit a lamp. After thinking of a bite to eat and rejecting the idea, she decided to go up to her room, close the door and forget everything for the night. The daylight would bring relief from her fears.

It always had in the past.

The faint aroma of perfume surrounded her shoulders and neck as she walked up the stairs holding the lamp. It smelled flowery, like roses or lavender, she couldn't decide which. She braced herself automatically for the screech of a loose stairstep around the corner.

As she turned to go up the second flight of stairs, something floated above her. She raised the lantern higher and a scream burst from her throat.

*A woman hung from the rafters by a noose.*

The body, dressed in a long white gown, swayed slightly, as though pushed and pulled by an invisible force. The long black hair streamed around her shoulders, the expression on her face contorted in pain, eyes wide and staring.

It was like looking into her own death throes, witnessing her own destruction.

*The face was her own.*

Jowanna swayed, futilely clutching the railing in one hand, the lamp in the other.

As she toppled backward, each edge of the stairs hit her body when she landed, lurching and bouncing all the way down. At the bottom, she lay for a long moment, the breath knocked out of her. Gasping, she raised to a sitting position, pushing aside the pain of her bruises as the darkness engulfed her.

Where was the lamp?

She rolled over to feel for the lamp, expecting to see a flame blaze up any moment from some part of the room.

The darkness remained unchanged. The remembered sound of glass shattering into pieces on the hard tile floor came back in a rush.

When the lamp broke, the flame must have extinguished.

In a strangling clutch of fear, she thought of what caused her fall. The hanging woman at the top of the stairway.

At first her legs refused to move, but finally, as she managed to stand, the sensation of eyes boring into her back pushed her forward toward the front door. Flinging it wide, she sucked in the cold fresh air of the desert night. By the uncertain light of the half moon, the stable door beckoned.

Jowanna made a terrified run for it.

She spent a miserable night wrapped in a smelly horse blanket, facing the unlockable stable door and praying for daylight. Every waking minute was a struggle not to see the agonized death grimace of the swaying, macabre figure at the top of the stairs.

For the first time, her total isolation struck like a fist between her shoulder blades. Off in the distance a coyote howled and soon an answer, more forlorn than the first, came like an echo back over the desert. Only a soft wind sifting through the salt cedar trees made a sound; the night was so quiet her ears rang with the silence.

At long last, daylight filtered down through a skylight in the roof of the barn. She stood and stretched cautiously, feeling each individual bruise on her body. Then she bent over, to hang her hair where she could see it, and pulled as much loose straw out as she could find. She brushed at her clothing, as well.

Enough stalling. She had to go inside the house and up the staircase to make sure of what she had seen last night.

Could it have been the ghost? Was that how the tragic Señora had died—suicide by hanging? What was the connection between them? She had felt a connection since first entering the house, and seeing Steven's portrait of the Señora had brought it out into the open.

When she cautiously pushed open the door and stepped into the front room, everything looked amazingly normal and in place. Only the broken bits of the lamp lay scattered, with the dark stain of oil marring the surface of the tiled floor.

Jowanna stood at the bottom of the stairway, not wanting to go up there. Not even in daylight. She made herself put one foot in front of the other, one step at a time upward. Her mind cringed at the thought of what lay ahead, but she had to see it again.

When she turned the corner of the staircase, the dormer window let in a flood of light that carried upward toward the top of the stairs. She forced herself to look up.

There was nothing there.

Forgetting her previous fear and caution, she raced to the top. Nothing. Down on her hands and knees, she searched every little corner, every inch of the steps for an explanation, a clue, a footprint.

She looked around for a chair to drag over to stand on. Her father's bedroom contained only a heavy-duty rocker. That was out of the question. Feeling like an intruder, she pushed open Kane's door and saw a ladder-backed chair that might do the trick. As she walked across the room, something on the floor just under the edge of his bed caught her eye.

She knelt down to pull out a large scrap of white satin material, torn as if someone had jerked it off a nail in a hurry. Traces of frayed rope clung to the surface of the glossy material.

Kane.

Her heart sank down into her boots as she thought of him playing such a mean bit of mischief on her. He had said several times he didn't want strangers around. Was this his way of telling her in no uncertain terms?

Determined to make certain of her suspicions, she dragged out the chair and stood teetering on it at the top of the landing. She ran her fingers carefully over the low rafter. Just as she was about to give up and get down off the chair before she fell again, her fingers traced over the beam and felt a nail hole.

Looking down she could see it was in the right place, with a nail in it, to suspend the hanging body. The hole was as big as her little finger tip. Why was it there?

Who had put the body there, and where had it gone? Was it a warning or a prophecy?

Chapter 5

During her first day alone at the ranch, Jowanna started out by brushing and talking to the horses, thinking she would read and nap when she wasn't out in the stables.

Troubled about going outside to face the warned-of hazards of the desert, yet inside the house listening every moment for squeaks and noises from upstairs, she finally made up her mind to do something to keep busy. She began to dust and tidy up, in spite of Kane's misgivings about her ability.

By the time she wrapped a towel around her hair and slipped on an oversized long-sleeved shirt over her clothes, she felt ready to attack the dust. The shirt had been draped across a chair in the kitchen, and judging from the size, it had to be Kane's. She sniffed the material, liking the masculine smell of horse, man and earth, all mixed together.

The dust rose in clouds as Jowanna moved purposefully through the living room in an effort to keep the night away as long as possible. It didn't take long to realize that nothing was happening but a redistribution of the brown chalky substance.

She spied a bunch of rocks lying about on a table and decided to get rid of them. Who cared about rocks when there were so many outside? She dumped the load in a wastebasket and looked for something else practical to do.

Her nose and eyelashes and any other exposed portion of her body were coated with dust—she'd spent half the time sneezing, and blowing her nose. Where did the dust come from? How did it get so pulverized, so fine?

As she worked she'd decided there was no reason not to sleep upstairs in her father's room. Her plan was simple. Lock the door and stay in the room until daylight.

When dusk began to settle, she fed the horses and shut the stable door. The tall ocotillo cactus seemed to lift fragile, spiny arms up into the darkening desert sky with spidery silhouettes. The stately saguaros, which by day stood peacefully majestic, now appeared like solitary sentinels, ringing the landscape, standing guard for the night. Far beyond, the dark, secretive mountains lay as if waiting. Jowanna shivered and hurried into the house.

Better to get upstairs before the shadows began to dance along the walls and ceiling of the narrow stairway. Get upstairs before those eyes that she felt piercing her back could gain her attention.

Inside her father's bedroom, with the door closed and the doorknob pushed in to turn the lock, the light from her lantern played softly over the walls as she made ready for bed. She stood at the window a long time, brushing her hair, looking out into the moonlit desert. From her vantage point, all the objects she thought of as threatening seemed softened under the spell of the moon, which had risen over the last peak.

With this view, it became a little more understandable, the appeal this country must have held for her father. The wonder had begun to grow within her as she watched the sunset over the far range of mountains sharding into a thousand rays of deep oranges and yellows and sinking down into the purple hills.

She would have liked to share it with her father. What made her momentarily think of sharing it with Kane? That was a curious notion, and she hurriedly pushed it away.

Her heart raced when she spied an eerie, elusive

movement out on the desert. Could be a coyote. Kane had said the puma wouldn't come close to the ranch house. She blew out the lamp and pressed closer to the window, trying to penetrate the pale light of the moon. Yes! A shadow flitted gracefully between the mesquite trees. She couldn't tell who or what was out there, only that the shadow was real.

In the darkness of the room her other senses took over and the perfume smell finally sank in, clinging faintly to the air around her. She had never smelled it in this room before.

Every time she smelled the perfume intensely, something happened. Did it come from the ghost of the Señora? Or the more prosaic possessions of Delia's left behind in her hasty departure? She hadn't seen a trace of a woman's things lying about or in closets, not even a hairbrush. Kane said he'd packed her clothing away in the locked storeroom. You'd think a husband would either leave the possessions in the room if he thought she might return or dispose of them if he was convinced she'd left forever.

Did that mean he still loved her and couldn't bear to throw away the few possessions his wife left behind? Or that he rejected her enough to hide them away? Jowanna turned to look into the dresser mirror. Every time she saw her face reflected, the image of the hanging woman returned to haunt her. Did Kane do that to scare her? The piece of fabric was in his room. There was no denying that.

She looked away, remembering that face and hair. It was her own, as if she had looked into a mirror. Was it real? Not in the sense of a real person, but an image created out of her connection to the ghost, perhaps. She and the Señora had to be connected some way. With their looks, they could have been twins.

If the hanging figure had been arranged deliberately, it was more than a prank. She might have broken her neck falling backward—or set the house on fire.

She walked toward the door, holding the re-lit lamp. It might prove easier to give up and go downstairs, but she didn't want to face those stairs at night. Each time she looked upward, she could still see the vision of a woman swaying in the shadows, her face a terrible grimace of suffering.

"There's no such thing as ghosts. Someone's trying to frighten me away. It won't work." As soon as she spoke the words aloud she felt a little better. She changed into her long, flannel nightgown, mentally thanking Bernice for including it in her suitcase. Even though the days were warm in the Arizona desert, nights turned chilly.

Her life back East had been very comfortable, but it seemed so far away now. Did her mother miss her? Did she miss her mother? Maybe, she admitted reluctantly. Dominating, rigid, humorless, her mother nevertheless had taken care to see that her daughter lacked for nothing her entire life. Nothing, that is, except love and affection and a sense of her own worth.

Funny, that it took all these years and a chasm between them to see the truth. Living in the shadow of her mother, she would eventually grow to be just like her. Did she want that?

Unable to sleep, she listened to the weird creaks and groans all around her as they echoed down the empty halls and stairways.

When she finally dozed off, she awoke, startled, and sat up in bed, her heart thumping in her breast. As soon as she awoke, she remembered what had awakened her. Slow, deliberate steps had resounded, coming up the stairs toward her room. Jowanna felt each step inside her crawling skin. Closer and closer, the slithering, dragging steps continued up to her door.

Cowering in the middle of the bed, covers pulled up around her neck, she knew without looking that there was nothing in the room to protect herself with.

She stared in stunned fascination as the knob turned slowly, first one way, then the other. Her mouth dried so that it was impossible to swallow, and her heart pounded in her chest. She wanted to close her eyes, but she dared not. Should she call out, or hope someone didn't know she was inside the room?

Then, the steps moved away, toward the back of the hall.

She leaped to her feet, and ran to lean against the bedroom door. She wanted to fling it open, to see who or what was out there in the dark hall. When she tried the knob, it didn't turn.

Was she locked in? Or was someone locked out? Did someone or something want her to stay inside the room for now? She sat on the edge of the bed, wondering what to do next. It wasn't a good feeling to be locked in a room, even if she had wanted to lock herself in. It wasn't the same.

Still jittery from her fears, she pulled open the bureau drawer to rummage under her things for her father's letter. She couldn't find it.

Pulling out the clothes and throwing them on the bed, she got to the bottom of the drawer, but there was no letter. Did that mean the sound she heard yesterday, the sound of drawers being pulled out up here, was real and not a ghostly sound? It had to be. The letter was gone.

The one and only letter from her father. Beyond the hurt of losing the keepsake lay the worry over someone else knowing the contents she had memorized. Maybe she should have told Kane about the noises upstairs yesterday. He couldn't have made them, since he was standing next to her in the stables right after it happened. Her silly pride had stood in her way. She hadn't wanted his ridicule.

Jowanna pulled out the second drawer. She might as well read the book she'd started. The opened drawer reeked of perfume, clogging her nostrils so that she choked, almost shoving it closed again.

Reaching in with her face averted, her fingers touched something cold and hard. She jerked back her hand but then explored further and realized the object was square, like a box. Curious, she pulled the drawer open wider and reached in to retrieve an exquisitely carved jewel box.

Funny, she had never seen that before.

*Leave it alone.*

Now she was hearing that voice again. A soft voice so close it stirred the hairs on her neck. Nonsense. She wasn't going to let wild imagination take over common sense. She sat down on the edge of the bed and tried the cover gently, only to stare down at the contents in petrified horror.

She screamed, instinctively flinging the box as far away as she could, frantically brushing the front of her gown as if they had been clinging to her. Her stomach roiled; she felt weak and nauseous.

Scorpions! The box had been filled with crawling, repulsive scorpions, the small, luminous yellow kind that Kane had warned her were deadly.

She closed her eyes for a moment, reliving the sight of them slithering and climbing over each other as they tried to get out when she opened the lid of the box.

Jowanna screamed again. They were loose in the room now. What had she done? She ran for the door, her long gown flapping between her ankles, tripping her. Sobbing in terror, she pulled hysterically on the knob and looked down in despair at the round brass object that had popped off into her palm.

She heard the other side of the knob rolling across the floor outside the door.

Against her will, because she couldn't help it, she turned to look back at the room, expecting to see all the scorpions crawling toward her, covering the floor. It was as if a nightmare she had been fighting off all her life had come to haunt her.

She tucked her bare feet in closer and pulled up the gown around her knees. She could climb up on the dresser, or she could smash some with her boots, but neither idea was a solution.

If she could make it to the window, she would take her chances with the low overhanging roof and the drop to the ground, but she discarded that idea right away. Nothing could make her go to that side of the room where she had flung the scorpions.

Oh, Lord! Was a ragged line of them making their way toward her, slithering past the end of the bed, tails curved upward in grotesque menace?

Screams tore from her throat until she could scream no more. She pounded on the door with one fist, keeping hold of her long gown with the other, knowing deep in her heart no one could hear her. She leaned her cheek against the hard wood, tears of fear and frustration running down her face.

It was then her ears picked up a different sound. She heard the door knob being fitted into place outside, and she almost fell through the doorway when it opened.

By then she didn't care who let her out. Blessed relief washed over her body. No one stood in the hallway. Cold chills spread in ripples as she slammed the door behind her and ran down the dark stairs, not caring about anything but to get outdoors, out of this house.

With trembling fingers, she unlatched the stable door and hurried to light one of the lanterns that always hung near the entrance. Flopping down on the straw near the horses, she drew deep breaths to calm herself. Every inch of her body still felt crawling with those vile creatures. She shivered and began to cry.

Something soft and furry nudged into the back of her neck. Her throat so tight and dry she couldn't have screamed again if she had to, she balled up her fist and whirled around to strike out. The big Appaloosa stood right behind her.

"Sorry, old boy. Didn't mean to scare you, but you gave me a fright." She lurched to her feet and ran her hand across his mighty flank, grateful for the comfort of his warmth. He flinched beneath her touch, the muscles rolled under her fingers, but he held steady. Reaching down into the leather bag hanging against the wall, she brought out a slightly dried apple, which he took delicately from her palm, nuzzling his velvety nose against her trembling hand.

The horse's warmth had a calming effect on her until, looking around, she noticed something was different.

Mirla was gone.

She searched through the stalls, nooks and crannies of the stables, but the mare had disappeared. Jowanna leaned her head against the big horse, needing to feel a sense of comfort from the sturdy normality of the animal. Without Mirla, she couldn't leave this place if her life depended upon it.

*Someone didn't want her to stay, and someone didn't want her to leave.*

Did that mean the same someone wanted her dead? Like her father?

Now, that was a crazy, irrational thought—what made her think it?

She should never have come here. Why did she? Certainly not only for the promised inheritance that now seemed as ethereal as the Señora.

She had come for answers, but had found only questions.

One thing was for sure: her father had not died by his own hands. Had her coming here precipitated his death? That was an unbearable thought that she had been pushing aside since arriving.

It was time she set aside her pain to examine it. Someone could have read his letter to her—to Jason—

before her father mailed it. That same person could have intercepted her telegram saying she would come. Whoever didn't want her here would have had to act quickly before she and her father got together.

What was her father about to tell? What fantastic secret had he been ready to impart that might have cost him his life?

She knew now—as if he had reached from beyond his grave to tell her—that there was a secret he had wanted to tell.

Her only thought in coming here had been to confront him with the bitter anger she had cherished through the years of her growing up. Anger for the loss of his companionship and that of her brother had eventually blended together until she couldn't separate them any longer.

That anger had not disappeared, but now it was focused toward her mother for lying to her, for conspiring against her father so that he couldn't come home to them.

He was dead. Period. Didn't that end her journey?

Should she consider staying a day longer at this remote ranch with only a trail leading into it, living with two men—either one of whom could have schemed to harm or drive her away?

Why would she stay a moment longer with two strangers—one with wary eyes she couldn't trust and one who was the last to see her father alive?

She answered her own questions.

It was too late to slink back home, admitting she had been foolish to leave in the first place. Too late to accept her place alongside her mother as a matron of society. She had tasted independence now. It was scary, frightening and dangerous, but she couldn't go back.

Not yet.

Now, more than ever, she needed to stay here, to discover why and how her father died. Her life depended on finding her father's grave at the base of the mountains. That had to be the start of unraveling the mystery of his untimely death, of Delia's disappearance, and of the strange things that had been going on in the house.

Her purpose in staying on now was more than to bid her father goodbye, it was to make peace with herself. She could no longer ignore the inheritance that he promised in the letter. How could she go back—forever a captive in her mother's house, robbed of the exhilarating independence she was beginning to enjoy?

There was only one solution. Follow the map to her father's grave.

That was the beginning and ending of it all.

Chapter 6

As soon as daylight came, Jowanna went back into the house. She crept carefully up the stairs and touched the doorknob of her father's room. It was intact, as if it had never fallen off. She pushed open the door, standing wide of the entrance in case any scorpions came her way. She walked inside and looked around. There wasn't a bug in sight. Where had they all gone?

No use to stand around thinking about it. She pulled jeans and a shirt out of the closet, holding them away from her while she shook them out as Kane had warned her to do.

Downstairs in the living room, she pulled on the clothing and headed back out to the barn. She hadn't formed any kind of plan, but whatever she did, it had to be done before Kane returned because he would just put her in his truck and take her out to Albandigos, she knew that for sure.

In the barn, Shambles greeted her, nodding his big head and pawing the floor as Jowanna ran her hand over his shoulder, in awe of his beauty. The muscles rippled in his chest, and his glossy coat of Appaloosa colors was like a blanket thrown across his back and rump. The bandage was gone from his leg. Kane had said he was nearly healed.

She stopped rubbing his coat to get him a scoop of oats from a bucket near the door. He ate delicately from her hand, as he had the apple, pressing his nose of velvety softness into her palm. Hanging on the wall were several of the back packs Steven had told her about. In case anyone had to leave in a hurry, they each contained a hat, water and a supply of the dried beef he called jerky. She had to use a pitchfork to bring one down from its hanging place high on the wall.

Encouraged by Shambles' greeting, she led him outside to a sawed-off ironwood root that looked as if it could serve as a mounting device. She stood on it to hoist a saddle blanket across his broad back. For a terrifying moment, his powerful muscles bunched. Nerves rippled beneath his skin, his ears twitched, and he snorted through distended nostrils.

She looked at the heavy western saddle Kane used and knew there was no way to lift it high enough to throw over Shambles' back, even if the horse would have permitted it. Mirla's smaller saddle hung nearby, but it wouldn't cinch around Shambles. Jowanna's spirits dipped lower.

Could she ride this horse bareback? The remembrance of another wild ride so long ago, and the taunting cries that turned into cheers, made shivers up and down her back. Her mouth went dry. But she was just a teenager then.

Besides, if Shambles threw her, she might lie here in the corral for days without care until Kane or Steven returned. She thought of Steven's mother, dying of appendicitis, without a chance to survive. Would something like that happen to her? Was that what someone wanted when he removed Mirla from the stables? Hoping she'd try to ride the stallion and get trampled in the attempt?

She clenched her teeth and set her shoulders. She wasn't giving up so easily. Determined to try, she fit the bit into the horse's mouth. The stallion reared and pawed the air with his powerful front legs.

"There, there old boy. How about a run?"

*Don't show fear.* She held back her panic as best she could, faced with the sharp hooves and teeth, knowing the horse would surely sense fear. Both Kane and Steven had warned that he bit on the least provocation.

Tears of frustration welled into her eyes, and she brushed them away impatiently. No time for that. He didn't bite her hand off when she fed him, and she'd have to trust he wouldn't bite her now. She patiently slipped the bit back between his teeth, taking care to keep her fingers curved away so he couldn't grab one.

"Come on, now, Shambles, honey-boy. Let's walk a few steps, and see how you behave."

This was madness. She hadn't ridden in years. Would it all come rushing back like riding a bicycle? Without a saddle, the big horse had her at his mercy. Would the attention she had paid him in the past days pay off?

She strapped on the back pack and stepped up on the mounting block, slowly stretching one leg over his broad back. He reared his head and snorted, pawing the ground. As she slid on, for a terrible moment she felt his muscles tense and contract beneath her legs as if he contemplated doing something drastic to get her off. She leaned down over his neck and talked to him, touching his ears, tickling gently under his mane.

It wasn't necessary to guide him around the corral fence. He stepped out with loud blowing breaths and arching neck, as if in anticipation, seeming to soak up the sunlight, dancing and high-stepping sideways. As she pulled the reins toward the corral gate, she saw with dismay that she had forgotten to open it. But by then Shambles was so excited to be free of the stall he took the bit between his teeth and broke into a long, graceful lope toward the gate.

"Oh, no!" she cred, gripping the reins tight. She grabbed his mane, twisting her fingers into the thick hair, and leaned over his neck, holding on as he soared over the fence and continued to gallop toward the mountains, as if he knew where to go.

Swallowing hard, she sat up, taking hold of the reins again, no longer futilely trying to hold him back.

She reveled in the glorious feel of the powerful muscles between her legs. Her hair, held back only by the velvet band, was whipped by the wind as they sped on.

By the time they reached the foothills and her father's gravesite, would he be tired enough to let her turn him around and head back to the ranch without any problem?

That was her hope.

She thought of the people who had died out here in the desert. The Señora's husband, disappearing forever. Had he been killed by gold seekers, strangers who didn't want him up here looking around? Did he fall into one of those bottomless mine shafts Steven had warned her about? He said they were dotted all over the mountainside and even on the desert floor.

Her thoughts were making her uneasy. Yet she felt empowered by what she'd already done. Was the fearful, timid Jowanna receding into her past? She fervently hoped so. She reached down to pat the horse on his neck, talking to him out loud.

When he showed no signs of tiring, she tried to slow him down, but he was enjoying his run. Jowanna looked up toward the eerie cliffs, growing ever closer. Shadows hid a great deal of the facade, so that she couldn't make out the caves Kane had told her about.

Shambles began angling off the flatland, heading toward the mountains. She pulled futilely on the reins, trying to turn him back to the desert floor. Finally, when they had reached a chasm she thought must be nearly the size of the Grand Canyon, he paused beneath a palo verde and stood in the shade of the huge, leafy tree, sides just barely heaving.

Was this his usual place to stop when Kane rode him?

She would have given anything to dismount and stretch her legs, but she didn't dare. There was no way she would be able to climb back on again. After a short rest, Shambles began to prance restlessly.

He was searching for Kane. She knew that now.

Looking back down into the valley, she could just make out the windmills on the ranch property, like tiny toys in the distance. They had traveled so far!

It was past noon. Could they make it up to her father's grave and back down before night? She thought of the dark silence of the desert, the saguaros standing like shadowy observers, each step of the horse menaced by rocks, holes and cholla cactus—and El Diablo, who always waited to strike out at humans. She shivered.

Yet Shambles knew the way home, and last night was a full moon. If the darkness caught them, she was willing to chance it, they were so close. She pulled the folded copy of the map out of her shirt pocket and spread it on the blanket in front of her. There was the saguaro in the shape of a praying man. Past that, turning away from the cliffs, it couldn't be much farther.

Just then a shadow scudded across the sun's face, as if to challenge her.

The wind against her back had been growing stronger by the minute. She looked up with sudden apprehension at the thunderclouds gathering ominously in the distance, flowing up from the valley below.

Steven had warned her about the sudden violence, the rushing water in dry washes. Even if she was sure he had exaggerated, she would stay away from gullies of any kind, and hopefully before the storm started she would have the horse back at the ranch, tucked safely in the barn.

They continued upward, toward the caves. She watched for landmarks on the map, feeling close to her father, who had so meticulously drawn it out for Jason to follow.

What had been his thoughts as he lay dying, alone in this huge expanse of emptiness he called home? Did he regret his life and his choices? Did he blame anyone for his death? How much did he trust Kane?

So many questions.

She looked up at the caves, but in spite of the time that had passed and the distance she and Shambles had traveled, they seemed as far away as ever. Her eyes strained to see each individual cave, which seemed almost possible, and then she caught a glimpse of a brief flash of light.

Was someone watching her approach with binoculars?

The idea made goosebumps rise on her arms. The terrain was growing rougher and the cactus and trees sparser, replaced with rock. If the path became any steeper she'd be forced to dismount and lead the horse.

They must be three-quarters of the way there. If she abandoned the idea of seeing her father's grave when she was so close, there was no telling when she would get another chance. The gravesite held the clues to what was happening to her, she was certain. Whoever was trying to frighten her away might grow impatient with a lack of progress, sooner or later, and do something drastic.

She could disappear like Delia. Die like her father.

A quick movement passed in front of them, causing the horse to freeze in place. She exhaled a deep sigh of relief, recognizing a roadrunner. Awkward like a chicken at times, it could rev up to a zoom of speed that made it a blur. She watched in amazement as it leaped up on a boulder, snapped at something behind and came out with a small, writhing snake in its beak. The long-legged bird slammed the reptile against the boulder once, then again, until it lay still. Satisfied, the bird trotted away with the limp snake in its beak.

"What a crazy place," she said aloud to the horse, needing to hear a voice.

At first the silence had been like a vacuum in her

ears, but she was growing to respect it, enjoying the peace it brought. Kane had said that would happen if she let it.

Lost in thought, she almost missed the beginning of the steep incline. This was the place to get off the horse and lead him. She pulled Shambles up to the nearest boulder and slid off, grateful to touch her feet to the ground.

She rubbed her backside and dipped into a few kneebends, getting the kinks out, knowing her rear and thighs would be sore for days.

No need to try and ride him here. Instinctively she knew that, in spite of her slight weight, the horse should be led. He followed along behind her as she pulled his reins. The trail was narrow, the footing precarious.

Up, up the ever-narrowing pathway. A deep ravine suddenly appeared to her right. To her left reared a sheer wall of cliff with the small openings of caves pocking the face of the stone. The dark holes made her remember the puma, and she continued upward.

For a time she began to wonder if she should have trusted Steven so implicitly. He'd said he copied the map exactly, from the one Kane had put away in his room, but why hadn't he brought it down to the kitchen table and copied it in front of her? That would have made more sense.

She followed the landmarks meticulously, knowing her life depended upon it. Not only hers but the horse's. If she lost Shambles, Kane would never forgive her.

Careful to note the peculiarly shaped rocks and cactus, she couldn't have made a mistake, yet...

Suddenly the trail stopped abruptly. Only after climbing to the top did she see it descend a short way to a flat basin.

That pile of stones below must be her father's grave.

Her pulse quickened and her heart beat faster as she realized how far she had come on her own, how much she had dared, and how unlike the old Jowanna she had become, the Jowanna who was afraid of everything.

She looked at the big horse and realized no way would she pull him along behind her on a descent like that—he'd run over the top of her—and she didn't trust herself to ride him down.

"Here, old boy. I'll tie you to this bush. I won't be long, it's getting dark too fast."

The only thing that could possibly harm the horse was the puma, and Kane had said he would put Shambles up against El Diablo any time. She hoped he was right.

Holding on to outcroppings of stunted trees and brush, she slipped and slid down the narrow pathway, thankful for Steven's long-sleeved shirt. Halfway down, she felt the hair on her neck vibrate—something tapped her shoulder, a strange premonition, a warning.

She looked up just in time to see a huge boulder hurtling down on her. Screaming in fright, she threw herself off the path, the brush and stones digging into her flesh and the side of her face as she fell and rolled.

Had she rolled far enough? A picture flashed through her mind of the boulder mashing into her body, crushing her. Dazed, she crouched with her arms around her head for protection while the boulder bounced down, shooting small stones off to the sides like bullets. After it passed, she sat up and watched it continue to the bottom and roll to a stop.

*Look up. Look up.* The voice in her ear caused her to do what it said in time to catch the fleeting perception, a blur of a figure running away.

The whinny of a horse invaded her confusion. Was Shambles in danger? Forgetting her own peril, she scrambled to her feet and ran back up the trail, grabbing onto rocks and brush to haul herself upward.

As she topped the path, her heart stopped a moment before re-starting.

The horse was gone. Along with the backpack she'd left on a rock by the horse.

She looked around, but there was no sign of another living being. Heart beating in her throat, mouth dry, she understood full well her ominous plight, stranded alone, without a horse, and dark clouds coming closer and closer.

Kneeling, she examined the bootprints at the edge and saw a large piece of rotting timber dragged forward and used to pry loose the boulder. Timber that might have come from a mine. Someone had deliberately pushed the rock down on her.

Who knew she would eventually come this way and spied, waiting for a chance? This was no prank, no attempt to frighten her. Someone wanted her dead. Wanted to leave her out here alone and helpless like her father had been.

Steven knew she was coming, but Kane might know, too. Could that have been Kane's binoculars she caught glinting from the top of the mountain pass?

But Kane couldn't have known she was coming up here, that she would dare ride his horse. Not unless he and Steven were allied against her father and had planned it this way, certain she would try to find the grave. The same person who pushed the rock down on her must have taken Shambles away.

"I'm not afraid of you!" She shouted the brave words into the silence.

Her only echo was the wind.

"The Señora's on my side," she shouted into the emptiness, feeling as lost and abandoned as she had ever felt in her life. Yet she was not alone.

For the first time since the adversities had begun happening, she accepted the truth that some entity was helping her. Whether a ghost of the tragic widow or her father's spirit left behind, she felt an invisible energy meaning her no harm.

Jowanna sat down on the ledge to examine her injuries. There were scratches. Her palms were abraded from the climb back up the steep slope, and her cheek felt scratched. When she put her hand up, it came back bloodied. She stretched sore muscles and let her feet hang over as her mind replayed the picture of the huge plummeting boulder crashing down on her.

The thought that her would-be murderer could have been either Kane or Steven caused a bitter bile to rise in her throat, choking off air so that she coughed.

It was hard to imagine Kane—big as the country he lived in, a bread baker, horse groomer, his eyes honest, his talk straightforward—hard to imagine him a killer. But then, it was no easier imagining Steven in that role, either. Could an outsider be involved? In her torment, she knew that was unlikely but not impossible.

What if someone from outside suspected Kane and her father had been hiding a mine full of gold? Everyone in Albandigos knew strangers weren't welcome out here. At some point wouldn't they have begun to wonder why? Kane had to have lied about the mine. Why else would her father say there was a treasure to be had and that it would all soon blow up in his face?

She forced herself to concentrate, her throat tightened with a need to cry, her mind bogged down with the struggle to make her world come out level. Everything was in disarray, like being inside a glass ball with snow swirling around when it was tilted upside down. And no way out.

What would her grandfather do? She straightened her back as if he had given her one of his light knuckle jobs in the center of her shoulders as he used to do when she didn't stand straight. The old tyrant. The thought gave her a little strength, and the urge to dissolve in tears disappeared.

Shielding her eyes from the overcast sun, she searched the valley for movement. There were dark, shadowy pockets where no light ever reached, creating an eerie patchwork effect.

The pile of stones—her father's grave—sat directly in the center of the basin, in the bright sunlight. Thankfully the land was flat with no towering boulders to push down on her. She slipped and slid down the trail and hurried toward her father's last resting place.

A flat stone beckoned, and she sat on it near the grave to catch her breath, gazing at the piled-up sand and stones with a hazy weariness while time passed. Someone, Kane no doubt, had carved her father's name on a board. There were no dates. No one out here knew when he was born or even the exact day when he died. She let her skin soak in the warm, soothing sunshine that only disappeared from time to time as an occasional cloud glided across it, pushed by the wind.

Struggling to replace the image of her father's violent death with scenes from her childhood, her thoughts clung to remembrances of him in New York. Playing with her and Jason, teasing, laughing. He had been such a delight to a quiet little girl overshadowed by her mother's stern authority. He was gentle, masculine, cheerful. She had missed him so much when he left them behind. After a patina of anger had gradually covered over the pain, she should have been able to forgive him, in time, but it never happened because there was no sense of closure.

Until now. Now she could tell him goodbye. She moved closer and knelt at the grave, tears blurring her eyes, coursing down her cheeks, stinging the abrasions.

"Goodbye, Poppa, I love you," she whispered aloud, the sound of her voice making it real. "I'm so sorry I didn't get to tell you."

She closed her eyes and when she opened them, raising her head to look upward at the nearest foothills, she caught a flicker. It wasn't like before, when someone with binoculars might have been spying. This was a stationary object and shinier.

Jowanna dried her eyes on her shirtsleeve and moved from her seated position to the end of the grave, but she still saw the flare of light. When she stood up, stepping a few feet to the side, it disappeared. All around the grave she walked, watching intently, seeing the shiny object.

More often now, a cloud scuttled across the sun's face. Dusk would settle soon tonight. She didn't want to be out here alone in the dark with no horse. Not with El Diablo roaming about, as well as whoever pushed the boulder down on her still in the vicinity.

She sat down and smoothed out the map on her knee. From her father's grave it didn't look too far to Kane's cabin, which was up a narrow incline, past a cave Steven called The Vault, and over the next ridge, on top of a flat mountain. Steven had drawn the shape of a pyramid in the middle of the piece of paper serving as the map. With the ranch house at the apex or tip of the triangle, Weaver's Needle made up the left side of the bottom length, Kane's cabin halfway between the two ends, the old mine next, and at the opposite end of the wide part of the pyramid he'd marked a T. What that stood for, she couldn't begin to guess. In the middle of the pyramid he'd printed High Plateau and Long Valley. The big X in the middle marked her father's grave, closer to the top than the middle.

Even if she found Shambles, she was past the point of no return as far as going back to the ranch tonight. She might make it to Kane's cabin, if it wasn't too hard to find. She wouldn't think beyond that. What if Kane was there? Did she want to be alone with him—give him a chance to finish the job? Had he killed Delia because he didn't want to share the mine?

Or in a jealous rage because she threatened to leave him? That meant he could have killed her father, too. Or left him to die.

Now that she saw the area, she could never again buy the story that her father had shot himself with his next-to-last bullet and left a bullet in the gun, instead of killing the puma. It didn't add up. He surely knew Kane would come looking for him, since this place was right on the trail to the mine and the cabin. Was he afraid Kane wouldn't have helped him?

If someone did push him, did he know who? A terrible thought, that at the last moment of your life, you realize someone you trusted was destroying you.

Somehow the thought of Kane doing this hurt more than anything that had come before. She didn't want to believe that big bear of a man was so evil. She wouldn't believe it.

*Go now. Follow the light.*

That voice again. It was so clear it rustled the tiny hairs on the back of her neck. Jowanna stood and brushed off her jeans, lifted her chin and looked up at the shiny object.

It was a long shot, but it was all she had to go on. Her father, whimsical at times, as she remembered him, was nevertheless quite logical when he needed to be. He wouldn't have wanted to leave a note causing Jason to dig up his grave, so he must have put a sign somewhere, and the shiny object was the only game in town.

He had felt threatened. Did he feel death near? When did he plan his burial? It was all so morbid. She had to get to the bottom of the mystery before whoever was out to frighten or kill her did it first.

Chapter 7

Moving along as quickly as her bruised body would let her, Jowanna began the climb upward toward the shiny object. The journey seemed to take hours. While she climbed, the object disappeared often, but she had noted a few landmarks. This gave her a twinge of satisfaction. The old Jowanna would have been totally out of her element, lost like a child in a New York blizzard.

What was it Kane had said? Oh, yes. "You have to become one with the elements, with the land, to understand it." She felt so close to her father now, so close to understanding the pain he must have felt when he left them behind. She was even close to understanding the pull this country had on him.

Jowanna hedged around the sharp spiny cactus, twisting her boots on rocks, plowing upward, keeping her eyes on the goal. Only once did she stop and look back. The mound of rocks looked very small, but she didn't allow time to think of her fear of heights. She figured that phobia had bit the dust already.

Here was that weirdly shaped rock and the crooked mesquite tree she'd made note of as she'd started her climb upward. She glanced uneasily at the sky, seeing the sun low, the shadows on the basin floor lengthening.

When out of the eerie silence a cry shredded the air into sharp little pieces, she nearly fell backward and the place at the nape of her neck prickled with a sudden chill. The puma! Was it tracking her? Which direction had the sound come from? It was impossible to tell, with the sound reverberating off the canyon walls. Where could she hide? How could she scare him away? She searched the ground for good-sized rocks to throw if the big cat suddenly appeared over the horizon. The thought made her surge forward, ignoring the scratches deepening on her fingers and hands as she scrabbled and crawled farther upward.

She stopped when she saw a faint glimmer ahead.

Creeping, almost perpendicular now, she held on to tough roots of brush and rocks, wishing, not for the first time, that she had taken Steven's gloves from the stables. She was growing very thirsty and trying not to think of a cool drink of water trickling down her parched throat.

Once, when she reached up without looking, a premonition warned her and she pulled back her hand just in time to avoid grabbing hold of a cholla, the dreaded jumping cactus. A handful of those thorns would have left her helpless and defeated, unable to use her hands.

There it was! The object was not large; a mirror of some kind. Suddenly she felt exhausted and discouraged at the thought that one of those big desert crows had probably brought it here out of curiosity.

All this time and effort for nothing.

But when she plucked it out of the rock cranny, her heart tripped forward a few beats as she recognized the old-fashioned mirror backed with a vintage celluloid cover. The youthful faces of her mother and father on their wedding day smiled back at her. She held it to her cheek for a long moment. The hard coldness of the object felt good on her flushed skin.

This old piece had been a favorite of hers when she was a child. She had wondered about its disappearance. Her father had had the picture inserted in the antique frame as a keepsake for her mother. He must have taken it with him when he left.

What did it mean? She sat on the ground, and

looked down at the grave, now a mere shadow on the basin floor. Her father had been trying to leave a message, then. The place he'd chosen to be buried had been important to him and, he'd hoped, to Jason, and now her.

If he imagined himself in danger, why did he stay? Had he trusted those around him too much? Was the grave and this mirror a sort of insurance if something happened to him?

Why hadn't anyone else ever found it?

Because no one was looking like she had been, she answered her own question.

She stood and stretched, her body aching from the fall and from riding the horse so many hours. She bent over to search, with no idea what she was looking for. Over near a large ironwood bush she spied a dark patch behind the clump.

A cave. She sniffed around the outside. Kane had told her you could smell a puma's lair a half mile away. This cave did have a musty odor, but not what she would expect from a large animal.

She reached in her pocket for the small flashlight she carried, blessing the leather case that had protected it when she fell. She peered inside, flashing the light, then moved forward, her heart thudding, pulse racing. The cave was shallow like the den of an animal, a large animal. As she bent to go in, a cloud of disturbed bats flew by her, shrilling in their fright. She stifled a scream, willing her legs to stop trembling and go on.

Afraid of disturbing more bats, she hesitated to flash the light along the edge of the cave. A natural skylight in the rocks above sifted rays of dust motes down to the floor. This must be near the top of a mountain. The climb had been steadily upward.

The cave was empty but for the pile of stones.

Disappointment diminished her elation at finding the mirror and the cave.

Was this all there was to it? A miner's old claim?

"That's it! What he wanted to show Jason!" Her excited voice broke the silence and another cascade of bats flew upward through the hole in the rocks, but she hardly noticed as she began to pull away the pile of stones.

Inside was a tobacco tin. She lifted it out and sat down to open the lid. Her hand trembled and she smoothed out the wrinkled piece of paper.

"My son," she read out loud. Tears welled up in her eyes so that for a moment she couldn't see. Her father had planned for Jason to find this letter.

"It is my last remaining hope that it will be you who reads this and not—not anyone else. I've written you and Jowanna faithfully in the years since I left, but I've never received a reply. I finally figured the Senator and your mother had told you about the missing money. I swear I never stole a cent from them. But I couldn't spend years in prison. Even now the loss of my children sucks at the marrow in my bones. But I made the choice. I had to live with it."

Tears blinded her, and she brushed them away. Her first thought was to hate her mother, but an understanding slowly intervened. Her mother had had her pick of the cream of society and chose unconventional, charming John McFarland over them all.

What a blow that must have been to the Senator, who doted on his only child. In trying to blend her husband into the accepted society, her mother had ruined everything between them and then refused to let him go.

Jowanna looked down at the letter again, continuing to read.

"I didn't think you would be in any real danger if you came here, you must believe me. Now I know I was wrong. Strange things are happening beyond my comprehension. That you are reading this now means I am gone. Something is going on. I dare not speak to either of them about it. In uncovering a treasure bigger than any of us has ever dreamed of, we realized it must be kept a secret lest it be our final undoing. These are my last words, since someone else may have found this: remember the games we used to play with your sister on rainy days by the fireplace. AND DON'T TRUST ANYONE!'"

Her voice died away as the enormity of what she had just read penetrated.

Did he know who plotted against him? Obviously not, or he would have said so, as a warning. Who was the "we" and "them"? She read it over to herself again, vaguely remembering the fireplace game, but the details were foggy. She'd have to give that more time.

The light from above had been steadily fading when a crack of thunder followed by a brilliant flash of lightning broke her reverie.

Kane, Steven and even old Charlie had warned her about being caught out in the open in a swift desert storm. She hurriedly stuffed the letter into her shirt pocket and the empty can back into the cairn, piling up the stones around it. Emerging cautiously from the narrow opening of the cave, she sucked in the fresh air before noticing the darkened sky and the strength of the wind as it smashed against her.

No matter her fears and doubts of Kane, she had to make it to the cabin before the storm struck in full force.

The sun had vanished behind the black roiling clouds that had stealthily swept up from the valley floor, pursuing her.

*Hurry upward, hurry upward,* a voice came from somewhere.

A warmth spread around her, enveloping her, soothing the goosebumps from the cold chill that came as she heard the voice.

"Who's there?" She spoke out loud. "Nerves. You've

got a case of nerves, but you survived the worst of New York's storms. What's so grand about a measly old desert storm?"

According to the map, there was a foothill to climb over, and then the terrain would level off again just before she reached the cabin. She was unprepared for the second crack of thunder, which hit with a mighty force, ricocheting off the canyon walls. Slipping, sliding, she nearly tumbled all the way down the mountainside to reach the trail that extended from the basin of the grave up toward the cabin.

Her heart pumped rapidly in her chest, and her knees threatened to give way with her. She hoped Shambles was all right. What if whoever had pushed the boulder down on her had merely frightened him away, and he was running loose now? In spite of her mixed feelings toward Kane, she didn't want anything to happen to his horse.

The pass led upward, worn by years of her father's and Kane's passage to their mine. She had no idea where the mine was, but Steven had said it was not so far beyond the cabin.

Bending her head into the sudden blasts of wind, she trudged slowly forward, pressing into the side of the mountain to keep her balance. As she climbed with an aching steadiness, the other side of the path dropped away to nothing, a deep chasm below.

The rain began to sheet down in malevolent fury, as if trying to dislodge her from the path. Suddenly it turned to hail, stinging through her shirt. She pulled the hat lower, grateful for the ties that she'd fastened under her chin. She needed to find shelter. Fast.

Remembering the map, she was sure that big overhanging rock they called The Vault was near. She could take shelter there until the storm blew over. Her growing terror didn't let her think beyond that. She needed to concentrate on one step at a time.

The thunder echoed sharply through the rocks.

Lightning zinged down into the canyon floor below, lighting up the fearsome drop-off and then filling the chasm with eerie, tortured shadows of the swaying trees. She imagined sliding down the slippery path, plunging off the side into painful oblivion.

No one would find her broken body. No one would ever know what happened to her. That probably had happened to many gold seekers over the years. The thought weakened her knees so that she barely crept up the incline in spite of the wind pushing against her back.

She saw the overhanging rock formation and dashed forward and into the recess. Above her head she heard a rush of water, but decided it was outside, not a concern.

*Get out! Get out!*

She ignored the voice. No way was she leaving this protection, scant as it was. Between lightning flashes she saw water first trickle, then spout from somewhere beneath the large flat rock that comprised the floor of the grotto, under her feet. She heard it rush across the path in front and watched it pour out over the ledge.

Jowanna leaned wearily back against the side of the rock and wiped the wet hair from her face. Lulled by the warmth of the remaining heat held by the rocks and the steadily pounding rain on the trail, weary from climbing and bruises all over her body, she closed her eyes, resting for a moment.

Suddenly she felt a grip of iron on her shoulder, and at the same time she heard the monstrous roar of water, starting from far up the mountain, the sound of boulders ricocheting off the sides of the rocks on the way down. Fear choked off the scream emerging from her throat. The noise in the little cul-de-sac was deafening as the water roared and rushed in.

Jowanna felt herself lifted up out of the muddy, swirling mass.

"Hold on, I'll get you out."

She looked up into Kane's grim face, streaked with mud and rain. His hat was low on his forehead, hiding his eyes. Then, unceremoniously, he threw her across his shoulder and waded through the melee of mud and rocks.

Outside, he slogged up the path. The wind had slowed to a gusting stage, and in a few minutes the rain dwindled away, with only the ragged remnants of a few lightning flashes moving off over the rim of the farthest mountain.

"You can put me down now," she managed to mutter against the roughness of his Levi jacket.

He ignored her and continued up the trail, kicking aside rocks and debris in his path.

At the top of the incline, he set her down in front of him, letting her feet touch the ground gently. He held his arm around her waist and when she stopped wobbling, he took off his jacket to wrap around her shivering shoulders. The temperature must have dropped twenty degrees.

"You almost shook me apart," she complained.

"I'll be damned! Is that the thanks I get for saving your life? What a dumb place to hide from a rainstorm."

"How could I know I was standing under a rain spout?"

He barked a mirthless laugh. "Any fool could have looked up and seen that arroyo just above the Vault."

She was too tired to argue. "Where are we?"

"About a hundred yards from the cabin. Come on, let's get dried out."

As they approached, Shambles, tucked away safe in a corral, whinnied a welcome. Gladness to see him safe warred with the question of how he'd gotten there. Just as she was beginning to relax with her rescuer, new doubts arose. How had he found her?

Kane took her arm and steered her up the last little incline. On top, she turned, and in spite of her teeth-chattering cold, and the residual panic from her ordeal, she viewed the spectacle spread out in front of her with breathless wonder. A solid sheet of rain visibly worked its way across the floor of the canyon, heading toward the far mountains. Lightning slashed through the gray curtain in steady intervals.

The cabin was tucked into the side of a mountain, just below the crest, with what could have been a lunar landscape spread out below. The height made her dizzy, and she leaned into a nearby bush, hands groping to hold on to something.

He stopped walking and turned to stare down into her face. She absorbed the caring, anxious look in his expression.

"What the hell am I thinking? You probably can't even breathe in this altitude." He swooped her up in his arms, holding her close. She murmured a faint protest before wrapping her arms around his neck, surrendering to the warmth and security that overwhelmed her.

Inside, he deposited her in an oversized hand-carved rocker while he hurriedly made a fire in the fireplace. Then he threw coffee into a tall blue-and-white enameled coffeepot and hung it over the edge of the flames on an iron frame.

"Now. Let's get you warm."

"How did you know where to look for me? How did you find the horse?" So many questions. Why had he saved her life if he wanted her out of the way?

"I got some questions of my own. How in the hell did you manage to ride my horse up here? And why? You could have killed him." His voice sounded gruff but not angry as she bent forward, laying her head against his chest and letting him take off the jacket. He picked up her legs one at a time and removed her boots, rubbing the cold from her feet.

Oh, that felt good. His hands were hard and callused, but strong and warm, too. She wanted it to go on forever.

"Let's get those duds off. You can wear one of my flannel shirts—it ought to come down below your knees, at least."

She tried to undo the snaps of Steven's shirt, but her fingers didn't want to work. She remembered a rock tumbling down, just catching her hand. It felt numb.

"Damn, you've hurt yourself." As if reading her thoughts, he picked up her scratched hand and held it toward the fire to look. Then he put his finger under her chin and looked closely at her face. "What the hell happened? You have a run-in with the puma? You'll have a dandy bruise coming up tomorrow on your hand, but it doesn't feel broken. He massaged the edge carefully, his big hands surprisingly gentle. "Are you hurt anywhere else that I should know about?" He touched her cheek. "You've a scratch there, but it doesn't look deep."

She wanted to tell him about the boulder pushed down on top of her, but she was shaking too much with the cold.

He began to pull away the snaps on her shirt and, before she had a chance to protest, lifted her under her arms as if she'd been a rag doll and shifted her toward the narrow bunk bed in the corner.

By now she had lost any sense of modesty. Her teeth chattered, while her body ached and cried out for warmth. Kane stripped away her remaining clothing and, holding her close like a child, he maneuvered a soft flannel shirt over her arms and began to button the front.

"Aw, to hell with it," he muttered as he wrapped the material around her, tucking it under her arms, and deposited her in the bed, pulling up the quilt around her. She lay quivering, knees up to her chin, a ball of freezing cold. Every inch of her skin felt lacerated with the stones and icy pellets of hail that had pummeled her.

A moment later she felt the bed shift and suddenly his body was next to her, forcing her legs down, pulling her close to be enveloped in his arms. For a brief moment she protested and then gave up when the blessed relief of warmth crept through her skin and into her bloodstream.

He held her for a long time. The steady beat of his heart next to her cheek lulled her so that she dozed, woke up and dozed again.

She awoke finally, realizing that the feelings that had come to her in her sleep were not very appropriate under the circumstances. The warmth from the outer limits of her body had spread to her midsection and had nothing to do with comfort. She felt his hard body close to hers, her legs were twined with his, and she might as well have been naked.

In fact, she nearly was. The shirt front that he had wrapped around her had come loose and she felt his hard arm against her bare breast.

Oh, she didn't want to move. The sound of his smooth breathing told her he was asleep. She tried to bring the material around her front, wondering what he had on. So far she hadn't felt anything but skin.

How did she get herself in such a predicament? She wanted to stay here forever, and yet she felt mortified to be so stripped of dignity that she could lie next to a man, a dangerous stranger, and enjoy it.

Kane must have felt her stirring, and he pulled her closer for a moment before he awoke.

He dug his hand into the thickness of her hair, touching the base of her skull and caressing the back of her neck, moving his fingers through the dark mass.

"Ah, Jowanna. I dreamed...but never mind. How do you feel?"

*I couldn't tell you the truth,* she wanted to say.

At that moment the tension released from the back of her head and the tingle starting from there echoed down the length of her body.

"Maybe you shouldn't do that." Her voice came out a shaky whisper as she tried to control the trembling that radiated down from the top of her head to her legs. She could hardly reject the soothing touch of someone who had just saved her life.

He pushed back a little, leaving a cold space between their bodies. "Does it bother you?" His eyes were dark, the thick lashes masking their expression. The flickering firelight danced through the sun streaks in his hair and turned his bare shoulders and arms to a soft burnished bronze. His shoulders were wide, his upper arms muscled from hard work.

She felt his hardness move against her thigh.

"You're so beautiful. You remind me of Mirla. Little blackbird."

She knew it was probably his highest compliment, being compared to a horse. A splendid, elegant horse.

Jowanna disentangled an arm from the covers and reached out a hand to touch his lips. Such a dear mouth. Long and sensuous, it felt smooth and unyielding under her moving fingers. What was she thinking? She barely knew the man.

He groaned. "Now you've done it." His voice broke with huskiness, and he pulled her closer. His hands, gentle and careful, pushed aside the material of her shirt and touched a breast, sending jagged shock waves into the pit of her stomach. He thumbed her nipple softly, and she thought the top of her head would explode.

Kane moved his hands down to her buttocks and pulled her close against him, her soft form melding into the hardness of his body. Twisting around with a graceful maneuver, he sprawled across her, careful to hold up his full weight. She looked up into his face and he leaned on an elbow to gaze at her.

Expecting to see naked desire, she felt a shock reverberate through her being when she recognized something else. A caring, a tenderness that went beyond passion. It was there in a moment, and then gone, leaving her wondering if she hadn't imagined it.

He touched his hand to her face, smoothing the damp hair from her cheek. He leaned forward and kissed her. The kiss felt as if it would last forever, and she wanted it to.

His warm tongue searched her mouth. She answered back, wanting him.

When they stopped for a breath of air, he rolled to her side and still holding her, kissed each closed eyelid, the tip of her nose, and let his lips just move across hers. When his tongue moved over her bottom lip in a gesture so sensual, so exquisitely erotic, it was all the more so because it was so unexpectedly gentle. He took her hands, encouraging her to explore.

She couldn't do that, and pressed her body closer into him until they blended together. Against her leg she felt his male hardness, but she didn't flinch away. She'd never even had a serious boyfriend in her life, but she was beyond fear of the unknown. Brazenly, she pushed aside the covers and rolled on top of him. Looking down into his face, she had to smile at his surprised expression. She leaned forward, her long hair tangling around his hands as they reached up to her. He spanned her waist and held her away for a brief moment, his eyes filled with admiration.

I've never wanted anyone like I want you." His voice came husky, deep in his throat. He let her body down to rest on top of him, and she felt every inch of his warmth, not knowing where her skin ended and his began.

He rolled from under her and again lay on top of her. This time his eyes were filled with fierce passion, and she knew that whatever happened had to happen because they had gone past the point of no return. He bent and bit her neck lightly, as she'd seen stallions do to mares. He spread her legs with his and took time to let his hands roam over her body before he lifted her just enough to begin his thrust.

Although he didn't push hard, for a second Jowanna thought the pain would rob her of any pleasure, and she cried out. He paused, looking down into her face, but she was ready for him and welcomed him into her body. His first thrust brought a wave of desire that was nearly unbearable. She threw back her head and pushed closer into his. His kisses became more demanding and her body felt heavy and warm, while her heartbeat hammered in her ears. Inexperienced as she was, she sensed his ardor was touchingly restrained.

Waves of ecstasy washed over her just as he moaned and she felt his pleasure mix with hers. He rolled off her and reached to hold her close. She felt the peace and contentment flow between them.

When they could speak, he pushed the hair away from her damp forehead and looked deep into her eyes. "Why didn't you warn me, woman? I never would have…"

She stretched luxuriously, feeling a throbbing still within her. "It didn't seem important."

He kissed her in a lingering, open-mouthed way that she'd come to love. "You have to be at least twenty-eight or nine. I didn't for a second think…"

"That you were deflowering a virgin?" She was shocked at her boldness but took heart from his seriousness. "It was beautiful, Kane. I'm glad it was you."

He snuggled her into his chest and they slept for a while. When she awoke, she watched him putting on his jeans and buttoning them. She continued to look while he pulled the white t-shirt over his head, feeling a stirring as the material molded to his body, stark white against his butternut skin. Now that the throes of passion had subsided, Jowanna realized nothing had been solved.

His movements were fluid, graceful for his build and height, and she thought of the shadowy movements outside her window the night she found the scorpions. She hadn't forgotten her father's admonition to trust no one. The warning just didn't seem to fit Kane, even though common sense dictated there weren't too many alternatives.

Wouldn't her guardian voice have warned her about Kane? She couldn't be sure.

"I'd like to get up and get dressed." She ran fingers through her tangled hair.

"If you're sure you're okay," he answered. "I'm afraid I didn't give your cuts and bruises much thought while we…"

She smiled. "Neither did I." She sat on the edge of the bed and fastened the big shirt edges together over her front. "I don't suppose you have a comb—or better yet, a brush?"

She discovered her arms were so tired and sore from climbing the day before that she couldn't get them up to her shoulders. She bent her head down to try and comb her hair with her fingers.

"Here, let me do that." He took a comb from the small table where he'd stashed his shaving things. "When I was a kid, my sister used to let me brush her long hair. I wouldn't do it when I got older, though. Thought it was sissy."

"Mmm, that feels delicious." She wanted to be angry with him because, even though he was pleasant enough, he had distanced himself, back to the remote Kane she'd first met.

He pulled the comb carefully through her hair, reaching into the locks to remove pieces of the debris the wind had blown at her.

"Do you want it in a braid? I reckon I'd remember how."

"Sure, that's good."

Who was this man she had made love with? Who

was this man who had claimed her body? Was it just for sex? She longed to tell him everything, to spill her guts about all the terror she'd been through since her arrival, about her suspicions concerning her father's death—but that thought brought her up short.

Her father's letter had warned to trust no one.

Jowanna felt Kane's hand slowly encircle her neck, the motion half frightening, half provocative. He could snap her neck with one twist of those powerful hands. A tremor began to transmit from the warmth of his skin, spreading down through her body so that she struggled to keep it from surfacing. A shiver of wanting, when he brought her untried senses to life, left her fearful but needing more.

Kane leaned forward, his cheek resting against the side of her head for a long moment, and his warm breath stirred the hair alongside her face. He turned her toward him and claimed her lips again, this time fiercely, as if he had lost the battle with his hard-held emotions.

She heard his low moan—or was it her own?—as she kissed back. The heady fire radiated from her center, spreading outward to encompass every inch of her body. Her fingers wrapped around a handful of his hair as she pressed into him. It was impossible to get close enough.

Breathless, they broke apart. He regarded her for a long moment, his eyes dark and unreadable. She looked away, waiting for her quickened pulse to subside.

"If you're looking for…I mean, there are a lot of things unfinished in my life. I regret now my hastiness in taking you. I'm sorry that I didn't realize you weren't.. you were…" He floundered and she refused to step up to help him.

"Go on," was all she said.

He laid down the comb and ran his hand distractedly through his hair. "There's something not right here. Something going on that I don't understand. But, and I don't see any easy way to put this, you still need to go back home. This isn't any place for you. "

His voice had hardened and he moved away to sit on the edge of the bed.

"Is it still Delia?" she asked.

He nodded, not looking at her. "In a way, but not like you probably think. I've no feelings left for her one way or another. We never closed it between us. I don't like unfinished business. But it's you, too. You know something that you're not talking about, and that means you don't trust me. I don't like that, either."

"Well, it seems there's a lot that you dislike. But I have to tell you not to worry overmuch about my virginity or the lack of it now. I was compliant and we made love together and that's that. What do you want me to do?"

"Like I said. It's time for you to go back home. You saw your father's grave. Did you learn anything from going there?"

She wondered why he would ask that. Unless he suspected she'd discovered something and needed to find out what. It was time to trust someone. She pointed to her shirt hanging next to the fireplace drying out. "Bring it here, please. I want to show you something." She would show him her father's note—and scrutinize his face to catch him in a lie. No one was that good.

He handed her the shirt and she felt in the pocket for the folded note.

It wasn't there. Neither was the copy of the map to her father's grave.

Stunned, she didn't know what to do next. He could have searched her clothing while she slept, found the papers. That meant he knew her father was hiding something and that eventually she might learn what and where.

Would that save her life or end it sooner? What if the papers had slipped out during the storm? That could have happened easily enough. She didn't know what to think, now.

She shivered, crossing her arms in front of her as if to hold in the pain. She didn't want Kane to be the one who pushed the boulder down on her. How could she believe this man was ruthless, scheming, when his eyes were so open, so honest? *You fool!* she scolded herself She hated her weakness.

Just because he appealed to her in so many ways. No—it was only a sexual thing, a fantasizing spinster's attempt to experience love—she assured herself. Just because she felt drawn to him as she had no other man in her life, that was no reason to give up her reasoning, her common sense.

If it wasn't him doing all this, it had to be Steven. Even though she didn't trust Steven, exactly, she wouldn't think him capable of double murder and nearly killing her, too.

After what had happened the day before, she was more than ever convinced that her father hadn't taken his own life.

"I thought I'd brought something with me," she whispered, not wanting to relinquish her closeness to him in spite of her doubts and the realization that he obviously still loved his missing wife, even while protesting it. What normal man would not prefer the beautiful, exotic Delia?

Tears slipped from her eyes and she let them go, turning her head aside, hoping he wouldn't see.

"It's warm in here now. Lie back on the bed and prop up the pillows behind you. I'll bring you coffee. Then we'll look at those scratches."

"I don't know how else to say it, but thank you for saving my life." Her voice sounded strained and cool, which was what she wanted—distance between them.

How could she think of letting Kane make love to

her, a man she didn't trust? Yet if he had wanted to, he could have left her out in the storm to be washed away. Unless he was looking for something he thought she might have. Or know. Her father had mentioned a secret treasure. Was it a secret even from his own partner?

"I'm sorry about your horse," she continued when he didn't acknowledge her thanks. "Was he all right when you found him? Where did you find him?" She hoped her voice sounded more casual than she felt.

He brought her the coffee and pulled the rocker closer to sit in it, his broad back blocking out much of the light from the fire. That was fine, she didn't want him to see the remnants of tears. She didn't need his pity.

"He trotted up just before the storm. I couldn't see who was riding him before. I knew Steven sure would never have gotten that close to him."

*I couldn't see who was riding him.* Kane just said those words. It was him spying on them—the glare of glass up in the mountains had not been her imagination. Had he seen her emerge from the little cave where her father had hidden the letter?

That cavern couldn't have been a secret from him. She'd be willing to bet if anyone knew every nook and cranny of this Superstition Mountain, he did. It was probably an abandoned mine, and her father figured no one would look there for anything. She felt confident no one could have seen the light from the small mirror unless specifically looking for something from the center of her father's grave, as she had been.

"Why'd you ride the stallion instead of Mirla?"

"Mirla wasn't in the stables when I left."

The flat statement lay between them for a moment as she watched his eyes. They betrayed nothing more than a flicker of surprise as he answered.

"The mare was likely somewhere in the shadows at the rear of the stables. You just didn't see her. She does that sometimes. It's a game with her."

Jowanna knew better. She had searched that stables from one end to the other.

"This rascal does cotton to women some, though, but I still don't get it, how you managed to ride him."

She struggled to keep her voice even. He either didn't want to believe her about the missing horse, or he knew why Mirla was gone.

"Shambles and I, we've been making friends since I arrived at the ranch. It didn't take more than a few dried apples and sugar cubes between us."

Kane grinned. "He's easy. Still, looks like you've got a natural feel for horses. That's rare. Most outsiders have to grow into the business of trusting horses, and vice versa."

Outsiders. Sure, she was an outsider, but it hurt to have him say it out loud. That meant he was trying to distance himself from her.

"Mmm. This coffee is good. Bet if you had a lake of it, you could walk across without a bridge."

He laughed, and the sound came from his midsection, rich and natural. "Cowboy coffee. Got some tinned milk and sugar here somewhere. Don't recollect where Mac stashed it."

She shook her head. "No. It's good this way. Did my father come here, too?"

His expression turned serious. The fine lines around his eyes flattened out and he swerved the rocker to look back at the fire. "Gotta bring in some more wood soon."

He didn't say anything for a moment, and she thought he wasn't going to answer.

"We shared everything. This was as much his cabin as it was mine, I reckon. We bunked here while we mined. He was quite a man, your pop. I—we—"

She sensed it was hard for him to form the words for feelings he couldn't express.

"Was he like a father or an uncle to you?" What

would it have been like to have her father all the while she was growing up? For a moment she felt jealous of Kane and Steven's closeness to him.

In spite of being sorry he was dead, she felt the familiar stab of anger against him for robbing himself and her of those missing years.

Kane shook his head. "More like a big brother. Like I am to Steven. Your pa and me, we argued a lot, both being stubborn and bull-headed, but we got along. Funny thing is, he didn't like Delia. Wouldn't talk about it. For some reason she didn't cotton to him, either. After I brought her home it was different between Mac and me."

"Jealous? Maybe he was jealous when he didn't have your full attention anymore."

"Maybe. Jealousy is a terrible emotion, eats a man alive."

The words sounded torn from him against his will. Had he been jealous of Delia? Delia and who? Steven?

*Do you really think Delia will come back to you after all this time?*

She was too cowardly to ask the question aloud.

"Mac was a special person. I'm sorry you didn't get to know him. He talked about you so much at first, it's like we were all the same family. Then when no one answered his letters he grew bitter and never mentioned his family again."

"When I found out he was still alive after all these years, I was consumed with anger," she admitted. "I came here, to confront him with my anger and bitterness—hurt him like he hurt my brother and me. Now what troubles me most is knowing that all those years he wanted to come back to us and couldn't. I think I hate my mother and grandfather for what they did."

Kane reached his hands to hold hers around the empty coffee cup and then lifted her chin with his fist to kiss her softly. "I know. I don't blame you, but that feeling will pass. Seems to me you've learned that anger and blame haven't helped in the past. It's not going to satisfy in the future, either."

"I guess you're right. It's hard to not be angry, though."

"You never did say how Shambles got away from you."

He switched subjects, as if trying to remove himself from the closeness that had developed between them.

"I've got a few questions to ask of you," she countered. "How did you find me? In that storm, I mean." Was there a subject they could talk about without emotion?

"I followed your progress up from the valley."

No mystery there. He admitted it.

"I couldn't tell who it was. With your clothes and hat, you looked like Steven, but when I recognized Shambles' gait, it threw me. Steven would never ride him. I didn't know what to think."

"I caught a flicker of binoculars in the sun, up on the mountain. Gave me goosebumps."

"Sorry. But you can understand my concern, wondering who was riding my horse. By the time the clouds began to gather, I figured it had to be you, and I knew you were in for it. It took me time to get down off the mountain, and by then you'd disappeared."

Should she tell him about the falling boulder? How to word it without accusing? Right now, sitting so close to him, she felt absurd thinking he would do such a thing.

"I was nearly killed." She blurted out. Then she told him about the near-disaster.

Before she had finished, he was kneeling in front of her, holding her shoulders in an iron grip. "My God, it's a wonder you're alive!" His look raked her body and she flushed, sensing he was trying to remember her bare skin, and whether she had cuts or abrasions that needed tending to.

"I'm all right. Just banged up some from rolling off the trail. It wasn't an accident, though. I saw a shadow up above, a person—that was clear enough."

He released his grip and rocked back on his heels. "Who would want to harm you?"

His expression went from disbelief to one of honest puzzlement. He was either innocent or an extremely good actor. Was this a good time to tell him about the hanging woman on the staircase, or the box of scorpions, or Steven's painting?

Before she could decide, his puzzlement turned to indignation. "You think I...you think I had a hand in trying to hurt you? That's plain foolish. Why would I bother to save you, then?" His jaw hardened with repressed anger.

"Is your mine far from here?" She changed the subject, feeling uncomfortable with all the emotions clouding the little room and knowing he felt the same.

He shrugged. She watched the firelight play on his lean features, across the taut planes of his face, touching on the sungold strip of hair that tended to fall over his forehead when he was agitated.

Which he seemed to be now.

"There's nothing in that old mine of interest to you. It's played out. We were going to give it up."

Not according to what her father's note said. Unless he'd been writing about Delia's grandfather's mine. Had Kane and Steven lied about that mine being worthless? She let it drop. "Well, what do we do now?"

"We? I reckon we go on down to the ranch, when you're able to ride. Unless you've got something more you want to see up here."

"I wanted to see my father's grave. That's why I came up here."

"How'd you know where it was?"

She swallowed. It wasn't fair to get Steven

involved. It was obvious there was trouble between them, and she didn't want to add to it.

"I—I went into your room, found the map, and traced it."

"It wasn't just lying out on the nightstand. You were snooping. The map was under some clothes in a drawer."

She looked away, not knowing how to answer.

"I don't get it. Why is it so damned important for you to see a little patch of ground? Couldn't you say goodbye to Mac without being right there? When I told you Mac's remains weren't buried at the ranch, I have to admit, that was a mystery to me."

"Isn't your sister buried at the ranch?"

"Yes. That puzzled me and Steven. Looks like he'd want to rest by her side, but he left instructions exactly where to put his earthly remains. Reckon he wanted to be near the mountains. I'm surprised he didn't ask to be buried all the way up to Weaver's Needle, but I'm thankful that wasn't his request."

"My father was a puzzle to everyone who knew him. He and my mother were so different, it's hard to see how they ever got together. Yet I think they loved each other in the beginning." She remembered hugs and snatched kisses between them before the arguments started. Most of the ugly times came after he went to work for her grandfather.

"I guess that's what undid their marriage, finally. The Senator—that's my grandfather, he wasn't a real senator, everyone just called him that—wanted my father to work in his office at the brokerage house. Even young as I was I knew how much my father hated it."

"That's Mac, all right. He couldn't stand to be cooped up inside for long, same as me, I reckon. He didn't like your grandfather much, either."

"What little I remember of my father was as a dear, whimsical man—a dreamer. He always made time to entertain us. I came here prepared to chew him out. Now I need some answers to why he never came back to us. Why he needed to stay out here more than he needed his own family." She moved the empty coffee mug in circles on the table, evading his scrutiny, not wanting him to see the hurt.

He banged his hand on the table so that the dishes jumped. "Dammit! You were so close to seeing him. We knew he had a family back East, but he wouldn't talk about it after a while. He did tell me about your grandfather, though. Hated his guts. I reckon it was mutual."

"They never did get on."

"Your mother and grandfather conspired against him, or so Mac said, and I've never known him for a liar. The Senator finally convinced her Mac was only after their fortune."

"I doubt my mother would have believed that."

"She *did* believe it. According to Mac, the old man had her twisted around his finger, being his only heir, and all that goes with it."

"You may be right. I never thought of it that way. I figured the twisting was mutual, both my mother and grandfather enjoyed the game of out-maneuvering each other."

"Mac always regretted leaving you kids. He had no choice."

"What do you mean?"

"According to Mac, the Senator shifted the books to look like Mac had embezzled a great deal of money. It was leave or go to prison. Knowing Mac, he wouldn't have lasted a month cooped up inside those four walls."

Kane's words drove into her heart like a knife. All those wasted years of not knowing him. Still, that didn't change the fact that her father had a serious problem here and had died for it. She turned to stare into the fire, afraid of giving away something by her expression. The grave, and from that the hidden cache with the letter, held the key to her father's death. The voice had told her, but she didn't really believe it until that same voice tried to save her life.

"Now that you've found the grave, are you satisfied? Gonna come back up here to put flowers on it?" The anger in his voice was thinly masked as sarcasm. "I don't want you hurt, can't you see that?"

By now she was confused, not knowing if his voice held concern for her safety or a warning not to snoop further.

"The way I see it, the boulder falling down on you had to be an accident. There wasn't anyone but me up here, and I damn sure didn't do it."

*There wasn't anyone but me up here.* Terrible words between them.

"You're wrong. I saw the piece of timber, I saw the trampled earth and boot prints. It was deliberate." She had to insist, if only to keep him from trying it again, knowing she was alert.

"I'm going to check it out. Might not be anything to see, after the rainstorm, so it might take a while. I'll be back by dusk."

"But can't we do it on the way down? I don't want to be alone," she protested.

He shook his head. "It could rain. It's clouding up again."

"It's already rained, remember? The footprints will be all washed away. Don't go."

He cupped one hand around the back of her neck, his other hand lifted her chin, running his fingers gently underneath to trace the bones of her face. She couldn't prevent the shudder that ran through her body, thinking of her neck twisting around with a snap.

He looked at her strangely, and moved away from her as if sensing her sudden fear. "I'll be back before you know it," he said curtly. "You'll be fine. Just stay put."

Looking up into that rough-hewn face carved from a slab of mahogany, into those coffee-with-cream eyes, she could believe a lot of things about this reserved man, but pettiness and ineptitude were not among them.

If he had wanted to kill her, he would have succeeded.

She swallowed, nodding. "Okay. Wait till I get dressed, and I'll see you off. I'll be here when you get back."

She hoped.

Watching Kane swing gracefully up on the horse, she admired the picture the two made together, the beautiful spotted horse and the tall, graceful man. The old time western painters, Remington or Russell, would have leaped at such a subject to paint.

Closing the door behind her, she searched for a latch, but it had none. What was this thing about Kane never wanting to lock doors? She pushed a chair in front of it, to give her warning if anyone tried to come in. Sitting in the rocker, watching the door, she knew the chair was of little consequence if someone wanted to get inside.

Her gaze wandered around the room, settling on the bookcase against the wall. She walked over to pick up the small, manila-colored tobacco sack with round gold labels on each end of the string tie. Also on the shelf stood a tobacco tin—identical to the one inside the cave.

She'd seen Kane roll tobacco out before. It wasn't that he smoked often, piling the tobacco on the little white paper seemed to be a habit thing, something to keep his hands busy in times of stress.

Like baking bread.

Was it that innocent, or was her father trying to tell her something he couldn't say in the letter?

Jowanna lay on the bed, pulling the covers up over

116

her head. She inhaled the masculine smell, and tears fell unnoticed from her eyes as she tried to push away her feelings for this man.

Who wanted her incapacitated or dead?

She prayed it wasn't Kane Landry.

## Chapter 8

Jowanna curled up on the bed, her mind a jumble of thoughts. What if Kane had been watching her all along and knew about the cave? If he had, that's where he was going. To see what she might have found. Maybe to destroy evidence.

She should have taken away the can, thrown it in the brush somewhere. When he saw the empty can he would know she'd found something.

Maybe he already knew—if he had taken her father's note from her pocket. But she could have lost it in the storm easily enough. Her mind was torn in two directions.

She dozed fitfully off and on, dreams of her mother and father mixed up with Jason, and the Señora, and Delia.

Waking once, she listened to what had startled her out of her restless sleep.

The agonizing cry of the puma.

Jowanna lay back and pulled the covers up high, but not before she heard the wind moaning through the scrubby trees and brush nearby, piercing the cabin walls between the chunks of dried mud. She sat up abruptly, straining her ears for the sound that crept beneath the wind. The steady clip-clop of a horse and rider.

Someone was approaching, slowly, with caution.

She looked around the room for a place to hide but there wasn't a possibility. The minutes stretched as she waited. The door latch lifted. A voice muttered, the wind swept away the sound.

Determined not be an easy mark this time, she

reached for the rifle hanging on the wall just as the chair slammed to the floor and the door swung open.

Kane bounded into the room, filling it with his masculine energy. He stopped abruptly when he saw her backed into the corner like a scruffy kitten, ready to do battle—the rifle pointed at his middle. He took a stride toward her before she demanded he stop. He looked furious, but behind that fury she detected something else in his eyes. Surely not amusement.

As she dipped the heavy rifle slightly, he swept across the room, grabbed the weapon and flung it on the bed as if it had been a toy. In one fluid motion he grabbed her shoulders with both hands and began shaking her as an adult might shake a small, unruly child.

"Good God, woman, that rifle's loaded."

Angry herself, she almost missed the puzzled, hurt expression in his eyes that quickly disappeared as fast as it had come.

He pulled her close to his chest, crushing her in a bear hug. She could hear him talking; the sounds came rumbling from deep in his chest where her face was pressed.

He held her away to look into her eyes. "Want to tell me what that's all about? Was someone here?"

She shook her head. "No, but I thought—you woke me out of a sound sleep, and it didn't sound like you coming." It was a lie. She had feared he'd found the cave and the empty tin and had come back to get the information, one way or another.

"Come, sit down," she said.

They moved toward the little table, and he poured coffee from the pot hanging over the red coals in the fireplace.

"I searched all over the area where you said the boulder came down. Didn't find a sign of anything after the rain, but I could see where you slid from, and the boulder below. That was a long fall; lucky you didn't break your pretty little neck."

"You didn't see the piece of lumber at the top?"

How could it not be there? Unless someone dragged it away. Was he lying? Staring into his somber eyes, impossible to read his expression, she sighed, looking away.

He shook his head. "The rain would have washed away the other traces you saw, but the timber would have been there. Maybe you imagined it. You'd been through a lot."

"Did you see anything else? Or maybe I should say, did you *not* see anything else?" She didn't bother to hold back the sarcasm, the thread of frustration from her voice.

"Like what?" He reached across the table and touched his hand to her cheek.

She couldn't pull away for the life of her.

"I like your hair loose, but I like it in one braid, too. You look like an Indian maiden."

"Thanks. Thank you," she managed. His compliments were so odd, as if torn from him without his consent.

****

Throughout the night, Jowanna wakened now and then from her cozy nest in the blankets to see Kane sitting at the table, drinking coffee. Once she awoke to watch him with his head on his arms, leaning on the table, asleep.

Her heart went out to him, and she wanted to slip out of bed to touch that lion's mane of hair, caress those hard planes of his face, smooth the tired lines from around his eyes. She tried not to remember the feel of his long, hard body against hers on this very bed. The way'd he kissed her, his gentle caresses, his fiery need—she even now wondered how he held back.

Creeping forward, she pulled off one of her covers and wrapped it gently around his shoulders. He didn't awaken.

Back in the warm bed, she lay a long while watching him, as if she could somehow guard him in his sleep, in his vulnerability.

But logic intruded into the emotion that clouded her senses. If he didn't see any evidence of foul play up there on the mesa, then either he took it away or someone else had before he got there. And there were still the note and map lost from her pocket—a loss that was unaccounted for.

The next morning she crawled out of the warm covers to make coffee while he slept. When he awoke, his eyes devoured her, his tongue touched his bottom lip in a way that spoke volumes. She knew he wanted to hold her, to kiss her, but he stayed still.

"Ah, coffee. Thanks for making it. Reckon I dozed off."

Did his trying to stay awake and alert all night mean he believed her? Had he seen more than he let on? Was his denial an attempt to protect her? Or someone else?

He looked at her, his eyes probing, but turned away when she didn't flinch.

"It'd serve you right to bob down the mountain on one of the burros," he said lightly, as if regretting his need for her. "But I won't do that to you—this time. I'll go saddle up Shambles."

When they were ready to leave, she turned to look at the little cabin and thought sadly of how close she had come to trusting him. She'd let him make love to her—and loved him back. But he apparently didn't think of himself as a free man.

Kane walked in front, leading the horse and she followed, content to have them set the pace. Watching his broad back, the surefooted grace of the man, it was easy to picture him in an old-time gunfight, but she couldn't see him stooping so low as to sneak a boulder down on someone or do any of the other things that had happened to her since she arrived.

Her heart and soul cringed at the thought. But who else could it be? And why? All the signs pointed to him. Was he playing some terrible game of cat and mouse with her? Saving her life one moment, threatening her existence the next?

For whatever Kane Landry's reasons, there was no one else to hold accountable.

When the foothills leveled out to the desert floor, he helped her off the horse to stretch her legs, and then when she'd walked around a bit, he climbed up into the saddle and pulled her up behind him. After they had gone a ways, she nudged his back lightly with her balled fist. "Hey. I don't remember coming this way."

He turned in the saddle, a wide grin causing his eyes to crinkle at the corners in an engaging manner. She felt her heart skip a few beats. She touched her fingers to her lips, remembering.

"That's paying attention pretty good—for a tenderfoot. Since you're so all-fired curious, thought I might as well take you on up to the mine with me. Some of Mac's gear is there. Thought you might want it."

"Thanks."

"And I left a few assay samples behind that need to go to Phoenix." He said the words as if guarding his macho image, not wanting to appear too considerate.

She could have said no. Maybe she should have. Anything could happen in a mine.

It was too late to worry about that now; she had probably gone past the point of no return. Whoever was after her wouldn't let her get out of the Superstition Mountains without finding out what she knew.

"I don't want to be in the way."

"Oh, I'm sure you will be," he said cheerfully. "It's okay, though. No one but me and Mac's ever been here, that I know about. It can get pretty spooky, 'specially at night."

*No spookier than that old house of yours*, she thought, but she didn't say it out loud.

"First we come down to level ground for a while, and then we have to climb up again. We'll have to walk part way in. With the burros you can ride some, but I left them at the mine."

"Are they safe there alone?"

He laughed. "No puma in its right mind would mess with an ornery burro. Not unless he could jump him from a tree or a ledge, and there isn't anything like that near the corral."

"How about coyotes? I hear them from the ranch house."

"They're harmless. Sometimes they run in packs, but even then they wouldn't bother a large animal unless it was sick or dying. Then they'd pull it down."

She shivered at the matter-of-fact way he spoke of life and death.

"Can Shambles manage it up to your mine?"

"Oh, yeah. He's as surefooted as they come, but I wouldn't trust even him to ride up that mountainside. 'Bout time we started walking."

He swung a booted foot over the top of Shambles' head and slipped down, holding up his arms for her.

He held her close so that she slid down the entire length of his body. The mischievous look in his eye when her feet touched the ground told her it was intentional.

She had to grin back.

"Think you can walk okay? It's kind of late to ask, but you're so game, I nearly forgot what you've been through since yesterday."

"I'll make it." Just riding the horse had started her entire body to protest with a dull aching. The bruises and bumps she'd received came back in a rush, so that her very skin hurt, but darned if she'd let him know.

"You can ride Shambles, if you need to. I can trust

his footing if I'm leading and he's without my weight on him."

Jowanna looked over the edge of the ledge they were traversing. Not on your life would she perch up high on that horse and look down. It was bad enough this way.

"No. Go ahead, and I'll follow along at my own pace."

At one point in the trail he swatted his horse's rear end to get him to move ahead and turned back to reach out a hand to her. The trail had gradually narrowed, and after climbing what she perceived to be the largest mountain in Arizona they were behind it and going downward into a valley.

"There's a mesquite tree coming up around the next bend. Let's sit for a spell." He smiled encouragingly.

She sighed, sinking onto a large rock under the welcome shade.

"You got sand, Jowanna. I'll give you that." His eyes were filled with undisguised admiration.

Too exhausted to answer, she felt a stab of pleasure at his spare praise.

"This is wild, beautiful country," she managed at last, after he had given her a sip of lukewarm water from the canteen he carried on his belt.

He nodded, looking around in satisfaction. "That it is. Takes an extraordinary person to see it, though." He studied her thoughtfully, until she turned away first, flustered by his probing look.

He pointed down to the valley below. "Outsiders think the desert is all browns and grays, but feast your eyes on that. The yellow are brittlebush, with blue lupine mixed in. Sometimes when we get a lot of rain in the spring and fall you'll see acres of Mexican gold poppies and orange globemallows. You can't see them from here, but on down toward the arroyo there are huge cottonwood trees and some sycamores. And I'll let you in on a little secret. There is a waterfall here in the Superstitions."

"Now I know you're teasing. What could make a waterfall here? Who owns this?" She spread her arms out to encompass the air around her.

He snorted. "No one owns it. God maybe did at one time, but He probably threw up His hands, not knowing what to do with it. Sometimes miners with claims think they own more than they do. Did Mac mention anything about all this in his letter?"

She almost asked which letter. That would have been a disaster. She wanted to trust him, more than anything in the world, but her father had warned to trust no one.

Was Kane fishing for information? She decided to play along and see if she could discover what he wanted to know. It might shed some light on all her unanswered questions.

"You mean problems with mining?"

He nodded. "Right. I wondered if in his letter to you he mentioned anything about mining problems. Old Jacob Waltz would be doing handspins down in Hades now, if he knew about how things were going up here in his backyard."

"You think he's in Hades?"

"Sure. Where else would he be? He was so used to 120-degree summers, he'd probably have to wear a coat down there anyway. Nowhere else would suit him."

They laughed. She felt relaxed with him, in spite of the notion that he was trying to elicit information from her about what she knew or what her father had written her.

"My father did mention a—a legacy. An inheritance, I think he called it." There, part of her secret was out. If he took the letter from her dresser, he would have known that anyway. When she hurried outside after hearing the noise upstairs, he had been in the barn, though. He couldn't have taken it unless he had an accomplice in the house.

"That's peculiar. I can't see where he came up with that. We aren't showing enough color to pay our expenses."

She felt gooseflesh rise on her arms as she began to worry how foolish it had been to come up here alone with him. He might be her mortal enemy. At the very least he was not telling the truth. Unless her father had made a discovery that he didn't even tell Kane about.

But how could that be? They were partners and friends. How could he hide anything from this man who knew this country like his own backyard?

Kane stood behind her with his leg nearly against her back. He would only have to give her a shove and she'd go soaring off into space, landing Lord knows where down in the valley. It was faint comfort to think that with Delia missing and her father dead under mysterious circumstances, anyone meaning her harm might have to be very cautious about adding another body or missing person. The sheriff had already been out to investigate once. And with only Steven and Kane living here, there weren't too many options for suspects.

But what if she was dealing with a madman? Someone totally illogical who didn't harbor a thought for consequences?

Kane's voice broke up her depressing reverie.

"Come on, it's not much farther. I want to get in and out again so we can make it down hill by dark."

"Scared of the dark, are you?"

"No. But I don't want that old puma sneaking up on us, either. Not until we get down and away from the ledges."

Suddenly he stopped and let the horse go so that it galloped into a clearing as if it had come home. Shambles went at once to a stream running down the side of the mountain and put his nose in to drink. Somewhere from the rear of the property came the raucous, squeaky-squealy sound of a burro.

The site was disappointing after her expectations of what a mine might look like. There was nothing sinister about the place. Sunlight dappled down through palo verde and mesquite trees. A few scattered pieces of machinery lay about, looking forlorn and used up.

"What's that thing?" She pointed at an odd-looking bit of machinery near the entrance to a cave.

"That's a dry rocker. Want to try your luck gold panning while I get my ore samples together?"

"Panning?"

"You did so good coming down here, I plumb forgot you was a city slicker, ma'am," he drawled with a long wink that made them both laugh.

He reached under a pile of odds and ends and pulled out a round metal pan.

"Come on, I can take a few minutes to show you how it goes."

He led the way to a bend in the narrow stream where a lively rush of water washed through. She knelt beside him as he crouched down and began dipping his pan and circling with a deft wrist movement that made the sand in the pan swirl around, some of it falling back into the stream.

"Here, let me show you how to move it." He took her hand. She felt a simmering flush beginning from inside, meeting the warmth extending from his big hand wrapped around hers. It felt as if it belonged there. Their faces close, they looked at each other, gray eyes meeting with brown, as if they would never look away again.

It was a heart-stopping moment in time, and she wanted it to go on forever. He leaned forward and kissed her, claiming her lips with such passion that she had to return it. They held each other close for a long time after the kiss, and she felt the thud of his heart within his chest, next to hers. She broke away first, with a sigh.

A muscle quivered in his jaw, instantly replaced by a rueful grin. "Okay, watch me now."

For a moment she lost track of the panning process, so intently was she staring at the muscled width of his shoulders, the way the curve of his back gracefully led to the bend of his hips, the length of Levi-clad legs tucked underneath his body.

He looked up suddenly, catching her staring.

"Are you paying attention?"

She nodded. *You bet I am*, she wanted to retort, hoping her face didn't reflect her flustered reaction. "How will I know when I find gold?"

He laughed. "You'll know. The greenest person alive can spot color the first time. Here, take this to use." He removed a handkerchief from his shirt pocket and unwrapped a round magnifying lens.

She held out her hand, but she didn't understand why she would need a magnifier.

"If you get any 'show'—something yellow in the pan—hold it up to the light if it's big enough. Turn it around and around, and if it's gold it'll stay the same color at any angle. Pyrites or fool's gold changes colors."

"I had no idea it was this complicated."

"It's not. Just have fun, and don't worry about doing it right. If you get bored, call for me at the entrance."

She wondered why she couldn't go inside with him. He answered that question before she could ask.

"The mine's not safe for anyone not knowing the whereabouts of the shafts. So don't follow me."

The lightly veiled threat. It wasn't the first time Kane had mentioned danger to her. Was he looking out for her, or did it have a totally different meaning?

"We keep a rolled-up blanket inside the tunnel for

emergencies. I'll spread it under that mesquite tree, and if you get tired, stretch out in the shade."

He walked over to the saddle gear he had removed from the horse and brought back the rifle, laying it next to her on the ground.

"Take care of this. I may be a while."

She looked up at him. "I don't know anything about a gun."

He smiled briefly. "It's a rifle, not a gun. And I know you don't. You tried to shoot me back at the cabin, remember?"

She did remember, knowing full well she couldn't have pulled that trigger on him no matter what.

"It's for signaling more than anything else. If you even hear a noise that could be the puma, shoot it into the air and I'll come running."

She swallowed. "Where—where would a puma come from? Does he sneak up on the ground? Climb trees? I've no idea what kind of sound you want me to listen for."

He cupped her chin in his hand and looked down into her eyes, and she felt herself drowning in the brown depths of his gaze. "I'm sorry I scared you. I wouldn't leave you behind if I really thought there was danger. I just want you to be careful, is all."

"Okay. I'll be careful." She watched him stride away toward the yawning entrance to the mine and disappear inside. The sun didn't seem as bright nor the air as fresh, after that. He had taken her enjoyment with him.

She shook her head. "Nonsense," she said out loud. He didn't want her, preferred his missing wife, so why should she moon over something she'd never have? She was learning new strengths—learning of a surprising new resilience in Jowanna McFarland that she never would have guessed was there. It didn't take long to lose herself in panning. A calm, peaceful silence filled the area around her. No bird sounds, no wind. Only an occasional soaring buzzard cast an eerie shadow from high above in the bright blue sky.

It was then she felt eyes boring into her back. Was Kane already here? She swerved around to catch a tall, exceedingly skinny Indian crouched down at the edge of the path, staring at her.

What should she do? Since it was only one Indian, it could be the one they called Apache Joe.

She swallowed. "Are you Apache Joe?"

He nodded and stood to move slowly toward her. "Kane here?" he asked.

She wasn't sure how to answer, but he didn't look menacing and she had the rifle close by. Pointing toward the mine entrance, she said, "He should be back any time."

"Who are you?"

He spoke in awfully short sentences, but that could be good. "My name is Jowanna McFarland."

With a look of pure astonishment on his hardened features, he came closer to peer into her face. She didn't step away but looked right back at him.

He seemed satisfied and nodded again. "Yep. Same eyes."

"Did you know my father?"

Apache Joe stared down at the ground for so long she thought he might have dozed off. Then he sat down in front of her, crossing his legs and getting comfortable. He brought out a dirty, well-used leather pouch and poured a pocket watch out into his hand and extended it to her.

"Oh! I recognize that from years ago," she exclaimed. "*From your loving wife*, it will say on the back." She turned it over and rubbed her fingers across the familiar inscription.

Apache Joe didn't seem surprised. She handed it back to him, and he put it in the pouch and tied it to his concho belt that seemed to barely hold up his too-large trousers. He must have been a good friend, for her father to give him the watch...unless... Forbidden thoughts began to nudge her, and she scolded herself for being so paranoid. *Everyone* couldn't have harmed her father.

"Did you know my father? You must have, if he gave you the watch."

The Indian looked into her eyes. "Everything is not always as it seems," he said mysteriously.

"Is that an old Apache saying?"

He laughed, teeth big and yellowish. "White man say so."

But the thought wouldn't leave about how he might have acquired the watch and she looked at him, wondering. Whether he saw the doubts in her eyes or just decided to leave, he stood and removed a small, tied bundle from his jacket pocket. "Burn this at ranch. Purifies." She looked down at the clump of sage in her hand, and when she looked up he had disappeared.

Time passed and she decided to get back to panning. While she leaned over, concentrating, she heard a noise behind her. She grabbed up a rock and leaped to her feet, ready to defend herself against the puma or anything else.

"Hold up there." Kane threw his hands in the air with a gesture of surrender. "Sorry I sneaked up on you like that, but I didn't want to startle you."

She grinned, self-conscious about her fighting stance. "It's a reflex. I've had—quite a time since I came here." She thought again about telling him of the hanging woman, the scorpions and the whole lot. But he hadn't believed the only thing she had told him, about the boulder rolling down on her. What would he think of the other mishaps? Probably that she was a neurotic, fearful, childish person who should go back home before another day had passed.

She didn't want that. For more reasons than she could count.

"Apache Joe came to visit."

"I'll be damned. He's mortally afraid of women. Did he talk to you?"

"Sure did. And what's strange, he showed me my father's pocket watch. I wonder how he came to possess that."

"No secret. Mac gave it to him one day when the Indian admired it. Mac was like that."

"Oh, thank goodness." She had begun to think the worst about poor old Apache Joe.

"Find anything?"

Jowanna shook her head, holding up the wide-mouthed jar he had given her to put her treasures in. "I don't think so."

He knelt at her side and took the jar to look solemnly at the contents, holding it up toward the sun. She had the greatest urge to kiss that upturned face.

"Nope. Nothing here, I'm afraid. Did you enjoy it? Get lonesome out here alone?"

"I appreciate being alone at times. I can enjoy my own company." After her father left and Jason died, she had always felt alone.

He looked at her, their faces so close together she could almost hear his heartbeat. "Where you been all my life?" His voice was light, bantering, but she sensed the seriousness beneath, and her heart contracted.

"In other words, it could have been different if you had met me before Delia—is that what you're saying?" She wasn't going to run from confrontation. She needed to know.

He frowned, pulling away from her. "One's got nothing to do with the other. You're different—with different qualities. Good, honest, qualities that a man wants in a woman. I've never known anyone like you…"

She waited, but he never finished the sentence.

Kane took the gold pan from her hands, set it down and pulled her to her feet, leading her to the blanket under the shady tree.

He threw his hat on the side and stretched out on his back, with his fingers laced beneath his head. She sat down gingerly, remembering what had nearly happened at the cabin.

"Hell, any man with a lick of backbone would be glad to have you—any way he could. But I'm not built that way, I reckon. I need..."

"What? What do you need?" She stared at him, loving the look of vulnerability that showed in his expression. It wasn't there often.

"Look at you. Your face is full of color, your eyes are sparkling, not to mention your hair is windblown and you've a streak of dirt across that pretty little nose. It's plain to see you don't belong out here. But you're trying to fit in."

She was tired, and his voice soothed her. She lay down next to him, careful not to touch. He didn't want her. He was waiting for Delia to return; he'd said as much.

He rolled over on his elbow to look at her. He traced a finger gently across her lips, making her heart race and her throat dry. The finger continued down her small, squarish chin and down to the pulse-beating hollow of her throat, lingering just long enough to feel her heart speed up.

He touched the buttons of her blouse and opened them gently. She closed her eyes, wanting him so bad it hurt.

"Oh, God, you're so beautiful," he groaned, burying his face in her neck, kissing her throat and moving downward, his lips trailing hot against her tender breasts. Breasts that felt near to bursting with a need for his mouth, for his hands.

She reached up and held his head between her hands, bringing him to face her. Right at this moment she admitted to herself that she loved him dearly. She pulled him to her, and rained kisses on his closed eyelids, the tip of his nose, and settled on his lips.

They clung together until they both finally felt that the wind had freshened and begun to blow hard. In the far distance they heard the crack of thunder, and a dark cloud scudded across the sky.

He scrambled to his feet, running to look off the ledge to the bottom of the valley and turned, his craggy face full of concern. "We have to go. Now. If we get caught up here in a rainstorm, it could mean we won't get down for days."

*Would that be so bad?*

As if he understood, he walked to the blanket where she sat and pulled her outstretched hands upward until she stood next to him. He put both hands on her shoulders. "We don't have food, we don't have protection from the rain—except for the mine, and that's not one hundred percent safe, because it's been known to wash out when the creek swells. Outside of that, I damn well wouldn't mind staying up here with you for days."

She looked at the little rivulet of water that she had just been panning in. Was it just fear that he wouldn't be able to control himself and his need for her if they stayed, or was he seriously worried? She couldn't take much more of this off-again on-again lovemaking. "I'm ready. Can we make it to your cabin?"

"Maybe. But I know a short cut to the ranch, if you're willing to take a chance. It would get us there in almost the same time it would take to reach the cabin. It's all downhill. In some places it may scare you. Biggest problem is, if the storm hits, there's nowhere to hide."

She closed her eyes, thinking. To get to the ranch and a warm shower, a night in a real bed, she'd be willing to risk it. With Kane at her side. "Let's go."

He looked at her with concern. "You sure? You've got some bruises and scratches. Do they bother you?"

Jowanna shook her head, gathering up the

blanket.

\*\*\*\*

He hadn't exaggerated. The trip was mostly downhill. Kane went first, with the horse behind him, and she followed. The trail was cut well into the terrain from constant use. As he explained, the Apaches had used it a long time before white men intruded on the landscape.

She looked up into the sky, wishing away the dark clouds that had begun to draw in toward the mountains as if magnetized by the peaks. Once in a while a low, ominous rumble of thunder sounded off in the distance, carried up by the current of wind from the desert floor below.

The wind rose to a shrieking crescendo, moving through the weirdly balanced rocks and natural caves they passed by. At times she could barely hold her balance, needing to lean into the rocks for protection.

Moving along behind the horse and man, she felt the hairs on the back of her neck stiffen and she stumbled, feeling as if hostile eyes pierced her back, following her progress. The mountain aura was sinister, threatening. The air and atmosphere surrounding her felt as if the Superstitions guarded centuries of secret shadows—of life and death—jealously protecting the memories.

She shivered and hurried to catch up, not knowing if she would ever make it down to safety.

## Chapter 9

By the time they got halfway down, Jowanna began to recognize a few landmarks. Looking down at the basin that held her father's grave, she paused to stare at the insignificant little pile of stones. Should she ask Kane and Steven to move his buried effects back to the ranch now? The reason for his wanting to be buried up here alone was finished, the elaborate scheme to hide his letter to Jason.

No, she answered her own question. As much as she'd like to ask them to move her father's buried belongings, it would take a full explanation of why and of what she'd found. Even if Kane had stolen the note from her father, he would only realize that she was on guard now, and the rest of the letter wouldn't mean anything to him.

Why would he keep it, then, rather than just read and return it to the pocket while she slept? Chances were the letter had fallen from her pocket during the storm.

She wanted to believe that.

Kane had been turning to check on her constantly while they moved along, to make sure she was still following. When he saw her stop, he came back.

Together they looked down on the pile of stones. The silence between them lengthened. His closeness and the grave of her father brought in her earlier apprehensions with a rush. Her father had warned to trust no one.

He put his arm around her shoulders, as if to allay her fears and doubts. "I wanted to bring you back to the stones. To let you see for yourself that there wasn't any timber or a sign of anyone else being there when the boulder fell."

Fell? Is that what he believed? Hadn't he listened to anything she told him? She stopped gazing down into the valley and turned her face up to him, staring into those deep brown eyes, shielded now by the low-worn Stetson.

The wind had died away somewhat, portending the onset of the rain she could smell in the air.

She was sure the earlier storm must have flattened the short, sparse desert grass, but someone had taken the big piece of timber away. Or he was lying. He couldn't have mistaken the mistrust in her eyes. She didn't bother to hide it.

"I saw where the boulder was. I'm not arguing that it didn't fall. But these freaky things happen all the time. A boulder sits precariously on the edge for eons of time and suddenly lets loose for no reason."

"But there *was* a reason. I tell you, I saw the timber and the marks where someone pried the boulder, and I saw the shadow of movement above." She reached up to push back his hat, looking into his skeptical eyes, the mellow chestnut color sucking her in until she was swirled downward by a vortex.

He grabbed her hand and held it a long moment before he released it.

She pulled away and turned to look back down on the grave.

"It could have been the horse moving around restlessly before he took off," he said with the soft reasonableness one would use to sooth a child.

That made her see red. *Let it alone. No need to pursue this track.*

She hated to believe he had anything to do with rolling the boulder down on her, but who else could have? What was the point of arguing? Either way she was out of luck because, even if he didn't do it, he didn't believe her story.

Who was the real Kane Landry? Was he a ruthless, bitter man who would stop at nothing to have what he wanted or this man walking along with her, a quiet, contained cowboy, a book reader, a strong gentle person who was her first love?

Jowanna shook her head, wondering if she would ever piece it all together.

"Come on, girl, the storm could hit any minute." He took hold of her elbow and propelled her forward. "I want to be on the desert floor by then, riding Shambles."

She had forgotten the impending storm for a moment, but the worry laced within his words jolted her back to the present. While they continued down the mountain, the skies darkened with the oncoming dusk and the threatening black clouds.

As soon as they were down past the foothills, he mounted Shambles and pulled her up behind him. Jowanna closed her eyes, leaning her head against his wide, warm back, and inhaled the essence of him.

"Put your arms here," he commanded, pulling her hands forward as far as they would reach. "Hold on, we're in for a bumpy ride."

Suddenly the horse reared. Above the noise of the storm she heard a crackle from movement in the brush nearby.

Kane pushed her leg away, reaching back for the rifle mounted on his saddle.

She screamed in fright as a band of javelinas ran across the trail from the brush at one side to disappear into that on the other side. Their grunts of irritation and fear mingled with Shambles' snorts and prancing hooves.

"Quiet, feller, that's a boy. It's okay. Just a bunch of crazy pigs."

He turned in the saddle. "Sorry I had to push you, but I needed the rifle in case it was El Diablo. Storms agitate the big cats. They get restless and come down from the mountains then."

"Is that puma like a spook or something? I've heard him a few times, or at least I think it's him, but I've never seen him."

"He's spooky all right. You may never see him—if you're lucky. He's older than anyone can remember, and his pelt is scarred from fights and bullets careening off his body. He's charmed. If it hadn't been for him attacking your father, I've never wanted to kill him. He's just part of this life, like the sky and the mountains and the weather."

"Maybe he didn't attack my father." That was as near as she'd come to expressing doubt about his death. She trod carefully, not wanting to say too much.

"'Course he jumped Mac. We found the spent shells and the blood from the wounds when the cat hightailed it up toward the caves."

"Do you really think my father killed himself?"

In spite of the threat of oncoming storm, he slid off the horse and circled her hips with his long arms, to set her on her feet and look into her face. "You got something stuck in your craw. Spit it out. What do *you* think?"

"I asked you first."

He shrugged and touched the restive horse on the neck, soothing him. "It doesn't seem like something Mac would do," he admitted reluctantly. "But how do we know what he was going through—his leg probably broken from the fall off that ledge, and helpless, with only a couple of bullets left? Would you rather have it end sudden, or be ripped apart in a slow and agonizing death by the claws and teeth of a 100-pound wildcat? It comes down to that, doesn't it? He couldn't have been sure his last bullet would kill the lion."

His words sounded reasonable, and she'd never approached it from that angle. If her father had killed himself, then all these things happening to her were just to get her to leave. Maybe someone already knew where the treasure was and wanted her to go.

Then it couldn't be Kane. Why would he have saved her life? Because three deaths and disappearances would be too hard to explain to the authorities? Maybe. Or it could be Kane and Steven were conspiring together. That would make more sense. One person couldn't be everywhere at once.

He looked up at the sky. "You ready?" He swung back up into the saddle and maneuvered the horse near a rock so she could get on behind him, then urged the horse forward.

The rain began to pelt them, and the skies opened up with jagged slashes of lightning which at times struck into the ground around them. Shambles galloped forward, as if he enjoyed it. She admired the horse, but with each hoofbeat she thought of the holes he could fall in, breaking a leg, tossing them off onto the hard desert ground. They could perish out here without protection.

By the time they finally made it through the back gate of the corral, the storm had passed and the dark clouds had moved on across the peaks, over to the next county. The sky lightened perceptibly, a pre-dusk characteristic of the desert.

Kane put his leg over the horse and leaped down. His hands wrapped around her waist—hands strong and powerful. He held her up a long moment, looking into her face and then let her down.

Steven ran out to greet them.

"Where've you been? You're soaking wet. I've been worried sick about you, Jo. You just disappeared. I ' thought..."

They all knew he referred to Delia's sudden departure.

"I'm okay. I took Shambles out for a ride and..."

Kane stood close, holding her arm for a moment, steadying her.

Suddenly she missed having her breast crushed

against his firm back and, in looking up at him, she saw in his eyes that he missed it, too.

"You took Shambles? I don't believe it!" Steven looked so astonished that both Kane and Jowanna burst into laughter.

"She's like your mom," Kane said, not letting go of her arm yet. "My sister was afraid of damn near nothing."

"It was lucky you found her up there. I mean, in all that country, how odd to run into her. I want to hear all about it."

Yes, wasn't it lucky, and odd. Too much of a coincidence? Now that she had time and distance to think about it, Steven's comments made sense. She waited for Kane to tell Steven about her near escape with the boulder, but he turned away without any mention of it.

Had Steven's use of a nickname for her irritated him? Why should it?

"Cold? Maybe you should go inside." Steven touched her shoulder lightly.

She shook her head, wanting to wait for Kane.

The after-storm air was thick with moisture, but clean-smelling and warm.

She and Steven leaned against the corral, watching Kane remove the heavy saddle as if it had been a piece of paper and begin to rub down the horse, checking his hooves in the process.

"He loves that mean bastard," Steven commented.

"Of course he does. And Shambles isn't mean, he just has a mind of his own," she added. It was a delight to watch the way Kane tended to the short, sparse mane and tail.

A very unusual horse. A very unusual man.

"That's right. You rode him all the way up the mountain. I still think you both are pulling my leg. No one but the big guy rides that horse. Ever. I'd make a gelding out of him, tame him down, but Kane wants to use him for breeding."

His words gave her a feeling of pride. She hadn't been afraid, and the horse knew that. Maybe it was that simple.

"He wants to make this into a paying ranch, you said."

Steven nodded. "He also wants to quit prospecting, or says he does. I don't know if a prospector ever can quit. It's like an obsession, like a gambling fever. Just over the ridge, just inside the next cave is the mother lode. They're all afraid that the day they quit, it'll be the bit of land left unchecked where they could have found the bonanza."

"That's sad. Did my father have that mentality?"

"I guess he did. It didn't bother my mother none, since my pa was addicted to prospecting, too, and she was used to it."

"You resented it?"

"Hell, yes. What kind of childhood do you suppose I had? Out here alone, the men always gone, tutored by my mother..."

It sounded pretty good to her, recalling the lonely years she'd spent away from her family, in a girls' boarding school. Even when she was home she never invited a friend over. Her mother didn't like strangers in the house and was very judgmental of her friends.

"...to have her die and I couldn't help her."

Steven's blurted words dragged her back to his reflections. The underlying bitterness in his voice caused a chill to zigzag up the back of her neck. He was a very angry person. Capable of doing almost anything to get his way?

"Of course, both Mac and Kane professed to having reasons for going for the gold, not like some who just search for the hell of it." His voice returned to normal tones, and the straight line of his mouth eased.

"Do *you* think Kane will ever make this a real ranch, with workers and a corral full of his precious horses?"

"He's got a start right here, if he'd breed the Appaloosa with Mirla. She's a little champion."

"He called her a mustang."

Steven laughed. "Yeah, I know. He's got a one-track mind sometimes. He bought her for Delia, but she's as good as he'll buy up in Oregon."

"I thought you didn't like horses."

"Don't. But when they're the only transportation..." He threw up his palms in a gesture of futility.

"So you don't think he'll make this a paying ranch again?" She persisted with the question.

Steven shrugged. "He's stubborn enough, if that's all it took. But he's got a lot going against him. First problem is this ghost legend. Then when Mac died and Delia came up missing...well...even if he had the money, it's impossible, the way I see it. Ranch hands are notoriously superstitious. He'd never get anyone out here to help, no matter what he paid them."

"Who keeps the story alive? With just you and Kane here now, looks like it would die down."

Steven looked evasive, for the first time avoiding her eyes. "Who knows? Old Charlie in town yaps constantly. Lots of people gossip for the lack of something better to do."

Jowanna could see where it could hurt Kane's chances at having a ranch if someone in town kept running off at the mouth about ghosts.

"You never showed him the portrait you painted of the Señora? The one who looks like me?"

"Oh, hell, no! He'd have a foaming fit. He thinks by avoiding the topic, it will eventually be forgotten."

They stood for a moment, not speaking.

It was a shame, the silence on this place. It was meant to be full of life. It wasn't hard for Jowanna to imagine the corral full of beautiful dappled horses, a delightful mixture of children playing in the courtyard, a bunkhouse full of men and a plump, sunny-faced woman in the kitchen bossing everyone and cooking up a storm.

What a strange notion. It was almost as if she saw through someone else's eyes. The Señora's? Her father's? She rubbed the chill from her arms.

"What do *you* want, Jowanna McFarland? Why are you still here?"

She jumped, startled at Steven's in-your-face question.

"I'm here because I wanted to denounce my father for leaving us. When I learned he was dead, that changed things. I had to make my peace with him. The only way I could do that was to see his grave, to sort of visit."

Steven turned her shoulder so that she had to look into his eyes. "And did you make your peace? Did seeing his grave tell you anything you didn't know before?"

What a strange way to put it.

She nodded, tears pushed from behind her eyes. Tears of weariness, of buried pain, of just missing her father by days. She thought of his note. How much could she tell Steven? Surely she could trust him more than Kane. Steven could hardly have been up there to roll the boulder down on her. Would he have had time to get there before her? He said he didn't ride horses. *Trust no one.*

"Did you hear me?" He touched her cheek to get her attention.

"No, I'm sorry, I was woolgathering. What did you say?"

"I asked if anything special turned up on your adventure. If you were hurt..."

He broke off to watch Kane come toward them, as if he didn't want to continue the conversation.

What did he mean, was she hurt? Why would he imagine she was hurt? The scratches on her face were barely visible.

Kane hadn't had a chance to talk to him alone yet—to tell him about the boulder. He would only know about it if they were in this thing together. Had he and Kane joined ranks against her father and now her? Were they both after the treasure mentioned in his letter? That would explain Steven's slip of tongue.

"Come on, let's get inside, get some dry duds on," Kane said.

They took her arm, one on each side, to escort her inside the house. They bantered words back and forth, friendly enough but with a faint trace of animosity buried beneath their voices. She wondered if they both had loved Delia. Steven spoke so highly of her, with none of the bitterness that Kane expressed. Was that the cause of the underlying hostility she sensed so strongly between the two men? Or was it her healthy imagination working overtime again?

After they changed clothes, they sat drinking coffee for a while until Kane reached across the table to touch her hand holding the cup.

"Tomorrow, early, I've got to head into Phoenix to buy supplies and take the ore samples to the assay office. I want you to come with me."

Steven stood, scraping back his chair. "I should leave, too. We can meet in Albandigos for breakfast before you go on into Phoenix and I go to Tucson for a gallery showing."

It sounded as if neither man wanted to leave the other alone with her. That was strange.

Jo can come with me if she wants to," Steven added, as if in afterthought.

Kane stood to face his nephew. Standing a head taller, he loomed over the smaller man, who didn't back down an inch.

"Jo? Since when did you two get so cozy?"

She was right before in thinking it irked Kane that Steven gave her a nickname, and it seemed as if

Steven used it to goad on purpose.

"I'm not talking about her *visiting* Phoenix. I'm talking about her getting on a bus and leaving. She needs to go home," Kane said.

"No!" Steven exploded and then looked down at his boots as if the loud word tossed into the room embarrassed him. "I mean, she may not be ready to leave yet. I know you don't like company, but she's Mac's daughter, for God's sake. She has as much right to be here as we do."

"I don't see it that way. What if something happens to her? I'd have a hard time explaining. The sheriff would haul me away and I'd never see the light of day again."

Is that all her disappearance or death would mean to him? That he was inconvenienced? "Shouldn't you two back off and let me speak for myself?" She stood, arms akimbo. She felt the flush of anger infuse her skin. The very idea of these two talking about her as if she were invisible.

They looked so surprised at her interruption that she almost laughed. She would have if Kane's words hadn't hurt so much.

"I've decided to stay here a bit longer..." she began.

"But why?" The words burst from Kane's lips, his brows crashing together with exasperation. "You said you needed to see the grave. You've seen it and nearly got killed. It doesn't make any sense for you to stay on longer."

Did that mean he believed her?

"Nearly killed? What are you talking about?" Steven interrupted. He leaped from his chair to stand facing Jowanna. "What's this?"

"I'm sure someone rolled a boulder down on me. I saw the tracks and the scuff marks. But when Kane checked it out, all signs of it were gone."

Steven turned to Kane, questions in his eyes.

Jowanna held her breath. What would Kane say?

146

Kane sat back down and sighed. "I didn't see anything. Not a sign of tampering. But what would be the point of her lying? Someone could have covered up his tracks. And the rain didn't help matters."

"Hard to believe. Why? And what did you see?"

When she'd finished telling Steven about the large board and the trampled grass, he walked toward the window, to look out.

"Then you *should* leave. I told you before, this place is cursed."

"Damn it, Steven, shut the hell up!" Kane bolted from the chair, knocking it over. Jowanna recoiled at the snap of the chair hitting the floor.

In an instant Steven was at her side, as if to protect her.

Kane scowled down at them. "This place isn't cursed. It takes fool talk like that to ruin things, and I don't want to hear it."

She moved away from Steven's hand on her shoulder and put some space between them. Was Kane jealous? Impossible idea.

"I don't believe the Superstition Ranch is haunted, either, Steven," she said. "But if it is, the spirit could be benevolent, not harmful."

"Either way, that's nonsense." Kane still fumed. He stalked to the window and pulled aside the white curtains to look up at the mountains.

"So many things have happened..." Steven began.

"I don't want to hear another word about a ghost. Sis loved it here. She died with appendicitis, but that could have happened anywhere. Mac had an accident. We know the dangers when we decide to prospect. As far as Delia... Well, I feel like she's out there somewhere, laughing at me."

Jowanna looked at Steven staring wide-eyed and open-mouthed at Kane, as if this was the first time Kane had ever expressed this opinion about his missing wife.

Steven recovered quickly. "I'd no idea you felt that way."

Jowanna thought he meant to reach up and put an arm around the bigger man but changed his mind at the last moment. That underlying vein of resentment between them, was it all coming from Kane? All because of Delia?

She didn't like to think that.

"I don't agree with you—on any of it," Steven said. "You know my feelings on the subject of people dropping like flies around here. Delia's down some sinkhole—fell or pushed."

That was the first Jowanna had heard of that idea, and it sent goosebumps up her spine. Kane had told her he received an annulment through the mail from her in Phoenix.

Kane spun around to grab hold of Steven's arm. Jowanna saw the smaller man flinch with pain, but he didn't try to move away.

"That's a lie! What's got into you? Delia never went out alone. If she's in some sinkhole, someone threw her in, and I damn well didn't."

"Ah—sorry, that just blurted out. I didn't mean it." Steven disengaged Kane's clenched fingers from his arm and stepped back.

Did Steven know something he wasn't telling anyone?

Jowanna needed time to sort this out. *Was* Delia at the bottom of a mine shaft? Had someone first tried to scare her off and then, when she didn't budge, killed her?

That scenario was coming uncomfortably close to the same thing happening to Jowanna. First someone tried to frighten her away and then he tried to kill her. Her father's death was another unexplained incident. He was at home in the desert, knew his way around in the dark. Why would he suddenly fall and break his leg? It didn't hold water.

There was still the possibility that someone had pushed him off a ledge and then shot him as he lay helpless. Or put his rifle out of reach and let the puma do the rest. She held her arms to keep away the shiver that ran through her body.

"I don't think Jowanna needs to hear all this from us," Kane turned to leave. "Reckon we can go together tomorrow."

"On second thought, I should put some finishing touches on a portrait. I'd hate to hold you up. You go on in, and I'll follow the day after. If I make it by the weekend, I'm good." Steven stood and stretched nonchalantly.

Kane shook his head stubbornly. "No. I'll wait. We'll leave together."

What was going on? It was as if Kane didn't want to leave her alone with Steven.

Somehow the petty emotion of jealousy didn't fit Kane. How odd, to be jealous of her when he apparently pined for the beautiful Delia. He was an enigmatic, mystifying man, Kane Landry. The more she was around him, the less she knew him. But the more she wanted to know him and know he wasn't at the bottom of anything terrible going on here.

She wished with all her heart that both Kane and Steven would go. She was anxious to figure out the game her father mentioned in his letter. If Kane had taken that letter from her pocket, there was no way he could know what game her father referred to. She hadn't even figured that out yet. Still, he couldn't know that, either. He had to assume she understood and needed privacy to look. Was that the real reason he didn't want to leave Steven alone with her?

Steven looked at Jowanna and shrugged, palms up.

"I'd say it's time to turn in. Jowanna's had a busy day." Kane turned to study her, his eyes somber, full of questions. His lips split apart in a wide grin and he touched her lightly under her chin. "Hey, you did fine today. You've no idea how different you are from the timid city girl who first came to the ranch."

Yes, she did know and was glad that he knew, too.

Steven went outside, Kane disappeared into the living room, and she sat a moment, enjoying the quiet. A thunderous bellow erupted from the living room. Jowanna rushed toward the sound of outrage.

"Who the hell messed up this room?" Kane demanded.

Jowanna stared at him with dismay. He was pointing a shaky finger toward the table that had held the rocks.

"I...I assure you...no one messed up the room. I did try to tidy up a bit, but..."

"What'd you do with my rock collection?"

"Collection?" Her voice rose in a squeak that she struggled to regulate. "I thought someone had just dumped some old stones on that beautiful table, and I..."

His glowering wasn't helping her to remember what she'd done with the damn things. "Oh, now I've got it. I gathered them into a wastebasket and dumped the lot of them out front near the porch."

"Woman, that's the..." Words failed him, and they glared at each other, neither backing down.

"If the silly things are so valuable, you should keep them in some kind of a case," she defended herself.

"Why? This is my house. I can keep them any damn place I want to. I've had that collection since I was a kid. There's some gold nuggets amongst them. I don't suppose you noticed?"

She shrugged. "No, not really. They looked quite dull. A rock is a rock, after all."

He snorted, a rude sound that she decided it was better to ignore.

"And what about this rug behind the couch? Did

you think you could hide the destruction of a valuable antique Navajo original?"

"Oh, that was a shame, and I am so sorry. I'll repay you, of course. Perhaps the bleach mixture was a little strong, but I was only trying to get that stain out of it."

"You put bleach on it?" The horror rose in his voice and his eyes sparked lightning flashes as his dark brows winged downward and his lips clamped together as if to avoid saying too much.

How can a person be so furious and still be so controlled? It was amazing, and she was impressed in spite of her defensive indignation. "I assumed since it was on the floor, it was only a rug."

"Only a rug?" His repeating her words began to annoy her.

"My, we are cranky, aren't we? I was just trying to help. This place is so full of dust one can hardly..."

"Cranky? You call me cranky? After tossing out a 20-year rock collection and ruining an irreplaceable antique Navajo rug, you stand there and call me cranky? Dust is a part of our lives."

Steven pushed open the front door. "What's going on here? I thought World War III had broken out, and we're barely finished with World War II." He looked from one to the other, his eyes full of questioning surprise.

Jowanna started to laugh, remembering how hard, how industriously she had tried to clean, and how useless it all had been. At first Kane hid his twitching lips behind his big hand, and then he began laughing, too.

Steven stood there watching as they laughed until they threw themselves down on the nearest couch. She had to promise to help him round up his precious rocks and also that she would never clean again without his supervision.

****

That night Jowanna slept as never before in the big house. There were times when she felt drowning in darkness, swept down, down, down into a vortex that she couldn't get out of. In spite of that, her tired body took over her mind and demanded sleep. Scratching and creaks in the hallway that had her imagination in an uproar when she first arrived barely caused an uneasy twinge now, she had grown so used to them.

Of course it felt better with someone else here. She knew Kane and Steven were close in their rooms. She dozed again, and then, not sure if she was dreaming or not, she awoke screaming into a pillow, struggling to push away the soft fluffiness across her face. To her horror, she felt gloved hands and scratched at them in desperation as the pressure continued downward until she couldn't breathe. Then suddenly the weight was gone and she sat up, wide awake now, throwing the pillow off onto the floor.

The room was empty, but a *presence* remained, surrounded by the faint trace of perfume. Was it a threatening presence or one that woke her in time?

"Open the door!" She heard Kane pounding and then Steven's voice outside in the hallway.

Unsteadily, she crept out of bed and hurried to the door.

They burst in and Kane swept her in his arms, sitting on the edge of the bed with her in his lap. Steven sat on the other side, staring at her.

"What happened?" Steven was the first to speak.

Jowanna gestured toward the pillow lying on the floor by the dresser. "Someone tried to smother me with that. I woke up just in time to fight it off."

"Oh, my God!" Kane's eyes showed honest concern, his mouth grim with anger. He pulled her closer to his chest. "Who would do that? It's just me and Steven here, and I damn well..."

"Me neither, so scratch that. Anyway, you must have had a nightmare. Your door was locked from the inside, remember? How could either of us have gotten in here?"

"Right. The locks don't have keys; the knobs just turn from inside."

She remembered the scorpions and the way the knob had fallen off. No, she knew how the locks worked, and she definitely remembered pushing in the knob to lock it before she went to bed.

Kane reached to smooth the hair back from her shoulders, and she flinched, her eyes wide with fear.

"Don't do that," he said, his voice soft with a thread of bitterness weaving through it. "Don't ever flinch from me. I'd never hurt you."

*How do I know?* she wanted to ask.

"You've had a bad dream," Steven suggested.

She'd had a lot of bad dreams in her lifetime, and this wasn't one of them.

Jowanna squirmed off Kane's lap and sat up against the wooden headboard, pulling the covers high about her as if she were cold. "I didn't dream it, and I didn't imagine it. Someone was in this room. Someone tried to smother me."

Kane stood, his weight releasing from the bed made it bounce, causing an odd expression of annoyance to cross Steven's features and then disappear. Steven's composed tranquility was irritating and it was gratifying to see a change, even so briefly, in his expression.

Much more open with his feelings, what Kane felt was expressed in his face or actions immediately. Walking around the room, he examined first the pillow and then went to the window. "Do you always leave the window open? It gets cold by morning, even in the summer."

"Not to me. Remember I'm from New York. I like fresh air. Could someone have come in from there?"

Kane shook his head. He leaned out and looked upward. "Not likely. The roof is steep under your window. A person could come from higher up, the attic, maybe, but no one's here but me and Steven."

He still held the pillow and she looked away, not wanting to imagine his big, strong hands holding it over her face. The gloved hands had felt smaller than his would have been—or was that just wishful thinking?

"You know, if either of us wanted to put a pillow over you while you slept, I doubt you could stop it."

That gave her pause for thought. Something didn't feel right here. Those hands would have easily succeeded that task before she awoke, with or without the Señora's whispered warning.

Did that mean he didn't do it? Or perhaps that he didn't want to kill her, merely to frighten her into moving ahead with her father's instructions?

"Leave your door open. I'll be close," Kane said.

"I—I don't think I can do that, not with what happened," she argued.

"Sure you can. Locking it didn't help, did it?" Steven said. "You've just had a bad dream. No wonder, with all you went through up on the mountain. Trust Kane, he'll watch out for you."

She looked at Steven, who for the first time seemed to agree with his uncle.

"I guess it's okay." What else could she say, since they were so sure she'd had a bad dream. By now she nearly accepted the idea. What else could it be?

Yet she knew the warning voice had come to her, waking her. Waking her up in time to save her life. Someone wanted her to leave, and if the scare tactics didn't work, wanted her dead.

There was no escaping that thought, no matter how hard she tried.

What would be his next move—and when?

## Chapter 10

When the first light of day struck the side of her bedroom wall, Jowanna stood looking out the window at the desert, serene and tranquil, so different from the day before when they'd outrun the storm.

The water in the old-fashioned pitcher and bowl was icy cold, but she put the washcloth to her flushed face, and it felt good. She could take a shower in the little bathroom off the kitchen after they were gone. Kane had rigged up an ingenious system to heat water using the sun.

Her door was open and she tried to be quiet. They were probably still asleep.

She stepped out into the hallway and tripped, falling into a pile of blankets a little aside from her door. Arms and legs flailed as she tried to disentangle herself from the covers.

"Hold on here, don't get your saddle cinched too tight." Kane's voice came muffled from the center of the pile.

She relaxed, waiting for him to come to the surface.

He managed to sit up with them still tangled together. He looked so different now, sleep clouding his eyes, his thick hair tousled like a boy's.

She wanted to kiss him, remembering the feel of his lips against her own.

As if reading her thoughts, he hugged her, impatiently pushing away the covers between them. He kissed the top of her head and then worked down to her closed lids and her nose and finished with that odd, tingling nibble to her lips until she couldn't stand

155

it a moment longer.

She reached up and caught a handful of hair, pulling him to her. Close.

After the kiss, her pulses sped through her veins in a zinging pattern that brought a flush to her face. A warmth started from the center of her body and spread like wildfire.

He groaned and held her for a moment, his warm breath sighing into her neck, his long, thick eyelashes moving against her cheek.

She didn't bother to analyze this feeling, this heady warmth that spread from the pit of her stomach up through her body, swelling her breasts so she thought they would burst with the pressure.

"Make love to me one more time, Kane," she felt her own whisper. The plea never left her lips for he had claimed them again with his.

"Well, well, what's going on?" Steven's voice intruded.

They came apart abruptly. She struggled to get up, and Steven leaned down to help her.

"Ah—thanks for watching my room, Kane," she managed, running down the stairs.

"I'll do it the next time," Steven offered, laughing at her retreating back.

**** 

Later, sitting at the kitchen table drinking Kane's coffee, she tried not to stare at him. She knew he must be having problems in that direction, too, for he stood up restlessly from time to time, striding to the window to look out.

Her feelings for him were so mixed up. Fear, mistrust, need, desire, all together. Instinct told her she could trust him with her life. Yet her father had warned not to trust anyone.

Trusting the wrong person could have cost him his life. Perhaps Delia's life, too.

"I'm fixing to ride into town. You get ready to

come." Kane looked at her, eyes dark and unfathomable. In spite of the doubts and fears of this man, a remembered warmth began its traitorous spread from her midsection up to her throat when he looked at her like that.

So in control, so formidable at times, yet she saw, in a brief flicker of expression in his eyes, a concerned tenderness that he so badly didn't want to show.

He had turned and moved away toward the stairs, confident he would be obeyed.

"I'm not going anywhere." She folded her arms across her chest in a gesture of finality. Not a moment ago she was considering dropping the whole thing, of going back to her mother with her tail between her legs, giving up. No! This was the new Jowanna. The old one had died the night her double stared back at her, hanging in agony from the top of the stairs.

"Damn straight you're going!" Kane, halfway up the stairs, bolted back down to face her.

"Is this ranch in both yours and my father's name?"

Kane looked at Steven and then back at her, disconcerted.

"Yes, but..."

"No buts. I told you from the beginning I didn't come here to claim any part of your ranch. But that mortgage does give me the right to stay here. I can't leave yet." She turned away and went into the kitchen, with both men following her.

"Why not? You saw the grave. Isn't that what you stayed for?" Steven's voice sounded strange, really interested in her answer.

Had she said too much? She backpedaled. "I mean, things aren't ever going to be the same at home between my mother and me." Were both Kane and Steven wondering if she had discovered something at her father's grave? When they didn't speak, she continued.

"My dear, sweet mother lied to me for eighteen years. I don't know if she knew about the Senator framing my father so he couldn't come back to us—I hope to God she didn't. I need time to sort that all out before I go back. I may never go back there."

Jowanna sat at the table. Her hand jerked, spilling some coffee as she moved the coffee cup around the oilcloth. She watched the soft brown rings form beneath. The color of Kane's eyes.

She knew now why she was willing to risk her life to stay and find out what her father wanted to tell Jason. Besides discovering the truth behind his sudden death, and being near Kane as long as she could, she needed her share of the treasure—if there was a treasure—to make a new life for herself. There was no way she could go back and be dependent on her grandfather's money for the rest of her life.

Kane came closer into the room, hooking a chair away from the table with a long leg and straddling it, facing her. His eyes were no longer hostile, his expression softened to understanding.

"I reckon you're welcome to stay here as long as you need. But you can't stay alone."

"Why not?" Steven asked.

"Because, if she's right, someone pushed half a mountain down on her. Didn't you have something to deliver to the gallery in Tucson? That's what you said last night."

They must have sat talking after she had closed her door and went to bed.

"Do you believe someone tried to smother me last night?" She watched their expressions.

Kane looked down and scuffed his boot on the tile, stalling for time. Then he took a deep breath and faced her. "I don't see how that could have happened. Your door was locked from the inside. You had a bad dream. That's why I hate to leave you alone."

So, the same way he refused to believe anyone had

pushed down that rock on her, now he had completely discounted last night's episode. It did look farfetched in the light of day.

Jowanna almost regretted not confiding in him about everything that had happened to her since arriving at Superstition Ranch. Maybe it would have been good to have it all out in the open.

"I can't believe anyone deliberately pushed a boulder over on her, either," Steven said with a hard edge to his voice.

"But..." she began to argue.

"Well, if you're not leaving, my business can wait," Kane said to his nephew, both ignoring her protests.

"You don't trust me to stay here alone with her?"

This was as close as the two men had come to airing their mutual distrust, and she didn't want to be the focus of it.

"Hold on. Don't I get to say something? You both go. I'd like some peace and quiet here alone. I can take care of the horses." She needed to be alone, to explore the significance of her father's letter about the fireplace game.

"She's right," Steven said. "If she's afraid of one of us—or both—then with us away, she can assume nothing will happen to her."

Jowanna didn't like the way he put that.

Kane ran his hand through the crown of his thick mahogany-colored hair, indicating his inner agitation. "You got a point." He turned to scowl at her. "Just so you stay put. And stay off Shambles. You almost got him killed the last time you took him without permission."

"Yeah, we still hang horse thieves out here, you know," Steven said sarcastically.

"Oh, hell, I didn't mean that, but he could have been harmed. He's..."

*He's the whole point of Kane's dream*, she knew that without his saying it with mere words. "I'll be fine. I'd like to catch up on some reading, stuff like that."

"And don't tidy up anything," Kane commanded, a twitch at the corners of his mouth.

Soon after, she stood by the gate and watched them roar away in their separate vehicles, the dust rising above the desert floor for miles.

Looking up at the house, there was that instant, as in the first day she came, that she felt rather than actually saw a curtain move upstairs. She had been on edge ever since she arrived, but no need to be now. The only thing left in the house was her and the Señora, and the lady had proved an ally, not an adversary.

Then why this heavy foreboding, this uneasiness that wouldn't go away?

****

When Jowanna went inside, the house crowded around her with a heavy silence. The air was cool and comfortable, while outdoors it was already getting hot.

The notion of spending nights alone in the eerie old house nagged at the back of her thoughts and she tried to take her mind off the prospect by thinking more about her father's letter. What did he mean about the game—the rainy day game?

She took her steaming coffee mug and stepped down into the living area, where she sprawled on the couch. How luxurious to lie about as disheveled as she pleased. Her mother never would have allowed it. Back in New York City, before she left her room each morning she had to have showered and dressed for the day. Jowanna laughed out loud, just to hear her voice.

"Tomorrow I won't even change out of my PJs and robe. So there! I'll come down and spend the whole day that way, if I want to." *Get a hold on your imagination, she can't hear you,* Jowanna scolded herself.

She pushed impatiently at the dark cloud of hair streaming around her shoulders, and a stab of irrational excitement zinged through her. No wonder her father had chafed under the family restrictions. She could see that he'd always been a free soul, a dear charming man who should never have been captivated by her mother's cold beauty. But he had been—a mistake they both had paid for.

It would be so easy to hate her mother, but damn it, it was also easy to understand her attraction for John McFarland's unconventional uniqueness. It was probably the only time her mother had strayed from her straight and narrow existence, and the prescribed life laid out for her since birth.

"I've grown up!" Jowanna said to the room, disturbing dust motes that sifted in front of the picture window over the couch. It was true. She had changed so much from the timid, self-effacing person who had come here. For the first time in her life she felt in control of her destiny. She was afraid. Someone had tried to kill her twice. But she was persevering. She had to find the treasure, make a life for herself, somewhere, somehow.

It was sad to think of leaving this place, even though it had proved so very dangerous here.

Jowanna stared at the fireplace. That was where to start. She closed her eyes, trying to imagine the family on a rainy afternoon. She, Jason and her father would have been reading a book or playing some game together, while her mother would sit in the sunroom, doing needlepoint and listening to her music.

The comfortable glide into her memory brought a bittersweet pleasure. The three of them had been so close. When she lost first her father and then Jason, she'd felt abandoned, like an ancient Eskimo put out onto the ice alone.

It wasn't that her mother wasn't caring—in her own way. She made sure Jowanna never wanted for anything material. Yet she had handled the loss of her husband and son with a typical control that sealed her off from additional hurt—not letting anyone else inside.

Jowanna didn't want to live that way. She was ready to take the hurts with the pleasures—if there were any in life. Her memory suddenly fixed onto a specific element.

That was it! The fireplace game. She remembered and hurried over to have a closer look. A big fireplace, it might take a long time to explore. When did Steven say they would be back?

She ran into the kitchen and found a towel to wrap around her head for protection from pieces of rock if any should pop out. Lighting a lamp and pushing the andirons aside, she pulled out the crisp, burnt wood with the little shovel.

Yes! It was nearly the same shape as the fireplace in the New York apartment. The one her mother considered too messy and her father used to insist upon lighting on those long winter nights. Large enough to walk into if you bent your head just so.

Inside the wall of the one back home were loose bricks here and there, where her father used to hide little trinkets and notes for her and Jason to explore and find. When it rained or snowed, it had been a delightful game and took the place of their usual outings. He left little songs or a loving poem, and once a gold locket waited for her behind a brick.

Jowanna hadn't realized how terribly much she had missed her father over the years; she had concentrated on being angry with him all that time.

Inside the fireplace, she turned to face the living room. It wasn't even necessary to bend her head. She ran her hands up and down the bricks, tentatively feeling—for what? Would her father have put the loosened brick up high, thinking Jason would be here to look?

Her fingertips would be cut to pieces—how would she explain that later? Impossible to use gloves, it was necessary to feel each brick. Armed with a screwdriver filched from the kitchen, she pried and searched. Her fingers were scratched and numb from moving over the rough brick surface. The steam from her breath made the area close and claustrophobic. It wasn't a game anymore. It had become hard work.

She bent down and emerged from the fireplace to sit on the floor. Just dusty enough to mess up the furniture, it wouldn't do to leave any telltale stains to cause questions.

Staring at the fireplace, she studied it as if to wrest the secret away by sheer will. Suppose one of them decided to return early? She knew Kane was worried about her staying alone.

What if, in discovering her father's cache, truths turned up that she didn't want to face? Truths about Kane, for example. He reminded her of a wounded animal, ready to go on but needing help and not knowing how to ask for it.

If only she could trust him. If only he trusted her.

The afternoon shadows slanted through the windows, and still she searched. Each separate brick had to be tested. To move hastily past one would necessitate doing this all over from the beginning if she hadn't found a loose brick when she finished.

Her stomach began growling, and she suddenly realized she hadn't eaten all day. Grimy and weary, she stumbled out of the lamp glow inside the fireplace to the gloom of the living room. The walls closed in on her. It had grown so silent that she could easily hear the ominous sounds of the creaks upstairs.

She couldn't quit now. If she stopped and ran upstairs to cower in her room all night, she would never have the heart to begin again tomorrow. And if Kane or Steven returned before she finished, it would be all over. She couldn't very well string out her reason for staying here beyond a reasonable time, could she?

In the kitchen, she cut off a thick slice of Kane's fresh bread and buttered it, sprinkling on a bit of cinnamon and sugar. That and a cup of coffee should hold her until morning.

She ate, looking out on the desert from the kitchen window. The moon rose gracefully from behind the eastern range of mountains, seeming to pause momentarily as if transfixed on a mountain peak. Then it moved upward, the moon rays swimming down over the desert floor. The nearby bushes swayed with a light breeze. She could hear the shwoosh-shwoosh of the tamarack trees close to the porch.

A feeling of tranquility spread through her, a feeling of soothing comfort. There was that weird intuition again, as if she looked through eyes other than her own. Was she really a reincarnation of the Señora?

"That's a stupid idea!" she said aloud. Maybe she looked through the eyes of her father, who must have stood here many times gazing out over the desert.

She set down her cup and, with a determined lift to her tired shoulders, headed into the front room to do battle with the fireplace once again. She lit another lamp and left one on the sideboard, taking one inside with her.

Working from as far up as she could reach and down toward the bottom, testing each brick with the screwdriver, she let time pass. Finally, one of the bricks made a dry, screeching sound and gave way under her prying. She wedged the screwdriver first into one end and then another and gradually worked out the reluctant brick, which fell to the floor. She breathed a sigh of relief when it didn't break. That would have been a tough thing to explain.

She held the light close and bent to peer into the long narrow hole. Imagining insects of every description was easy, but common sense told her none could have gotten in behind the brick. Maybe, maybe not. Steven had mentioned that scorpions had been known to live years trapped without food or water.

She sighed. Nothing to do but put her hand in.

Holding her bottom lip between her teeth, she reached her arm into the long hole in the wall. Back, back until her shoulder was touching the firewall, her cheek mashed into the harsh brick.

There! Her fingers barely touched something soft and spongy. Ugh! She imagined everything from a tarantula nest to a dead mouse, but knew she had to follow through. This was no time to indulge in her old phobias. She made a tremendous stretch, afraid for a moment that she had pushed the object even farther away, but no, she pulled it back toward her with trembling fingers.

Emerging from the fireplace, the object clutched in her hand, she could see beneath the light that it was a leather pouch, smelling faintly of tobacco and mildew. She stuck it inside her shirt and then, tired as she was, began tidying up the fireplace to eradicate any sign of her snooping.

Without warning the front door pushed open.

"Steven! You startled me. What are you doing back?"

The darkness from outside met with the lamplight to silhouette him in the doorway.

"What are you doing up at this hour of the night?" he returned. "Housekeeping? I thought Kane forbid that." His voice had an edge of puzzlement behind the attempt at humor.

"Ah—no, not exactly." Her head wrapped in a towel, holding a dustpan full of crushed cement, she knew he must be puzzled at her appearance.

He came closer, pushing his foot backward against the door to close it.

She could see he was waiting for an explanation.

Stall, she thought. Stall long enough to come up with something plausible. An earthquake, maybe? Kane mentioned they had them from time to time. Especially up in the Superstitions.

"Did Kane come back with you?" she asked.

Steven shook his head and flopped down on the couch, still watching her face. "Nope. Last I saw of him, he was heading down the freeway toward Phoenix. I called the Tucson gallery from Gila Bend. Good thing I did. They wanted another painting that I'd left here. Had to come back and get it."

Sounded reasonable. A lot more reasonable than what she could come up with on the spur of the moment. Should she trust him? She had to trust someone.

As much as she hated to admit it, Kane was just too conveniently in the wrong places at the wrong times. She didn't think they could both be plotting against her.

She took a deep breath and made an irrevocable decision.

"Steven. There's something I should have told you."

*Don't trust anyone.* Her father's note said not to trust anyone. Was that the memory of her father's letter or a voice whispering in her ear? She decided to ignore it.

Jowanna told Steven about the scorpions in the dresser and the hanging woman, and repeated about the boulder that had crashed down on her.

As she talked, she watched his face. His expression reflected surprise and concern, which allayed her fears somewhat, although he might have been a good actor. He would be naturally better at it than Kane. He didn't interrupt.

When she'd finished, he leaped to his feet, and before she had a chance to react, grabbed her and held her in a hug. A friendly, brotherly hug.

"I'm so sorry you've gone through all this, Jo. I'd no idea. Something's going on here. Has to do with Mac's death and Delia's disappearance, I know that. I hate to think Kane would have anything to do with either one, but who else?"

She couldn't tell by his voice if he felt sorrow or grim satisfaction at the idea. Her spirits dipped, she hadn't wanted her suspicions confirmed. She had wanted Steven to heatedly deny his uncle's involvement.

"I don't know. Could outsiders be trying to..." She broke off at the pitying look in his eyes. "I found..." she was about to tell him about the pouch she'd just found in the fireplace but changed her mind abruptly at the quickened look of interest in his expression.

"What'd you find? Is that why you're tearing up the fireplace? You're looking for something?"

He took her hands and pressed her fingers open with palm up. He held the light closer.

"You've cut your fingers. How'd you do that?"

She pulled her hand away, not caring for his touch. Not after Kane's.

"Never mind that. My father left instructions—near his grave..." How much could she say? Had she gone past the point of no return?

Steven waited, his eyes narrowed in speculation.

Had she made a wrong decision to confide in him?

"He left a note behind that said to look for something in the fireplace. I can only suppose that's why someone rolled the boulder down on me and tried to smother me, to get at the note or to stop me from doing so."

"How would killing you help find anything?" His voice was steady, his words reasonable.

"I thought of that. With the boulder, someone may have surmised I'd already found something and decided to take it off my dead body. That or he could have wanted me to stop looking."

"And with the pillow?"

"Something's not right there. It was as if this person wasn't really trying. Maybe wanted to rush me along in my discoveries."

167

"You're probably right there. If, for instance, Kane tried to hold a pillow over your face—I doubt you'd be here today."

His words brought in the image of that happening, making shivers run up her body. She didn't want to hold that idea. "He couldn't have. The door was locked."

Steven's raised eyebrow told her there were ways. She decided to ignore the bait to pursue that direction.

"Do you have this note you found at Mac's grave?"

She shook her head. "No. It was taken—ah—lost in the rainstorm."

"Poor little one, what you've been through. Have you figured what it's all about?" The note of caution in his voice made her edgy and she pulled away from his arms.

"Maybe. I think—I don't know for sure—but I think it concerns assets my father knew about and wanted Jason to know about, too. Then it got out of hand."

"But how could your father have a treasure without Kane knowing? They were partners and close friends."

She hadn't said anything about a treasure. Assets and treasures were not necessarily synonymous. "I don't understand that part, either." Caution claimed her, and she quickly decided not to tell everything. "All I know is I didn't find anything in the fireplace, and I checked each brick, believe it or not."

She saw the look of skepticism, the guarded, secretive look in his eyes, the look she first saw the day they met. She could hardly blame him; it was all so bizarre. And she was a terrible liar.

He pushed her gently down onto the couch and sat beside her, pulling off the towel turban so that her hair fell around her shoulders.

"Such lovely hair. Someday I'd like to paint you. Would you let me?"

He had an upsetting way of changing emotions or subjects, like a chameleon. It was as if he had dismissed all that she told him before about the treasure and the near-misses on her life.

"You already have."

He shook his head. "That wasn't you. That was the Señora. I want to paint *you*."

"Maybe. If I'm around long enough," she hedged.

"Oh! That's right. How stupid and insensitive of me. Your life may be in danger—although, my dear, I think you've exaggerated some of your fears."

"What do you mean?"

"The scorpions probably crawled into that container and had lived there for years. The hanging woman, well, what can I say? You had just seen my portrait of the Señora. It was probably a trick of lighting. The lamps give off eerie glows, especially on these shadowy stairways at night. You admitted how many phobias you had."

Yes, she did say that at the beginning. But she didn't believe a word of his patronizing attitude. Had she misplaced her trust in him? Thank goodness she hadn't told him about the pouch.

"I've got to leave for Tucson early in the morning. Come with me. It'll be safer for you," he coaxed.

Jowanna shook her head. "No, but thanks for asking. I'll stay and rest. I've worked hard today, and all for naught." She laughed at her small attempt at a joke. She was on her own now, more than she had ever been in her life. Trusting only her awakening instincts, she had to discover what her father had tried to communicate in his last desperate letter.

It was the clue to everything good and bad that had happened to her since arriving at The Superstition Ranch.

Chapter 11

Telling Steven goodnight, Jowanna ran up the stairs to her room, wedging a chair against the door for some reason that she didn't stop to analyze. Once inside the room, she set the lamp down and plopped on the bed face down, too exhausted to worry about dirtying the comforter. She pulled open the leather bag and spread the contents out in front of her.

Disappointment rose into her throat like bile. There was a chunk of stone. She held it in her palm. Heavy enough to be gold, the lamplight refracted off it in multicolors of deep yellow.

A stone and a small scrap of paper.

She sighed, smoothing open the tightly folded note. At the very least, she was hoping for a detailed letter from her father telling her everything.

The paper was covered with a very precisely drawn map. The meticulous drawing showed a triangle, with the ranch house at the apex and Weaver's Needle at one corner of the base while a large, firm X marked the other edge of the base.

In line between Weaver's Needle and the large X he'd written The Cabin in tiny letters and beyond that, along the same line, he'd written The Mine. In the middle of the triangle, closer to the base, was a shaky circle that could only have been his gravesite.

He had known, even then, before he died, where he wanted to be buried.

The thought chilled her to the bone.

It was coming together. The large X wasn't the mine that belonged to her father and Kane. All along she'd supposed he referred to their mine, the one everyone knew about. No secret there. She should have known better.

Then what was the X? How could it remain a secret right under Kane's nose? Why couldn't her father trust his own partner with whatever he had found?

Suddenly the silence was shredded by low, heartbroken sobs. Jowanna sat up on the bed, her heart thumping in her chest. Chills ran up and down her arms and raised the hair on the back of her neck. The terrible cries sounded just outside her door!

Where was Steven? Had he heard it, too?

Cautiously, she stood, debating whether or not to investigate. She grabbed up the pouch, cramming in the stone and map, stuffing it between the mattress and springs.

If challenged, she didn't want anyone to find the map. Whoever her father hid it from would not hesitate to kill her once they knew everything she knew.

The sobs had died down to pitiful whimpers and she put her hand on the doorknob.

*Stay in the room. Wait.* The now-familiar voice pushed past her panic to command her attention. She sank back onto the bed, unsure of what she was feeling and hearing.

The darkened room closed in around her, like a tomb.

Suddenly a loud whinny came from the stables. Her bedroom window was open to the night air and she ran across the room to lean out, trying to see past the gables and the low-slung roof. Was that a flash of light in the stables? Maybe Kane had returned. Or maybe something was after the horses.

She thought about it, listening to the yip of coyotes in the near distance. What if El Diablo leaped the corral to get at them? Just because he had never come this close before didn't mean he never would. The last time she'd heard the puma's scream, it had sounded alarmingly near.

Hesitating only a moment, she ignored the warning voice and slipped open the door to run out into the hallway. She could hurry down to the stables, check on the horses and run back up before she had a chance to be really scared.

"Steven! Something's bothering the horses." She lit a lamp and held it in front of her as she progressed down the dark hallway. The lamplight threw threatening shadows all over the walls and ceiling, making the stairway look dark and ominous.

His door was ajar—Steven was not inside.

She opened Kane's room, holding the lamp high to avoid tripping over anything. His window had a different vantage point and she might be able to see the stable door. If the double door was closed, she'd leave well enough alone. She paused to lift her chin, inhaling Kane's essence of horse and man. It was a good smell and somehow reassuring.

At the window, she leaned forward to peer out. The stable door was wide open. In her preoccupation with the fireplace, had she forgotten to close it? Steven wouldn't have bothered to look in on the horses before retiring for the night.

But she felt certain that after feeding them she had closed the door and lifted the latch into place.

Just as she put a hand on the stair rail, determined to go downstairs to check it out, the sound of voices reached her, and then footsteps on the porch.

Her first thought was of Kane and Steven together, but the feeling of a gentle, insistent hand on her shoulder stopped her headlong flight down the stairs to greet them.

*Wait. Wait and listen.*

Something about the whispers, the stealthy scuffling noise of the steps, finally got through to her. It didn't sound like a ghost, that was for sure. She blew out the lamp and crouched at the crest of the stairway, waiting.

The front door creaked open slowly. The voices continued, the hushed quality causing a sense of foreboding to crinkle up and down her spine, raising the fine hairs on the nape of her neck. She didn't recognize the speakers, couldn't pinpoint how many there were, but one of them could be Steven. It definitely wasn't Kane. She would know his deep rumbling baritone anywhere, under any circumstances.

Not Kane! The elation sang through her blood, fighting with apprehension as she began to understand that she had trusted the wrong person.

Whoever it was knew she was upstairs and didn't want her to hear them.

Her first thought was to confront them, find out who was skulking about—until she thought of the box of scorpions, the crashing boulder, the smothering pillow and the horrible memory of the hanging woman that was still imprinted on her mind.

The map! She had to get the map. She crept toward her room, waiting each step to hear a loud protest of the hardwood floor. She reached under the mattress to retrieve the pouch.

The rock was too heavy to carry. She put that back in the pouch and removed the folded paper, her fingers trembling in her haste. Below, it sounded as if the voices were arguing. Stepping across the threshold of her room, she saw their lamplight flickering as someone made a sudden movement toward the stairs.

They were coming up!

For a moment she considered barricading herself in the room and then changed her mind. Even if they didn't crash open the door, she would have to come out eventually.

She stashed the map deep in the pocket of her jeans and stealthily climbed the stairs. She hated going up into that dark, shadowy place that resembled a black mouth, waiting to devour her.

Climbing slowly to keep the stairs from squeaking, she looked upward at the narrow attic steps. With a sense of desperation she tried the door of the locked storeroom.

It was open.

Hurriedly, she pushed inside and leaned against the closed door, heart pounding so that she couldn't hear if they were up the stairs yet or not. She took a deep breath, her nostrils clogging with the heavy scent of perfume, and struggled for calm. If they went past this room, she might dash down and outside while they searched the attic.

Her bedroll, along with her flashlight, was out in the stables alongside Kane's. He'd made one up for her when they got back from the cabin. just in case she ever needed it again, he'd commented, with that stern look that said he hoped she wouldn't. Why would he think she might have need of a bedroll?

Her only hope now was to get away and follow the map. Whatever lay at the end of the X was her only salvation, and the answer to everything.

She had blown out the lamp but carried it with her, unable to part with the promised light. Her eyes slowly adjusted to the gloom as the shuttered window let in ghostly slivers of moonlight to spill across the floor.

There was a jumble of old furniture piled around. Any one of the pieces would gladden the heart of a collector. She shivered. Why was the perfume smell so strong here? Was it the Señora trying to tell her something? Why was this room kept locked when nothing else in the house was?

She strained her eyes to look into the dark corners. Women's clothing hung in a narrow closet, some piled in boxes on the floor. Yes, Kane had said Delia's things were stored in this room.

Something nagged at her, something out of place.

The cot. There was a cot near the window, with a sleeping bag that looked definitely used, as if someone had crawled out of it in a hurry.

She sensed a presence in the room, a threatening presence. She put her head against the door to listen. The odor of perfume surrounded her like something alive—something with tentacles—reaching, reaching. In the stillness of the waiting house she heard doors slam. They were getting closer. Had that been her bedroom door? She leaned against the door, listening, hardly daring to breath. Surely they could hear her heart thudding in her chest.

Slowly someone climbed the stairs, footsteps approached the place where she stood trembling. She closed her eyes tight, praying that whoever it was wouldn't notice the storeroom was not locked as usual.

The steps came closer and closer, slithering, stealthy now, the voices stilled. They stopped in front of the door she leaned against. How many were out there?

Then, miraculously, they moved away, up the stairs to the attic above her. They carried a lamp that spread a flood of light under the door. She fought down an urge to step out and confront them—to find out who it was out there. Immediately she knew this was not a good idea. The old house felt saturated by a malevolence, the atmosphere thick with menace.

Pushing the storeroom door open cautiously, she stepped out and gulped fresh air.

*Get out. Get out.*

The voice again, urging her to move from her frightened stance, frozen in place like a rabbit in headlights. The steps above her on the attic floor were no longer stealthy, they sounded angry, stomping across the creaky floor.

They were coming out! Coming down the steps.

She'd never make it down the two flights of stairs

and out the front door before they caught her. Remembering the little dormer window on the first landing, she ran forward and tried it. Stupid of her! It had always been stuck tight with paint. Her heart sank down into her boots. She gave one last frantic tug and felt the latch move beneath her fingers.

It was opening! "Thank you, Señora," she whispered.

Jowanna crawled out onto the roof, closing the window behind her. The cold desert air struck like a blow after the dank closeness of the storeroom. The roof tilted alarmingly in places, and the moonlight twisted around the shadowy gables, lighting part and leaving part dark. They had only to look out the window to see her.

She crawled forward, toward the pigeon cage, and slipped inside it, letting the screened door fall silently back in place. Trembling, she lay as flat as she could, while the musty, ammonia smell of old, dried pigeon droppings gagged her and she frantically fought back a sneeze.

The reassuring feel of the map, crinkled in her pocket, lessened her terror. She wouldn't make the mistake this time of putting it in her shirt and losing it.

Why hadn't she just let things be and gone back to New York? Better yet, she should never have made the trip out here in the first place. Someone had to know her father left instructions, and now whoever it was must realize she knew where his treasure was. Someone had gotten rid of Delia and most likely caused her father's death.

One thing was sure. They were the ones who were walking in the hallway just now. Jowanna had the greatest urge to climb out of her hiding place and confront her enemy, get it over with and learn the truth. However, the continual feel of a light pressure on her shoulder, keeping her low, confirmed the recklessness of this idea.

She drew a deep breath and held it as they passed the window and then—moved back to stand in front of it. She wanted so badly to lift her head, in hopes of seeing them. She strained her hearing but still didn't catch Kane's rich baritone; she was sure she would know it, even if he had been whispering.

The sound of them trying the window latch turned her blood to ice. If they opened the window and stuck a head out to look, she would be helplessly exposed in the cage.

The latch held in place. The window didn't budge. The edge of the lamplight passed as they moved downstairs.

She felt the protective warmth surrounding her and gave thanks again to the Señora.

After counting minutes, which would take them off the stairway, she slithered out of her confinement and crawled toward the window. It was locked tight. Either they had re-hooked the latch or the Señora didn't want her to go that way.

Ear pressed to the window, from a long way off she heard the clink of glasses and the angry clang of a cast iron frying pan slammed down on the stove. They must assume she was hiding and had decided to wait her out.

She rolled on her side to look over the edge of the roof. A long way down. Her fear of heights came back to haunt her, constricting her breath, drying her throat.

Closing her eyes tight, it was hard to recall how far the edge of the roof was from the ground. At least ten or fifteen feet.

She had conquered most of her other fears. She might as well get on with facing this one. There was no way she dared wait until morning, when they would catch her here in the open like a butterfly pinned to a mat.

Who would come to save her? Kane? He wasn't due back for days. When he returned, she would have disappeared like Delia, only much more explainable. Steven would say she'd returned to New York.

Had Steven killed her father, then? Or was that an accident that played into his scheme? Had Steven's obsession to leave this place and make a new life for himself obliterated everything else? Was it so important that he had to have that treasure no matter what? That might explain the ghost story circulating in town. Steven wanted Kane to leave the ranch. He needed it closed and empty.

She must locate the treasure first and then find a way to warn Kane.

Jowanna slid down the sloping roof, trying to brake her descent by clutching the icy cold Spanish tiles as she slipped downward. She felt her blouse tear and the sharp tang of scraped skin. By the time the edge appeared, her palms burned, and her nails were bent and broken.

Aiming for a clump of dry grass in front of a huge cottonwood tree, she let go.

For a moment she sat stunned, the air knocked out of her. The noise of her slide across the roof and the fall to the ground had sounded like a thundering herd of runaway cattle, to her ears, and she sat still, listening, trying to catch her breath.

No one ran out the front door. The night as still as a graveyard. She shivered at the idea. Being in the dark was another of her phobias that must be conquered if she wanted to get away from here in one piece.

Jowanna stood up, feeling for any part of her anatomy that might be out of place. So far so good. Only her hands were raw and burning, and the place on her stomach where her blouse had torn open felt bruised and scratched.

The map! She dug her hand into her pocket and

felt the reassuring crispness of the paper. At least she hadn't lost it this time. The thought brought visions of Kane, and she gulped, not wanting her thinking to go that way. Kane, saving her life in the washout, holding her close and warming her icy cold body, the feel of his strong arms around her, his lips. Their bodies melting together...

She let the tears course down her cheeks, holding her arms across her chest as if to contain the pain, keep it from spreading. At that moment the realization struck her. She had fallen in love with Kane the first time they met, when he stood in the kitchen, bigger than life, looking at her with those somber brown eyes edged with telltale laugh lines.

And now her gullible belief in Steven had put Kane in extreme danger. When he returned, if Steven and his accomplices found her and the map, Kane would have to be done away with, too.

A chair scraped across the tile in the kitchen, and the lamplight wavered toward the living room. Someone was coming near the front door.

She crouched down and ran to the stables, her heart up in her throat all the way, expecting to hear a shout from the opened door.

Inside, she rushed to her bedroll and retrieved the flashlight. Mirla nickered a welcome, and Shambles walked forward to touch her shoulder.

The stallion would be quicker and more sure, but if Kane came back in time, he would need his horse. She wished there was some way of leaving a message, but it was important that no one suspect she knew the whereabouts of the mine.

Besides, what could she tell him for sure? Her suspicions? Not for anything would she have named Steven as an accomplice to this evil scheme as long as she didn't know for certain. They were family, all that was left.

****

Riding the mare out on the desert, Jowanna sighed with relief as soon as the ranch house disappeared from view behind a rolling hill. She sniffed the cold desert air, forgetting her danger for a moment, and became lost in the magic of the moonlit night. Every rock, bush and cactus took on a shimmering pale yellow iridescent light. The shadows swayed in a mystical dance with the wind as a partner.

What a pity she couldn't have shared this with her father.

She clucked the mare along briskly, afraid of making a noise that would carry back to the house in the unearthly still night. A sense of foreboding crept over her, spoiling her earlier sense of beauty in the landscape, causing her to raise her eyes to look at the shadowy face of Superstition. How many men had died trying to wrest the secrets from this mountain? How many, like the Señora's husband, lay in unmarked graves—sacrificial trophies to an unmerciful destiny? She imagined the mountain watchful—secretive—indifferent to human suffering—patiently waiting.

Waiting as a lover waited to unite with another forever.

Waiting just for her.

## Chapter 12

"Buck up, girl. This kind of thinking won't get you anywhere." She spoke out loud, skittering from under the heavy gloom of her thoughts. "Come on, Mirla. Watch where you're going."

They had been gradually climbing while the moon sank lower and lower, casting shadows on the desert floor that surely hid prairie dog holes, coiled rattlesnakes lying next to rocks, and tarantulas hiding in the brush. She held Mirla's reins with a tight grip, ready to pull her back if she startled. The little quarterhorse had stamina, but Kane said she wasn't as surefooted as Shambles.

Jowanna began to shiver in the cold, predawn air. She reached back and undid the bedroll, thinking to wrap it around her shoulders, and found herself looking down in dismay to watch the little flashlight roll out and tumble on its way down the rocky mountainside.

She needed that flashlight. The idea of traveling through the night chilled her even more. Pulling out a Levi jacket from the wrapped sleeping bag, she blessed Kane for being so thoughtful. It was as if his strong arms wrapped around her when she put it on.

What would Kane think of her when he found out she had trusted Steven and told him almost everything? It was easy to imagine the bitter line of that sensuous mouth, the wary look in those brown eyes meant for laughter.

"Kane could have killed Delia in a fit of jealousy," she said out loud. Her only answer was a twitching of the mare's ears. The way Steven spoke of Delia, the painting of her hidden away in his room, could mean they had been having an affair right under Kane's nose, and he might have suspected. Had he actually found out about it? Or had Steven done away with Delia when he got wind of the treasure, not wanting to share it?

One thing she was certain of: Kane was not a killer. Of course he could have been furious or hurt if he found out Steven and Delia were lovers. That could be the basis of the animosity she had sensed between the two men.

None of this introspection helped her now. The intruders figured she was hiding upstairs. When would they realize she was gone? They would follow. It was too late for anyone to turn back now.

At the top of the first major crest she paused to wait for the sunrise. The sun burst open like a ripe orange between two mountain peaks, flinging the golden liquid rays down on the shadowy desert so that everything was bathed in an iridescent brilliance. Awakened birds, startled from their nests, erupted like black sticks sweeping across the sky.

"Oh!" She sat in awe, struck by the raw beauty, then turned to look back down on the valley. The house and outbuildings were like toys in the distance, as yet in deep shadow.

Jowanna slid wearily off the mare and stood stretching her aches away, letting the sun warm her chilled body. She wished she had one of her hair bands in her pocket to slip over her head, to keep her hair out of her face when the wind began to blow. The thoughts of wind in her hair were only to stave off the more appalling thoughts that threatened to weaken her resolve.

What if she became lost? Disoriented? Would she die of thirst? Would the puma come on stealthy paws to stare down at her as she lay dying—as it might have done to her father? So many doubts assailed her now.

She wanted to turn back the time, leave this place and go back to New York—to hide in safety the rest of her life.

She led the horse to a large rock and crawled up on her back, straightening the blanket beneath her legs. Her salvation lay in finding the treasure. How she knew that, she didn't stop to figure out.

Before long the sun beat mercilessly down on her hatless head. She felt as if her dark hair sucked the rays into her brain. It was difficult to remember how cold she had been not long ago. A huge chuckawalla sunned on a flat rock. Otherwise nothing moved.

The air was still as death.

The brush and cactus began thinning as they climbed higher. Landmarks passed, ones she recognized from the map, raising her hopes. There was the giant saguaro bent in the shape of a U. The map showed that oasis of palo verde trees. As they moved along, she raised her eyes to see a huge hole in the rock looming high over the canyon wall. Everything was going right according to the map.

Mirla drank from several small streams coming down from the mountain. Jowanna wondered if they came from the fabled waterfall Kane told her about. Hard to imagine a waterfall in all this aridness. Once in a while shuffling bits of gray clouds moved across the pale blue sky causing deep shadows. The gradually increasing wind brushed through her hair, lifting it up from her shoulders. The clouds gave a temporary relief from the sun, but that was tempered by the threat of rain.

She shivered, in spite of the heat. Any one of these washes coming down from the mountain could hold tons of water in a rainstorm. She knew that now, and the knowledge made her so afraid she nudged the tired horse on with her knees.

Reining Mirla over to the skimpy shade of a windswept mesquite tree, she turned to look back on the valley below. Her breath caught in her throat; her chest felt as if all the air had been crushed away. She stared in stunned fascination at the thin trickle of dust rising up from the desert floor.

*Someone was following her.*

Glancing up at the sky, the clouds appeared darker, rolling with turbulent winds. The sun didn't feel quite as hot, and she sensed an element of ominous waiting, as if the desert and mountains expected the onset of the storm.

Moving ahead at a faster pace in spite of the tired horse beneath her, Jowanna let Mirla pick her way through a sparse trail of cactus and rocks.

There! As marked on the map, the stand of five ocotillos were straight in a row as if some demented Johnny Appleseed had come up here to plant them. She took the map out and spread it on her thigh to check the distances. It was becoming more critical now, as she began to search for an approach to the narrow green valley shown on the map. It was hard to believe in any green valley. Her eyes had grown so accustomed to sere browns and grays.

After traversing the long basin she should come to a dead end and, if she was doing it right, a hidden access to a passageway leading from the valley up to a mesa and a secret cave, which was the X.

Shielding her eyes with her hand, she looked out over the desert.

A lone rider approached at an alarming speed.

She kicked her heels into Mirla's sides and, lying down across her neck, urged the horse forward to a gallop.

The edge of the canyon loomed, and she prayed her father had drawn the map right. Between two boulders lay the trail. She unhesitatingly turned the mare between them and for a brief second headed downward into thin air. The horse faltered, stumbled, and, before Jowanna could scream out her fear, recovered her footing, and after the moment's frightening plunge, the green canyon emerged below.

Several times Mirla leaned back on her hindquarters, braking the descent. Jowanna bent low on her neck, clutching her fingers into the horse's mane to keep her seat.

When they reached the bottom, Mirla stood on the lush green canyon floor, sides heaving, bubbles of white foam coming from around the bit in her mouth.

"Good girl, good girl," Jowanna crooned to the sweat-coated horse. "Look, sweet baby, I know you deserve a good long rest and some of this delicious grass to roll in, but you've got to help me. After we find the cave and hide, I promise you something to eat and drink."

Taking a deep breath, she urged Mirla on, trying to stay in the shadow of the cliff to be less conspicuous when the rider topped the ridge, as she knew he would.

Looking ahead, it seemed like miles to the end of the canyon. Poor Mirla couldn't be pushed much farther.

Above the sounds of her heart as it beat in her throat and Mirla's hooves thunking in the soft loam, she heard the echo she'd been dreading—the sound of tumbling rocks that meant her pursuer had found his way down the canyon wall to this valley.

She choked off a scream, burying her head in Mirla's streaming mane, their long dark hair blending together in the wind, as she cajoled and pleaded with the horse to keep going.

*Hurry. Hurry.* She didn't dare to look back now. Her heart pounded, louder than Mirla's hoofbeats on the soft green grass. Her breath hurt in her chest, as if she were doing the running, not the horse.

She caught the sound of a warning shout behind, saw a blur coming at her from a rock overhanging the canyon at the same time Mirla stopped in midtracks,

185

throwing her off in front of the rearing, screaming horse. The last thing she heard was the sound of a rifle crack, and she knew she must be dying.

****

Jowanna swam through blackness, trying desperately to surface. Bit by bit her memory returned, bringing a surge of elation tempered with panic.

She wasn't dead. Where was she?

The icy terror at being followed relentlessly, the fear of not knowing her enemy, the remembrance of the leaping puma and the sound of a rifle crack along with the helpless sensation of flying through the air—it all came back in a rush.

Dimly she tried to bring back the voice she heard talking to her, calling her name over and over. Let them keep the map. She didn't want any part of this. She wanted out.

Opening her eyes cautiously, all she saw at first was shadowy darkness. Then in front of her she made out an opening, like a gigantic round picture window.

Kane stood silhouetted in the pale light of dawn.

She was lying in a cave, must have been here all night.

"Are you all right?"

She swallowed, her pulses racing at the sound of his deep voice.

At once Kane knelt at her side, looking into her face. He bent and enveloped her in his arms, kissing her tenderly. His lips paused, his warm breath hovered over her lips until she wanted to pull him closer, but she felt weak and disoriented, unable to move.

"Where am I? Did you bring me here? I remember a shot and..."

He sat on the edge of the bedroll and pulled her onto his lap, cradling her against his chest.

"Why did you run from me? I followed you all the

186

way from the house, trying to catch up with you. Shambles was favoring his sore leg again. I thought he was almost over that sprain, but he's had a little too much exercise on it too soon, I guess, so I didn't want to push too hard."

"Did you see Steven at the house?"

She felt a tremor run through his body that could have been shock or surprise.

"So. Steven's behind this. I didn't see his truck. He was supposed to be in Tucson."

"Steven's behind what?" He had probably hidden his vehicle away in the wash somewhere so no one would know he was at the ranch.

"I'll explain later. I want to know for sure you're okay. That was a pretty rough fall."

"But how did you know to follow..."

"I didn't like the way you sounded when we left, so I thought it over and doubled back."

"And?"

He smiled. "Ever the impatient one. I didn't see anyone at the house, and lamps were lit all over the place. I saw Mirla missing, along with your bedroll, and put two and two together. I rode Shambles on up to find you."

"I could see the trail of your dust from up on the ridge. I didn't know who was following me. Was that El Diablo ready to spring on me? I heard a warning shout and saw the movement, but..."

"I caught up with you just in time. I shot at the old devil, but he's like a spirit. I'm sure I missed him. Granted, it was a hurried shot, no time to aim. He would have got you by then."

Her head throbbed and her throat felt dry as if she had been screaming. "Is Mirla okay?"

"She's with Shambles, and they're safe. Hidden in a grove of cedars a little away from here, toward the rear of the tunnel."

How could she tell him about Steven? Had he

guessed? What could she tell? That she was sure she'd heard his voice? She had only hunches to go on. Had he hired assassins to help him or...what if it was outsiders, someone from the town, or even Phoenix, who had heard about a treasure?

What if Steven wasn't even involved and was in danger, too?

She pulled the jacket closer around her chest. She hadn't been wearing the jacket when she fell.

"Cold?" His voice was roughly tender, as if he couldn't express the words he might have said.

"There's something I've got to tell you..."

"Wait. I want you to see this." With little effort he picked her up and carried her toward the gradually lighting sky.

"Oh, my Lord!" The exclamation was wrung from her as she clung to him in alarm. It was as if she was on the edge of the world.

Her empty stomach rebelled, her fear of heights coming back suddenly. All he had to do was toss her forward, and she would end up lifeless on the floor of the canyon.

"Ah, you're trembling." He held her tight against his body. "I'm holding you, sweetheart. You're safe now, don't be scared. Enjoy the spectacle."

Peering cautiously over the edge, she saw the verdant canyon floor with huge cottonwoods looking like little toy trees. The cave faced west, so the sunlight was indirect, coming from behind, not as brilliant as the morning before but, instead, creeping across the landscape in delicate apricot-colored tendrils. Soon the light bathed everything below in a soft hue of morning.

"It's beautiful. Thank you for showing me. Now, I'd as soon back away as not."

"That's the beauty that has to be kept unspoiled."

What did he mean?

Her heart had nearly stopped when she saw, off to

the side, a ragged boulder with a heavy rope tied around its base.

A narrow ledge led to this boulder, and zigzagging down the mountain were steps. Some looked like natural outcroppings and some were chiseled in the hard stone. Is that how he'd brought her up here? On those skimpy steps?

He grinned and kissed the tip of her nose lightly.

"The only way to kill off a fear is to face it. You've been doing that right along, haven't you? I doubt your mother would recognize her baby daughter." He took her back to the blanket and set her down gently, sprawling beside her.

"You've been away so much, I'm surprised you noticed." She wanted to smooth the unruly hair back from his forehead; her hand itched to do it.

"I notice a lot more than most people give me credit for."

Was he talking about Steven and Delia now? Had he harmed Delia? The old doubts flooded back, and her mouth went dry.

"How did we get up here? You didn't bring me up those steps, did you?" She looked at his broad shoulders. She'd seen the hard muscles in his arms that morning at the cabin while he was still in his t-shirt.

"Never mind that. We need to talk. I want to know where you were going in such a damn hurry. Why you ran away."

It was light enough to see most of the inside of the cave and into the dark tunnel behind.

"Yes. Talk. That's what we need to do." How could she tell him she had suspected him of being a cold-blooded killer and thief until last night? How could she tell him that it seemed as if it was Steven now? Just get it over with, no other way. She began to tell him everything that had happened to her since she arrived.

When she came to Steven's portrait of the Señora

and her own resemblance to both it and the ghostly figure of a woman hanging at the top of the stairs, he touched her shoulder, the groan wrung from his lips stopping her in mid-speech.

"Why didn't you tell me any of this before? You knew most of it when we were alone at the cabin. There was plenty of opportunity to confide in me."

She looked away, but he turned her chin back with his big hand. Gray eyes staring into brown, she couldn't look away.

"I—I thought you might be the one—the one who..."

Jowanna hated the hurt look that flickered in his eyes, but she continued. "You were the only one around when that boulder came down on me," she said defensively. "I found a note from my father—it's a long story. I told Steven about it. I thought you stole it out of my pocket when you brought me into the cabin. It was gone, and..."

"I never saw a note. Probably it fell out and got washed away. You trusted Steven before me."

The accusation stood like a wall between them.

"There were so many coincidences I couldn't explain away. You seemed to always be there at the wrong time."

She gripped his arm, as if needing to keep from tumbling off into a vortex. "Kane, I saw the piece of torn dress under your bed after that thing with the hanging woman. What was I to think?"

"Steven put it there, then. Why would I have saved your life in the storm if I'd wanted you dead?" There was a bitter edge to his voice.

"I don't know. I just don't know. Evidence seemed to pile up. I didn't trust Steven enough to show him this, though." She pulled the folded paper from her jeans pocket and handed it to him.

He unfolded it and spread it out across his thigh. The look he turned on her made it hard to swallow the despair in her throat.

"So that's why you were heading here—to our mine. Where did you get this map?"

"My father drew it for Jason and hid it away. I figured out how to follow it. Whose mine is this? Is this Delia's grandfather's old claim?"

"No. That one's played out. I went to Boston to make sure that old claim was free and clear because this one, that we found much earlier, was adjoining it. We knew we had something good here—even before we found—well, what we found. We didn't want any legal problems cropping up."

"This cave and that tunnel, they took a lot of work. How could you have kept it secret?"

"We didn't do it. There must have been an earthquake, we get 'em up here, but not often. The Superstitions had the last bad one in the 1800s. Nearly cracked old Weaver's Needle half in two. Anyway, Mac and I were plundering around, and we stumbled upon the back opening and followed the tunnels. It was dug out maybe a hundred years ago."

"It'd been hidden that long?"

He shrugged. "Could have been the Lost Dutchman Mine of old Jacob Waltz. There was also a group of Spaniards known as the Peraltas rumored to have secreted a mule train of treasure here that they took from Mexico and never came back for."

"You and my father discovered it?"

"That's right. We owned it together, Mac and me. After I went back to Boston and bought Delia's grandfather's claim, we—hell, what am I going on and on for? I don't expect you to believe me. You've doubted me ever since you came here. Just like your father, neither of you believed in me."

He leaned his head forward on his palms, his appearance so tired, so desolate, she wanted to cry out to him, to hold him in her arms, to rain kisses all over his dear face, but she knew he wouldn't accept her touch.

Not now, perhaps never again.

"*She* preferred Steven to me, did you know that?" His voice was torn out of his body. "From the very beginning I could see the attraction between them. What hurt most was that it looked right—like they'd be good together. Not like with her and me. As soon as I brought her back here, I knew it was a mistake."

"Why did you marry her, then?" Foolish question. The woman was beautiful. Steven's painting of her reflected a cool, distant beauty with a curious exotic edge that for many men would have been enough.

There was a cold edge of irony in his voice. "It was a hasty decision, I admit." He threw up his hands with a gesture of resignation. "She said she was broke and wanted to leave Boston. She also said..."

It was hard for Kane to continue, but Jowanna waited, not wanting to hear but having to listen.

"She said she fell in love with me at first sight. I had a hard time believing that, but I wanted to. Remember what you said when you first came here, about kids running around and...well, I had that dream, too. Sometimes in the afternoon I'd doze on the porch and wake up hearing them. It was downright spooky."

"I know. I heard them, too. Or thought I did."

"I wanted the ranch to come alive again, and I thought she was the answer."

Kane was right. Delia probably had schemed to follow her grandfather's claim. She may have sold any rights to Kane and then married him only to keep hold of it. That sounded pretty farfetched, especially when she didn't know the woman.

"Then you really don't know why or how she disappeared?" She needed to believe him.

"No. As much as we grew to dislike one another, I wouldn't want anything to happen to her. I hired a detective to check in Boston, but she never returned.

It's like she vanished off the face of the earth after she sent me that annulment paper."

"Did you talk to Steven about it?"

"Yeah. At first we talked about it, but he seemed to be as confused as I was. He never admitted to—ah—loving her, but I know he did. I won't ever believe he's hurt her in any way."

"If they had become lovers, maybe she became pregnant, or maybe something else complicated things. Maybe she realized the mine wasn't worth anything." She searched Kane's face for an expression of pain at her blunt words, but he only sighed. A tired sigh that made her want to hold him close.

"Sounds like a soap opera. Steven has big plans for his future that probably wouldn't include anyone but himself."

"Do you hate them?"

"At first I did," he admitted reluctantly. "But Delia and I could never have made it together. I just want to find her and get things settled between us. Our marriage is over, the annulment took care of that, but still I'd like to know she's alive."

"But what did my father mean about a treasure? Why did he warn me not to trust anyone? Why did he say something was about to blow up in his face?"

Kane looked angry for a moment and then sad. "He could have compromised everything by sending that letter. We found a strongbox filled with gold nuggets, way inside the mine. The finest, purest gold either of us had ever seen in our lives. We hid the box and decided to blow up the mine."

"But why? If someone took gold out of here, there's bound to be more."

"Oh, there is. Plenty. That's the problem. A find of that magnitude would turn this place into a hell on earth—bulldozers, dynamiting, every treasure hunter in the world trying to wrest that gold from the ground. Can't you see how that could ruin everything here?"

The new Jowanna could.

"We decided to take the box of nuggets, use it for what we needed, and get rid of the rest. At least I thought we had decided that." His voice had turned harsh. His eyes closed, and he tilted his head back in a gesture of tiredness.

She reached to touch his hand, and for a moment he held still, letting her try to comfort him.

"I'm sorry I thought you were my enemy..."

"I am, too. I'm sorry as hell Mac stopped trusting me, too. Let's drop it. For now." He stood up. "I have to look for Steven—get some answers. I've suspected something wasn't right for a while."

"But you didn't believe me. You said so."

He looked shamefaced. "I thought the less you knew, the less trouble you'd be in. I believed you—for the most part."

"Thanks," she said dryly.

"You stay put. You'll be safe here. I'll be back when it's settled."

"Wait. Don't leave. There are so many questions. Why did my father mention the treasure in his letter to Jason and in his note that I lost in the storm? Why did he, when you both had agreed to get rid of it?"

"I have no idea. We agreed not to tell *anyone*. Not even Steven. That still hurts—that he didn't trust me. He, Delia, and now you. None of you trusted me." He tilted his hat in that sardonic mocking way and began to descend down the face of the mountain.

"Wait! Do you have to do that? Is that the only way out of this place?" Her panic-filled voice stopped him in his tracks, and his look softened. She saw the regret deep in his eyes.

"No, there's a back way out the tunnel, but it takes too long. I'll be back for you, after I find Steven and get some answers."

Jowanna crept close to look over the edge at his disappearing form and then changed her mind, nausea rising in her throat.

In the corner of the cave lay a canteen and her knapsack holding some dried beef jerky. She wasn't hungry, only thirsty. In the midst of a long swig of deliciously cold water she stopped, almost choking. Beyond her knapsack lay a miner's hat with a stubby bit of burned candle, like the one she'd seen in Kane's cabin.

She felt a desolate sadness at the thought that in discovering her feelings for Kane, she had also lost him. He had been hurt by Delia. Her father's mistrust, coupled with her own suspicions and the fact that she had turned to Steven instead of to him, had to have been a bitter pill. Now thinking that his sister's child, his only relative, might be behind all that had been happening at the ranch had capped it.

Kane was in danger, too. Surely he must know that.

Steven was involved in all this. He must have brought in an accomplice; not hard to imagine, since he went to Phoenix and Tucson all the time. He could have hired someone to help him. Would Kane believe that? Did he go to find Steven still trusting in his innocence?

She felt so foolish, believing in Steven's portrait of her as the reincarnated Señora. He could have used the picture on her father's dresser any time he wanted to. Skilled as he was, it was nothing to make her older, mature, to guess how she would look now and add years to that image.

He probably made up the hanging figure, since sculpting her likeness in clay wouldn't have been a problem for him. That meant he deliberately left the scrap of material in Kane's room, knowing she would probably find it and blame Kane.

Oh, what a fool she had been.

What should she do? Sit here like a fly captured in a spider's web, waiting for something to happen?

Surely the old Jowanna would have. But not the new one.

A blinding hurt caught her unprepared as her memory snagged on a picture of Kane's tanned face, eyes crinkling at the corners in amusement and the glint of gold running through his straight brown hair. The way he tilted his hat up a notch when he was puzzled, his slightly bowed long legs striding across the kitchen, hard hands touching her, his lips...

Was this all a bad dream? What if her father's death had been a dreadful accident, and Delia actually ran away to Las Vegas, to find work in the chorus line? What if most of the things that had happened to herself were just pranks to frighten her away from the ranch? Would Kane have helped Steven just to be able to keep possession of the ranch and to hold on to this secret he still held the key to?

No! It was Steven all along. It had to be.

What troubled her most, and what she still didn't understand completely, was why her father didn't want Kane to know he had confided in someone about the treasure that seemed to belong to them both. Why had he needed someone else to know about the secret that they'd agreed to keep together?

It could have been that her father had sensed something going on, and when he thought Kane had changed his mind and possibly taken Steven in on it, he decided to confide in someone, too.

She set the dusty miner's cap firmly on her head. It was too big, so she put her hair up in two braids and wrapped them around her head to take up room inside. Only two matches left in the cardboard holder. What she wouldn't have given for her little flashlight that had tumbled down the mountainside yesterday.

Some instinct of preservation warned her to hide all signs of her presence. She grabbed up her belongings and stashed them behind a large boulder just inside the darkness of the tunnel. Kane said there was another way out of here, and she was going to find it, catch up with him, and tell him...tell him what?

It was too late to tell him that she believed in him now.

Jowanna continued cautiously down the narrow path. The size of the tunnel varied from being just wide enough that she could reach both arms out and touch each side wall to widening out so far in places that she felt lost.

How long would the little candle stub last? At one point she nearly lost her balance kicking a large stone out of her path. When it rolled away, she heard it drop off into what must have been a deep shaft in the floor of the tunnel. She leaned against the cold, hard wall, her legs buckling as the rock bounced from side to side down the length of the shaft, the noise echoing until it subsided with a pitiful little splash at the bottom.

That was close. Before her heart returned to a halfway normal beat, she heard a restless, rustling noise come from a dark recess off to one side.

She screamed in fright, and then she heard an eerie, frightening animal cry—the puma?—that tore apart the silence in the cave. She listened, heart pounding, while the echo bounced off the walls and ceilings of the cavern. Where did the sound come from? Was it close? Behind or ahead? It was impossible to judge. Maybe Kane's shot had wounded the animal.

She dared not try to return to the cave entrance now. She had passed the point of no return with the candle stub. Putting aside the thoughts of shaft holes, snakes and tarantulas, she hurried in a headlong flight down the path.

Once she stopped to look up at a crack of sunshine a long way above. Dust motes danced through the rays that reached halfway down before petering out in the darkness.

With every step came the worry that a sudden blast of air or a stumble on a stone would cause the candle to go out as the tunnel stretched on and on.

Suddenly the tunnel made a sharply angled turn and she walked into a small, round room hollowed out like the inside of a cave. In the corner, a pile of stones told her it was a mining claim like the one she'd found earlier, the one her father had left in the other cave. At last, answers to her last remaining doubts.

She rushed over to remove the rocks to look for the tobacco tin she knew must be there, but a scorpion slithered across her hand, its tail lifted threateningly. She brushed it away with a sweeping motion, as Kane had shown her how to do, and watched it scurry away down the tunnel.

Holding the hat with the flickering candle in front of her, she found the tobacco tin and flipped it open. A shock wave hit her when she pulled out a well-folded paper and recognized her father's handwriting, with both his and Kane's name, laying out the claim. Kane wasn't lying to her. This mine belonged to them both. She put it back, undisturbed. All she wanted to know was the truth. She piled the rocks up again.

Sudden darkness enveloped her as she felt a push backward by an unseen hand, and her fall extinguished the candle.

It was then she heard the voices.

## Chapter 13

Voices drifted toward her from the tunnel. Jowanna held her breath, straining to hear, to make out the speakers. The approaching footsteps kicked carelessly at stones as the sound of boots tapped along the pathway.

*Hide. Hide away.* Jowanna hadn't realized she held to the spot, mesmerized by the sudden intrusion. She felt around frantically for a place to hide. In the opposite corner of the cave she remembered a large boulder. She skinned her hands and arms moving along the edge of the wall, trying to find the place. Her ankle twisted on a protruding stone and she stifled the urge to cry out in pain. The boulder had barely enough room to crouch behind it.

She didn't have long to wait. The glow of a lantern sifted around the bend in the tunnel and suddenly the cavern was awash with light. Jowanna ducked her head, hardly daring to breathe.

A woman's voice filled the silence.

"Can you believe it, Steven?" The voice had a sultry, low-pitched quality filled with smug satisfaction. "This must be their claim. The little twit led us right to it, like you said she would."

Jowanna's first reaction was relief. It was Steven—not Kane. Even though she knew in her heart of hearts Kane couldn't be involved in all the scheming, she was grateful for having it confirmed.

Unable to bear the suspense any longer, she cautiously peered over the edge of the boulder, then covered her mouth with her hand to stifle the cry of shock. Even in dusty denims, her long golden hair tied back carelessly, there was no mistaking the lovely, exotic Delia.

She and Steven were sharing a long, lingering passionate kiss. Jowanna thought of Kane, of how the two had conspired against him, not caring if he suspected and what that would do to him— unconcerned that their betrayal had left a bitterness in him that might never heal.

How could she ever compete with this woman's beauty in Kane's heart? Jowanna's fingers clenched convulsively, as if she had to hold back to keep from slapping that smug face.

Delia's voice broke into Jowanna's thoughts. "Let's see who filed the claim. But we already know that, don't we, love?" Delia made a commanding motion toward the pile of rocks, which Steven began tearing apart in careless haste.

"I thought Jowanna would never find her father's map. Do you see now why I wanted you to let her come to the ranch?" Delia's voice fairly purred.

"Yeah. That was a great move when you had me intercept Mac's letter. I still can't believe they held this treasure in their hands and wanted to blow it up. What were they thinking?"

"You're so gullible, Steven darling. Kane probably just told Mac he wanted to blow it up. When Mac began to suspect that Kane might go back on their agreement, he wrote to his son for help."

"Maybe. But to give the devil his due, I've never known Kane to cheat anyone. I think Mac became suspicious of us, and that confused him."

"So what? It doesn't matter. That stupid ghost legend helped more than anything. Good thinking to spread the rumor around in town, keep it alive. That way no one offered to come out and work for Kane."

"I've missed talking to you, Delia. With her in the house, I haven't been able to see you in weeks. There's so much to say..."

"After it's over, we can be together. Patience," Delia said.

"Odd she never suspected you stayed in the storeroom."

"Why should she? That old house creaks and groans all night long. I came and went as I pleased at night. She was too frightened of her own shadow to peep a head out of her door."

They were laughing at her. That galled. Instead of hiding away like the twit Delia called her, Jowanna wanted to pick up a big rock and hit them both with it, she was so angry. But she knew she'd never be a match for both of them at once, so she held her fury in check.

"You should have seen her face when she looked at the portrait," Steven laughed. "I only wish we could have been there when she ran into the hanging figure on the stairs. I did a good job of sculpting that head."

Jowanna listened to Steven's jeering voice, full of contempt. Her cheeks burned with shame. To think she had trusted him over Kane. So the storeroom was Delia's bunk. Had she continued to use her perfume, maybe in a sick attempt to taunt her husband? Or to put in doubts about the ghost? Or had it truly been the Señora's method of warning? Either way, the perfume that Kane so plainly tried to ignore had been an added twist to his heartache and her own fears. A double bonus for the two conspirators before her.

Delia must have been responsible for most of the mischief, except for the boulder. She couldn't have managed that alone. Steven had probably followed Jowanna that day, waiting for a chance to do harm. Steven, who let everyone think he didn't ride horses.

Delia was the one who put the pillow over her face. Jowanna knew it couldn't have been anyone very strong, or she'd never have been able to push the hands away. How easily they had sucked her into their tricks with all her neurotic phobias—a city slicker, putty in their hands.

Steven raised the lamp and shone it around the cave, and Jowanna ducked her head just in time.

"There it is, Delia! There's the fault line, plain as day. It's got to be where the mother lode comes in. We'll be rich, sweetheart. So rich we'll never be able to spend it all in a lifetime."

Jowanna peeked around the rock to see him rub the rough cave wall with tenderness. They must not know about the strongbox of nuggets Kane had hidden away.

"Aren't you forgetting what's-her-name and my dear husband?" Delia asked.

Steven paused in his preoccupation and turned to face her. "I suppose we have to do something about them. They won't disappear, will they? I mean on their own."

Delia shook her head, wiping dust from her cheek with her hand, the nails tipped red as blood. "God knows we tried to get them to leave. But no, they won't go away any more than Mac would."

"I still think you had no call to shoot him like that. Wasn't it enough we pushed him off the ledge? El Diablo would have taken care of it for us if we had left him there."

"Oh, no. That's where you and I differ. You're weak, Steven. You need me. Never leave anything to chance. He could have crawled away and hid, waiting for Kane to find him."

Jowanna wanted to leap out and wrap her hands around that neck more than she had ever wanted to do anything in her life. Delia—Delia!—had shot her father while he lay helpless. She closed her eyes tight, willing calm while pressure on her shoulder increased as if someone pressed her down, holding her in place.

"I didn't count on her being smart enough to take the map when she ran from the house last night. If she'd left the map in her room, we could have copied it, tormented her a little more, and then without Kane around she would have run back to her mommy with her tail between her legs."

"Yeah, I agree," Steven said. "But it didn't work out that way. She was tougher than we thought."

Delia's voice grew sulky, provocatively clinging. "Love, we must get rid of them both, what choice do we have? We've gone too far. We can't turn back now."

Jowanna watched as Steven examined the rocky wall in silence. Then he spoke. "You're right. Neither Kane or Mac had any right to keep this mine a secret. They should have cut us all in. *We* are family. She only came to get her share. Mac as much as offered it in the letter."

"Do you really think she came all the way out here to see her father? Hell, she wanted a part of that treasure. No, they've both got to go."

"Ah, sweetheart, it's been hard for you, hasn't it?"

"I hated it out here from the beginning. I never would have come with him, but it was the only way to get to the mine. My mine."

Delia's voice took on a hard edge that Jowanna felt certain Steven missed in his infatuation. She would turn on him like the black widow spider she was, when she got control of the mine and didn't need him. Foolish, misguided Steven. As soon as the thought came, she pushed it away angrily. He let her father be killed and he stood there agreeing to their murders. There was no reason to feel sympathy for Steven.

The two had deceived Kane almost from the beginning, while he had tried to believe in them even though he must have sensed their betrayal. Poor Kane, torn between despising himself for what he probably thought was mere jealousy and knowing deep inside that he could be right. When he found out about all this, he would never trust another woman.

He probably didn't now.

Jowanna had cramped up from her watching

position and leaned back against the boulder, listening. She peeked out again and saw Steven run his fingers through his usually perfect hair, an odd imitation of Kane's habit.

"I don't like it, Delia. Too many bodies piling up."

"That's the beauty of my plan. There won't be bodies left to explain when we get through. We'll use that dynamite you found in Kane's cabin. Rig a trip wire across the entrance and blow them to pieces. It shouldn't bother back here where the gold is."

"And then?"

Her voice sounded impatient, as if she were explaining to an idiot. Steven didn't seem to notice, he was so infatuated. Reality would surely come later.

"When the dust is settled, you'll tell the authorities that Jowanna and Kane ran off together. He was such a loner, no one will miss him. In a few weeks I'll come back from Boston, and we'll be on our way to riches."

"Sounds okay. But how do we know they'll come back together? I hate like hell to bring that dynamite up that rope ladder."

"Don't be simple. It's the only way. Remember when we lost her trail at dark? She probably took another route and is already back at the ranch. She'll spill her guts to him about the map, and they'll have to come back, knowing it all starts and ends here."

"God, you must really hate him," Steven said.

"I saw them talking together. It didn't take long for the grieving husband to forget his wife, did it?" The woman tried to keep her voice light, but malice crept in, poisoning every word.

Jowanna saw her eyes narrow and the vindictive hate mirrored in the face of the tall, willowy blonde. She must have enjoyed Kane's worrying about her disappearance, and when he was nearly blamed for that, it was the frosting on the cake. She clenched her hands, wanting so much to smack the twisted face in front of her.

If Steven had turned to look at his beloved Delia now, he might have caught the cold, implacable look of cruelty that would set permanently on her features once her beauty faded.

As if in answer to Jowanna's wish, Steven swung the arc of light around to look, but Delia had already smoothed her expression into a sweet mask.

"What do you care?" Steven's voice was sharp for the first time. "You never loved him, you said. Damned if you didn't sound jealous just then."

"Nonsense, Steven darling. But it does go against a woman's ego to be forgotten so easily." She smoothed his hair with her fingers, lingering over his cheeks in a caricature of tenderness.

They deserved each other, Jowanna thought bitterly.

"Come on, let's go set it up. We don't have to hurry. They won't be here before evening, I'll lay odds on it." Delia's creamy voice was like the sound of fingernails on a blackboard to Jowanna, and she listened to their footsteps retreating toward the front of the tunnel, waiting to be sure they were gone.

She had to get out and warn Kane. He wouldn't find Steven at the ranch, and he'd turn around and come right back here, only to fall into their trap.

No matter that Kane wanted to live out his days as a bitter, untrusting recluse, she knew she loved him with all her heart. She might never work up the courage to tell him that, but she owed it to him, to her father's memory and to her newly emerged feelings to get back to him, tell him of Delia and Steven's plan, so they could fight it together.

Would he believe her?

Jowanna knew the first thing she had to do was find the other entrance to the cave, the one that only Kane knew about. Then, if she could get out, she must hope Kane had left Mirla behind, find the horse and ride back to the ranch. That's where Kane had to be now. Looking for Steven.

It was all a long chance, but the only one she had.

She stood and stretched painfully. Crouching so long had strained the sore muscles from her fall the day before.

A rock fell, knocking against the pile in the darkness. The sound echoed through the tunnel and she stopped in dismay, expecting to hear the sound of running footsteps. When nothing happened, she took a deep breath of relief.

She lit the remaining match and touched it carefully to the tiny stub of candle on the hat. It wouldn't last long, and then total darkness would claim her. The thought was enough to make her want to stay put until someone came back for her. But she knew it would be too late for both of them then, if she waited.

Placing the hat gingerly on top of her head to keep the flickering candle steady, she entered the tunnel and turned toward the rear of the mine, in the opposite direction from where Steven and Delia had disappeared. Soon she came to a complete dead end. She swallowed through a tight throat and leaned against the cold hard wall, thinking of how terrible it would be to die alone in darkness. When the candle went out it would be all over for her. And for Kane.

Thinking of her father's sad death sustained her. They couldn't be allowed to win!

Crouching down to look at the floor, she saw the shadows of two separate tunnels veering off in different directions. Down on her knees, ignoring the pain of rocks sinking into her legs in spite of her jeans, she searched the mouths of the tunnels, looking for signs of one being used more than the other.

It was her only hope.

Jowanna took off the hat gently and held the candle closer to the ground. If she took the wrong path, she couldn't return to the other one. The candle would be gone by then.

Where was the voice of the Señora when she needed her? Maybe the evil in Steven and Delia had blocked her in some way. There could be too many spirits left behind in this cave to allow for another entity. Jowanna had only felt her warning while hidden behind the big boulder.

Her heart beat rapidly in her chest as the feeble candlelight bounced off a small round yellow object lying in the middle of the right hand path. She picked it up and recognized the paper pull-tab from a tobacco sack, the kind she had seen Kane use up in his cabin.

Memories flooded back when she thought of opening her eyes after nearly drowning in the flash flood to see him leaning against the cabin wall, watching her sleep and rolling a cigarette. The thought of that dear face gave her courage.

Jowanna would have to trust her life—and Kane's—to this small sign.

She began to walk as rapidly as possible down the low, narrow tunnel, scraping her hand along the side to be sure of her footing. It would only take one stumble to lose the light.

The ceiling began closing down on her, and she could touch both walls with her outstretched hands. Her heart tripped and her throat dried with fear. Had she made the wrong choice? Blind terror threatened to turn her legs to jelly, to smother her breathing, until she felt a breath of fresh air. She raised her head, sucking in the cool air greedily, and saw daylight in the distance.

Rushing forward, she looked out of the tunnel, blessing the light that filtered through a gnarled tree growing tightly against the opening. She took off the miner's hat just as the candle sputtered out its last light. Unmindful of the scratches, she pushed forward, forcing her way through the mesquite branches and out into the open.

Glorious sunshine and blue skies! She had never seen anything so beautiful. Did Kane leave Mirla behind, and could she find her? Time was running out. Steven would be halfway to the cabin by now, to pick up the dynamite.

Making her way down to the canyon floor, she slipped and slid in her haste. Surely he hadn't had time to get to Kane's cabin and back with the dynamite yet, had he? What if she missed Kane? What if, not finding Steven at the ranch, Kane was on his way back to her already?

She had to intercede, to stop him.

At the bottom of the rough trail, she found the grove of trees and smiled at the sound of Mirla's welcoming nicker. "Hey, little girl. Hope you're rested. We have to ride."

She smoothed her hand across the velvet nose and leaned her body against the horse in a sort of a huge hug.

It wasn't easy crawling up onto the horse when every inch of her body cried out in protest. She had ridden so hard and fast the day before, and the fall didn't help. Was it only a day ago when all that happened? It seemed like weeks had passed.

Which direction was the ranch? Would Mirla know? Mountains and sheer peaks loomed over her shoulder, casting eerie shadows over the floor of the canyon. Lacy palo verde trees blending with stately saguaros greeted her as she climbed up a faint trail out of the canyon. The horse seemed to know where she was going. Jowanna let her go.

After a while the sun beat down on her hair, soaking the hot rays into her skull. She saw a shady place under a sweeping mesquite tree and reined Mirla over so she could climb down on a large boulder.

She tied the horse loosely and leaned against the tree trunk, wiping the stinging sweat out of her eyes with the tail of her shirt.

Suddenly she felt the earth tremble beneath her boots and a moment later heard the pounding hooves and the dust coming toward her, so close!

"I should have known it was too easy," she said out loud, the bitterness strong in her throat. They would catch her now and kill her, and Kane would be lost, too. She looked for cover, but only an outcropping of rocks showed any possibility. Once there, it would be impossible for her pursuers to follow her on horseback.

She began to run. If she could reach the bottom of the mountain, there could be some place to hide.

By the time she got halfway to the rocks, her chest burned unbearably and her legs wobbled beneath her, no longer wanting to hold her up. The sound of hooves hammered in her ears, blending with the pounding of her heart. She couldn't take the time to look back, to see how close they were.

Tears of angry frustration filled her eyes, blinding her so that she stumbled, nearly falling. A rough hand grabbed her shoulder and spun her around and she felt a sharp stone cut into her leg when she fell.

She struck out with her fists, kicking and yelling at the top of her voice. Big, rough hands gripped her wrists, holding them. Too exhausted to fight anymore, Jowanna waited with closed eyes for the blow to come.

## Chapter 14

Strong arms held her tight and Kane's deep baritone rumbled in her ear as he crushed her to his chest. Her trembling legs felt like spaghetti when he picked her up, still holding her as if he never meant to let her go again.

Jowanna turned her head against his broad shoulder, feeling the strength of his hard muscled frame sustaining her own flagging body. He leaned his chin over to her cheek to lightly wipe away the tears. Was he a mirage? Was he only a figment of her panic? Would he disappear if she opened her eyes?

She reached a hand up to feel his face, the roughness of his unshaven jaw, trailing her fingers across his lips.

"Kane," she whispered. "It's really you."

He sat down on a flat boulder, pulling her down next to him. "My God, woman. You scared the hell out of me. Every time I see you, you're in trouble. You need a keeper." He tried to sound angry, but she felt the grin beneath her still exploring fingers. "There's blood on your pants. Let's see to it."

Jowanna looked down, but the stain didn't seem to be spreading. "Let me rest a bit, and it will probably seal up itself." Her knee hurt like hell, and she wasn't sure she could walk on it right now, but maybe later the pain would recede. No good letting him know. She wasn't about to stay behind and wait for him to do whatever he would have in mind when she finished telling him.

"Why are you always running away from me? I'd never hurt you. Haven't you learned to trust me?" His words and the tone of his voice echoed a bitter hurt.

"Oh, Kane, I didn't know it was you. I thought it was one of them." She pushed away and sat apart, hating to let go of his rugged strength. "There's so much to tell you. We have to hurry."

How could she tell him that Delia was alive, had been hiding away under his nose, and was conspiring to kill everyone in her way to get the treasure? How could she tell him his own nephew loved the woman and had helped with her scheming? How much could this man take before he broke?

Wanting to get the hurtful words said, she began telling him about Delia and Steven in the tunnel. As she spoke she looked away, not wanting to see the betrayal deep in his eyes.

"You mean Delia's here?"

A chill spread through her body, blocking out the sun's sullen heat. It was hard to read the meaning in his words. Did he still love her?

"Yes. She never left." Jowanna told him about the locked storeroom.

"God, how blind I was. Steven told me that was where he put his paintings, and that he didn't want anyone to see them in an unfinished state. I believed him."

"No reason you shouldn't have," she consoled. "I believed you when you said you kept Delia's possessions locked in there."

"That's where I put them."

"And then you never went back inside?"

He shook his head. "No. That was when Steven took over the room. I gave him all the privacy he needed." His voice was bitter, harsh.

She knew he was thinking of Delia and Steven making love up there on that little cot, right under his nose. Well, maybe not when he was home, but he was gone so much.

"I can believe it about her, if I have to. But

Steven? You're sure of what you saw and heard?" He
reached down and pulled her roughly to her feet,
staring into her eyes with the look of a lost soul.

She ignored the pressure of his hard hands
clenching her arms.

"I'm sure. And there's more. A lot more. But they'll
be back with the dynamite, and we have to have a
plan."

"We'd better go. Got to beat them to the cave—
stop them before they do any more damage. Can you
walk yet?"

She struggled to her feet, pushing aside his
helping hands, and fell back on the boulder, wincing in
pain. "Just give me a little bit longer."

"Neither one of them are good riders. It'll take a
couple of hours for them to pick up the dynamite and
get back with it. I don't want to leave you here alone,
and I need more answers." He took her hands and held
them between his.

"Answers?"

"You thought I killed Mac? And that I was trying
to kill you? Did it ever occur to you how that didn't
make any sense—that I'd know where the treasure
was?"

She swallowed past the lump in her throat. "I
asked you about the treasure. You denied there was
one, remember?"

"Reckon I did."

"Why did my father write about the treasure
behind your back? I thought my father must have
found gold on his own and didn't want to share it with
you. I didn't know what to think," she cried out. "Who
could I trust?"

"You trusted Steven enough to tell him about
Mac's note," he accused.

"I did. I had to believe in someone, at that point,
and he was there. But I never told him about the
map."

"How'd they know about the cave?"

"They tracked me, saw you carry me up to the cave, and decided that was the missing mine. They waited, and when you went back to the ranch, they followed your steps and came inside. By the time they caught up with me in the tunnel, you were already heading back."

He took off his hat and laid it on the rock nearby, and then, elbows on his knees, he put his hands over his face. The gesture of such weary anguish tore at her heart. What a terrible blow to learn your beloved wife and the nephew who was like a brother to you plotted to take away everything, and to kill you, in the bargain. It was a tough pill to swallow, and she recognized his need to talk before he formulated a plan.

"How is it that you women can be so treacherously sincere? I thought she loved me, wanted to be with me, when all the time she only married me to keep track of her grandfather's mine."

"Not all women are treacherously sincere, as you put it," she flared and then understood, beneath his anger, the pain he was feeling. He had lost everything at one stroke and possibly his beloved ranch, too. There would have to be a re-opened investigation into her father's death.

"You came here for the treasure Mac told about in his letter," he reminded her.

"Not at first. Oh, I don't expect you to believe me, but I truly did come to have it out with him."

"Delia and Steven." He shook his head. "It's still hard for me to believe."

"They knew you wanted to blow up the mine."

He looked shocked. "How'd they know that? Mac must've let something slip."

"Steven opened my father's letter before he sent it on. He spoke of a treasure blowing up in his face, and I guess they put two and two together."

"Sure. I remember now, Steven took the letter to Albandigos to mail it for Mac. Poor sod, that sealed his death warrant."

"But what happened between you that caused my father not to confide in you about contacting his family?" She persisted, needing to know.

He shrugged with tired resignation. "It's hard to say. We both got to thinking what a big gold strike would do to the ranch—to our way of life. In the past, a rush like that has started entire towns on the site. Neither of us wanted that."

When he didn't continue, she feared he wouldn't. She sensed he was about through talking.

"And then?"

"We agreed to use the gold from the trunk for Mac to hire lawyers to clear his name. Take some out for Steven, so he could go back to the art university, and some to get the ranch back on a paying basis, help me get the ranch going again."

"How would that help? Wouldn't prospectors and gold hunters still come up here looking when the word got out?"

"Don't think so. We weren't going to use any more of it than we needed. We planned to go to Texas or New Mexico to exchange it for money. Then blow the cave and tunnel up so no one would ever find it again, at least not in our lifetime."

Jowanna sat, wide-eyed and stunned. Steven had been telling the truth. Both her father and Kane had decided to blow up a fortune. It was a concept that took a little time to accept.

In a way, she didn't blame Steven and Delia for disbelieving that anyone really intended to blow it all away. Because they were crooked, they probably figured each man was doing a double-cross on the other to have it all for himself.

"It looks like Mac had some second thoughts, and when peculiar things began happening around here, he sent for your brother to confide in him—give him a say in our decision."

"He thought *you* might have changed your mind first and wanted to keep it all. Or maybe that you'd cut Steven in without telling him."

Kane's lips stretched out with grim bitterness. "That's about it. Seems like it runs in your family, not to trust me."

"Ah, that's not true. My father was confused. I was confused."

Kane raised his head and looked at her as if she were a stranger suddenly intruding on his private thoughts. His voice was calm and coolly polite when he answered.

"Your pa had no need for the gold beside going back and straightening out his life. We talked, and he admitted it was the searching he liked best about prospecting. He knew your grandfather had taken care of his family."

Standing so tall and straight like one of the noble saguaros, Kane seemed as much a part of the terrain as the boulders and brown earth covering the desert floor. It hurt to watch as he looked around with quiet possessiveness.

"See all this?" He swept his arm to indicate the desert. "Imagine it filled with mining rigs—equipment of destruction—desecration. See that?" He pointed to the cloudless blue sky. "Imagine it filled with dust and belching black smoke from the diesels churning up rock."

She saw it in a fleeting moment and recognized it for what it would be—a nightmare.

"Time's running out. They could be stringing the wire by now. We've got to stop them. I can leave you here, if your leg is too bad."

"Then what?"

He drew his rifle from the scabbard attached to his saddle. "Take care of that when it comes up." He looked down at her, regret deep in his tawny eyes.

"Would you shoot them?" She felt her eyes widen with surprise.

"Hope like hell it won't come to that. But I have to get them down the mountain."

"Kane, I..." She tried to make the strength of her feelings for him come through, without laying the irretrievable words out for him to reject.

He reached for Shambles' saddle horn. "You stay put. I'm going up there."

As he swung up on the saddle, she ran in front of the huge horse and grabbed hold of the reins. "Oh, no. You're not leaving me behind. I uncovered the truth for you, whether you like it or not. I'm going to be there when it's over, too." She kept her face straight, not showing any pain from the stone cut.

He thumbed his hat back and searched her face for a moment with guarded eyes, his look of vulnerability gone as if it had never lingered.

"Reckon you're right. But they're serious. I can't doubt that now. You'll be in danger."

*Does that matter to you?*

She felt as if her heart was as brittle as that dried-out piece of driftwood Shambles stepped over. Kane would never trust another woman, especially not her, the one who had turned away from him with suspicion and fear. He would go to his grave loving Delia and regretting what had happened, she was sure of it.

As much as she was sure she loved Kane Landry with all her heart and soul.

"Okay. But you have to stay put up there when I tell you. I won't have time to worry about you."

*Worry about you.* The words gave her a glimmer of hope even as she told herself she was foolish for putting more into the spare words.

"Leave Mirla here under the trees. Tie her good. She's skittish when you leave her alone. I don't want you that far away from me. They won't give up easy.

Too much is at stake for them to let us stop them now."

He hauled her up behind him, and she clung to his waist.

She felt a deep sorrow for what he must be thinking. He had treated Steven like a younger brother. The two people he had loved most in life had betrayed him, and added to that was her father's mistrust, and her own.

She leaned lightly against his broad back. The air smelled clean and the wind blew softly through the lacy palo verdes. The brown seed pods danced in the breeze like Christmas tree ornaments.

It struck her how much she would miss this when she had to leave.

An explosion shattered the quiet. Shambles reared and when he came down began a nervous sidestepping. Jowanna felt Kane's powerful muscles tense with the fight to hold the horse steady.

The blast, muffled but still loud, issued from the direction of the mine. After a moment, they heard a second, weaker blast.

Kane shouted for her to hold on as he urged the stallion toward the sheer canyon wall, away from the sound of the explosion.

What was he doing? She used all her concentration to hold on.

He reined up short and sat staring up at the canyon wall. She followed his look and saw the cave opening high on the ledge. Or what used to be the cave opening.

The rope ladder hung by a thread and the mouth of the cave was no longer a dark shadowy hole—it was choked with stones and large boulders. Dust still rose from it like smoke from a fire. On the floor of the canyon huge boulders lay like popcorn from the force of the explosion, a few still rolling to a stop.

He spun Shambles around toward the hidden entrance at the back of the cave. He didn't stop to help her as he leaped from the horse, but she was right behind him, scrambling up the side of the mountain.

A horse whinnied nearby and they turned to look. Two saddled horses moved away toward the desert, frightened by the blast. As Kane and Jowanna climbed closer to the entrance, they could see rocks of all sizes piled in front of it. The dust had barely settled, and the hole was almost completely closed.

Kane bent and began frantically pulling away the debris. They worked side by side, but he didn't seem to notice her.

She concentrated on the job at hand, her muscles strained, her hands becoming bloodied and fingernails broken, some to the quick, as she pulled on the rough rocks. At the end of a half hour it seemed as if they had made little progress, judging from the pile still ahead of them.

Kane stopped to rest, rubbing his sleeve across his dusty, sweat-streaked forehead. The sun-bleached forelock fell in a curve across his eyes, and he brushed it back impatiently with bloodied hands.

Jowanna felt him regarding her as she leaned against a boulder, catching her breath.

"Why punish yourself like this after what they tried to do to you? Let me look at your hands."

She put her clenched fists behind her, but he reached around her easily and held them out between them. The warmth and strength from his fingers sped through every part of her body, soothing the scratches and scrapes so that she no longer felt them.

He bent and touched his cheek to one hand and she reached the other up to his hair, so gently that he probably didn't feel it.

"God, how did this happen..." The words were torn from his throat in a groan. He dropped her hands and turned away to pull at the rocks again.

When they had dragged enough rocks away to crawl inside, he paused. "Hold on. I'll get the lantern we keep hidden for emergencies." He walked over to a bush and, kneeling, pulled out a lamp from behind.

He lit it, but before he could crawl through the space, she touched his arm to stop him.

"Wait, could this be a trick?"

He straightened to look down at her. "What am I thinking? They could have set off a blast to lure us in and are waiting for us. It'd be a desperate tactic. They could have blown everything up, but we know they're desperate. Wait here."

She hesitated barely a second before she disobeyed his terse order, scrambling into the opening behind him.

They picked their way through the debris, and he held the lantern high. She nearly ran into his back when he stopped short.

They'd found Delia first.

Her beautiful neck was twisted in an unnatural angle. Even before Kane knelt to touch her, they both knew she was dead.

A wave of nausea broke over Jowanna. It seemed a waste.

Kane dropped Delia's wrist and stepped over her body, moving toward the front of the cave. There wasn't the amount of rocks and boulders scattered over the floor that should be after a blast. Long fissures appeared in the roof of the tunnel so that at times he didn't need the lantern.

"The dynamite didn't go off here. They set it up front. Delia must have been running away when the second blast caught her." His quiet voice sounded unnaturally loud as it echoed down the tunnel.

He turned to look at Jowanna, his face grimly unreadable by the light of the lantern. "Sure you want to go on? Maybe you'd better wait here." He brushed the hair gently from the side of her face.

She reached up to hold her hand over his for a brief moment. The touch was comforting, and she hated to part with it. "No, I'll go with you."

His eyes reflected respect that he didn't put into words. He took hold of her hand.

Now the way was filled with stones and boulders. He supported her elbow and steadied her stumbling, halting steps.

They rounded a curve in the tunnel and stopped. A huge boulder nearly blocked their way. To her horror she saw Steven's boot protruding from beneath.

It was then they heard the low moan.

"Oh, dear Lord, he's alive," Jowanna cried out, and they ran around to the other side.

Steven lay pinned like a butterfly beneath the weight of the heavy rock.

Kane knelt and took the hand that reached up to him. Steven's eyes reflected the awareness of his impending death. The mockery of his old sardonic grin made Jowanna's eyes fill with tears.

She leaned forward to catch his words, and her hair, freed from its binding, trailed across his face. She reached to push it away, but he held a lock gently between his fingers.

"I didn't want to hurt anyone. Most of all you two." His words came from somewhere deep inside him, and blood seeped from the side of his mouth as he gasped for air.

"We know, Steven. We know." Kane's deep voice filled the cavern, as Steven seemed to absorb some of his steady strength.

"Delia?" He managed to ask.

Kane shook his head. "She's gone. Happened in an instant. She never knew."

Steven closed his eyes, tears seeped from beneath the black lashes so dark against the pallor of his skin. "I didn't mean to fall in love with her. I knew it was wrong, but I couldn't help myself." Steven's sigh was like the whisper of the desert wind.

"But why take over the mine? We were going to

share some of it with you." The cry was wrenched from Kane, and he smoothed Steven's hair back from his forehead with an unsteady hand.

"We didn't know. It wouldn't have mattered. I had to be with her. I needed all of the gold to keep her. Oh, God, I've made such a mess of things."

Jowanna thought for the second time of the dreadful waste. She watched, heart filled to the brim with pity, as Kane wiped a sleeve in an angry gesture across his eyes to brush away his own tears.

"She...she went back to where your father lay and—and shot him." His eyes pleaded with her for forgiveness. "I wouldn't have let her, if I'd known."

Poor Steven. He'd never had any control over Delia. Her father had been right in suspecting a plot against him. But how could he have imagined Delia behind it? So he centered on Kane as the most likely, the same as she had.

"El Diablo...he finally beat us." Steven's voice trailed off, and they both leaned forward to catch his last words along with the death rattle low in his chest. Kane reached to close his sightless eyes.

Kane pulled Jowanna to her feet and they turned to look at what was left of the tunnel.

The puma lay barely a few feet away, stretched out like a giant mastiff sleeping at his master's side. Kane lifted the lantern higher and they saw the animal's hind leg tangled in wire. The battle-scarred old cat had triggered Delia and Steven's trap.

Jowanna looked at Kane. She knew that, beside his grief, he was thinking of the investigations, the people crowding up here, the attempted explanations of Delia's disappearance and her reappearance. He'd have to tell about the gold. If he didn't tell the authorities, none of this would make any sense.

She reached up and touched Kane's grime-streaked cheek.

"Dynamite it. Leave them in peace. They deserve

that, at least."

He raised the lantern. His hand beneath her chin let him look deep into her eyes. "You sure? The gold Mac and I removed and hid away is only a pittance compared to what's here."

"I'm sure."

"How will we explain where they are?"

Jowanna shrugged. "Who is going to ask? Anyway, since you have her annulment papers, they could have gone away together. Actually..." She paused and looked back down the tunnel. "They did go away together, finally, didn't they?"

Kane straightened his shoulders as if a heavy load had been lifted away. He took her arm gently, firmly, and propelled her back through the entrance. As they passed Delia, Jowanna averted her eyes and Kane stared straight ahead. She felt him tense but he never looked down.

"She almost made it to safety. True to form, she was running away, leaving Steven behind. She almost made it, too," he said tersely.

As they crawled through the small entrance, sunshine and waves of heat engulfed them, warming their blood, which seemed to have frozen in place from the cold tunnel.

He led her to a shade tree and then went to the hidden cache where the lantern had been and brought out a wrapped bundle that turned out to be dynamite.

He looked at her, a long searching look, his eyes dark with questions unspoken.

She returned his look, trying to hold back the pity and compassion. He wouldn't have any patience with that. "It's for the best, Kane. You know that."

The silence of the desert enfolded them as they stood close together, yet miles apart.

He started for the cave and then turned back and whistled. Shambles appeared as if by magic. "Ride him to Mirla and get far enough away for safety. He's used to noise, but hold the mare, she'll be scared."

He helped her into the saddle, and for once she obeyed his instructions without question. At the bottom of the hill, she held the mare's reins and waited for Kane.

It was taking so long! Where was he? What was he doing? What if life had turned so ugly he didn't want to come back out? Her leg throbbed, but she ignored the pain and pressed her face down into Shambles' mane, seeking comfort. When she sat up, a sense of relief flooded through her. He would never take the easy way out.

Her heart began thudding in her breast. He was running down the trail toward her.

She would be gone soon enough, never to see him again, but at least she would always know he was safe.

They watched as half the mountain rose up into the air with a mighty roar. She clapped her hands over her ears, and Kane reached out to hold her steady as the earth trembled beneath their feet.

Mirla's terrified scream tore the air, an epitaph for the dead puma buried within the mountain.

Steven and Delia were left with their gold.

She felt Kane shudder when the rocks and boulders slammed back into the earth, covering everything.

What was he thinking? Was his heart disintegrating inside the wreckage? In the days to come, when she left and put this place and Kane behind, her life would lie in rubble like that mountain.

Would either of them ever get it back together again? She'd bet on Kane, on his tenacity and spirit, with what he had left to love—the ranch.

Tears blurred her eyes and she pressed closer, desperately seeking the comfort of his strength.

Chapter 15

They rode in silence, for a while, each lost in thought. The soft evening had turned to black night in the desert. Overhead, a canopy of brilliant stars, accented by a sliver of a moon lit their way.

Kane began talking, as if thinking out loud. "I figured something was going on between them almost from the beginning, but I cursed myself for being a jealous, unreasonable fool. When she left and Steven stayed, I was convinced of my stupidity and tried to make it up to him in every way I could. Steven's the only family I have...I had."

The words were torn from Kane with such torment that Jowanna could hardly ride so close without reaching out to touch him, but she sensed he would reject her attempt at comfort.

"Why? Jowanna, why didn't you tell me about all these things that had happened to you?" The words escaped his mouth in a low, hurting moan.

She turned toward him in the saddle. "You didn't believe me about the boulder, or the pillow. I was afraid you were a part of it. I'm sorry, but that's what was in my mind."

He swallowed, visibly taking hold of his emotions.

She could see he was unused to sharing his feelings with anyone, and she felt sad and at the same time proud that he would be so open with her on this, his most hurtful time.

"I can see how you might have thought that way. I figured something strange was going on in that house, but I never could put my finger on it. I didn't want you to stay there alone. You saw me watching you one night. You stood in the window, brushing your hair," he admitted reluctantly.

"I saw a shadow on the desert. Did you take Mirla away as a prank?"

"Hell, no! I found her down in the ravine, tied to a tree, and brought her back. Figured only a tenderfoot would take a horse out and forget about her, especially with El Diablo skulking around."

"I'd never do that," she answered.

"No, don't reckon you would. Did they—did they kill Mac, then?"

"She did."

Jowanna was glad she couldn't see Kane's expression in the dusk. "They talked about it. She as much as admitted it to Steven. He didn't approve, but he was weak."

"Poor Mac, he was so close to going back and claiming his lost family."

"We were never lost to him. I was angry and bitter, but neither Jason or I would ever have believed he could steal from his own wife and my grandfather. I wish he would have taken us with him. Jason might be alive today. So would he, probably."

"Ah, Jowanna, we can't know any of that, can we?"

"Why didn't my father confide in you about writing to Jason? Why did he beg for his help? Why go in such a roundabout way to tell him—or me, as it turned out—about the treasure which belonged to both of you?"

Kane looked across the desert, as a drowning man might search for a ship in the ocean. When he turned to face her, his expression was grim, and the hard planes of his face looked carved in stone.

"Delia must have thought the mine belonged to her grandfather. They probably tried to scare Mac off like they tried with you. From that, Mac must have decided I had changed my mind about destroying the mine. He probably thought I was in on a conspiracy against him and that he needed some outside help. I'm sure he didn't realize his danger until it was too late."

"Do you have any idea who did all the original mining? Who might have owned the mine?"

"I—we thought for sure it was The Lost Dutchman Mine. It's become a legend in the Southwest ever since I can remember, with thousands of people looking for it over the past century. Old Jacob Waltz found the mother of the ore veins. It probably took him years and years to tunnel it out, and he didn't dare trust anyone to help him. The story is, he went down to Phoenix over the years, trading just enough gold to buy what he needed. Everyone knew about his gold, but he died with the secret of his mine untold."

"That's a miracle of survival. Imagine what it must have been like to work all week way up here alone and then go all the way down by horseback or mule into Phoenix to spend a few dollars at a time."

"Well, the old fellow had to be a little off. Maybe that's why the Apaches left him alone." Kane looked up at the mountains hovering so close, shadows caressing their facades with the slightly blowing wind. "This was part of their stronghold. The Apaches were thick in here, and not many strangers left alive. That's part of the legend, too."

"The poor lost souls. Don't you suppose that spirit is what causes chills when you look up here sometimes?"

He nodded. "You can feel it, for sure. I've felt that way, too, more often than not. That's why I was glad when Mac and I hooked up partnership together. This can be a damned spooky place."

The miles passed quickly, and as they approached the gateway, the nearby trees swayed with a ghostly rhythm. The house sat shrouded in a dark hush. Instead of a sinister watching and waiting, however, she felt the serenity, the harmony surrounding the house.

*As if evil had gone and left peace in the vacuum.*

"Do you want to talk more?" she asked, knowing he wouldn't. Not now, perhaps not ever.

He shook his head and helped her down. Her legs felt weak from the long, steady ride, but she was toughening up. She went with him to the stables, where he found two lanterns and lit them.

"What the...?" Kane exclaimed when he held up the lanterns. A third horse stood patiently eating from a stall near Mirla.

"Where did that horse come from?"

Kane shook his head. "It belongs to Apache Joe. Sometimes he brings it in while he goes on one of his shaman journeys." He turned and touched her shoulder. "Tomorrow we can sort it out. I'm bushed. I know you are, too. I'll take a look at your leg." His voice sounded heavy, full of sorrow.

They closed the stable door and headed toward the house. In spite of each of them holding a lamp, the stones on the path caused her tired legs to buckle a few times.

Kane took her arm as a stranger might help another stranger and propelled her forward.

Inside, he steered her toward the kitchen and pushed her gently down in a chair.

Jowanna watched him rummaging around in a cupboard until he found a bottle of what looked like whiskey. He knelt in front of her and took a knife from his pocket and sprung it open. He managed a tired grin. "Sorry I have to cut your jeans," he said. "Unless you want to shuck them off for me."

He might have been teasing, but she didn't want to be that close to him again. Nor to remember lying in bed next to him with barely anything between their bodies, or the love they'd shared so briefly. With no comment from her, he slit the side of her pants.

She cried out and grabbed onto his shoulders as the fabric stuck to the dried blood. He pulled it away carefully. "Mmm. Not too deep. Let's pour some whiskey on it, and I'll wrap it to keep it clean."

"Like you did with Shambles?" She tried to keep it light but the feeling of his strong fingers pressing against her skin, of his big hands rubbing the back of her leg to see if she had any muscle pulls, made her heart race uncontrollably. She hoped he wouldn't see the pulse jump in her throat.

"Keep holding onto me. This is going to hurt like hell." He poured the alcohol down the length of her leg, and she whimpered but tried to keep the scream of pain inside. She knew her fingers dug into his shoulders, but he didn't move away.

"Whew! Glad that's over," she said.

"Me too, woman. You almost took some chunks out of my shoulder. Didn't realize how strong those little white hands are. Now, when you can walk, head for the stairs. If you need my help…"

She leaned forward and kissed the top of his head. "You wrapped it good and tight. I'll be fine. Go do what you have to do with the horses for the night."

He leaned back on his haunches in front of her, his eyes holding her transfixed, his mouth curved with tenderness before he covered it with a bleak, tight-lipped smile. "I want to apologize again about that night up at the cabin. I took something from you and had no right to do it. I'm ashamed, and it's hard for me to talk about."

She opened her mouth to tell him it took two to make love, but he put a finger across her lips to shush her. "Night," he said, and while she closed her eyes against the hurt, she heard the front door shut behind him.

When Jowanna felt able, she walked out of the kitchen and started up the stairs. She inhaled, expecting the faint odor of perfume, but found only the usual faint dusty smell, the essence of the old house. All traces of Delia's perfume had disappeared. Had that been the Señora's way of trying to warn them? Not even Delia would have been so sure of herself, so arrogant, as to go into hiding under their noses and wear perfume.

Some things were better left unexplained.

\*\*\*\*

Jowanna slept restlessly that night, in spite of her weariness. Her dreams were filled with terrifying explosions and shrilly screaming pumas leaping off cliffs at her. Finally she sat up and concentrated on Kane's presence in the room next to hers. He hadn't closed his door, and she hadn't closed hers, either. The comforting thought led into a light sleep.

The next morning she awoke early to the smell of coffee and baking bread. He was in the kitchen. All was well.

She stretched and looked out the window at the blue sky. Closing her eyes, she could imagine his long-legged stride across the large kitchen, filling the space as if it were a closet. He would bend over the stove, putting wood in the round opening, the firelight reflecting off the sharp planes of his cheekbones, lighting the gold of his hair against the mahogany of his skin. She saw his sleeves rolled up to expose muscular, brown arms, wrist deep in flour and dough, making his bread for therapy.

Her heart was heavy at the thought of leaving forever, but she knew he had no thought of asking her to stay. He'd as much as said he would never trust anyone to be close to him again. Not after what Delia and Steven did to him, and then both herself and her father in a lesser but hurtful way, not trusting him.

She flung the covers off, suddenly in a hurry to dress and get downstairs, needing to bask in the warmth of those eyes for as long as she had time left.

Out in the hallway, Jowanna sniffed the air appreciatively and looked up toward the next landing. Were the phantoms of Delia and Steven exorcised, or

229

would they come back to wreak their vengeance on the house and its occupants? A steady sense of warmth and peace engulfed her in answer as she looked upward. The Señora was still here, would probably always be here, but she was alone in her haunting watchfulness.

Alone and protecting.

"Morning." She entered the warm kitchen, still shrouded in early morning shade.

"Sit before you fall," Kane said, pulling a chair out for her.

Someone sat on a chair close to the window and she could only see a silhouette.

"Apache Joe?" she asked when Kane poured out steaming coffee into the cup on the table in front of her.

"Jowanna, girl, is that really you?" The figure rose, and she saw a bandage around his head and his arm in a sling, but she would have recognized her father anywhere.

She leaped to her feet and ran to him. "Oh, my Lord! Am I dreaming?"

They came together and she hugged him, careful of his arm. Tears streamed down both of their faces, and when she glanced toward Kane, his dark eyes look suspiciously moist.

"Come, both of you, and sit. Drink some coffee and catch your breath, and then maybe Mac will tell us how he resurrected himself. I asked him when I first came into the kitchen and saw him sitting there, big as life, but he wanted to wait and tell us both at the same time."

"There's blood on your head bandage and on your arm. Are you okay?" Jowanna asked.

"Kane fixed me up, but it might have started bleeding again. I'll let him look at it in a minute. He's pretty good at doctoring. Right now I got a lot to say." He held the coffee close and smelled it with obvious appreciation. "Apache Joe's place lacked a lot in the way of creature comforts, and cowboy coffee was one of them." He reached to take Jowanna's hand. "I 'spect you've had time to discover that I didn't abandon you and Jason. I wrote every day and went all the way to Apache Junction to mail them once a week. But when I didn't hear, I knew she'd destroyed the letters."

"I came here especially just to give you hell," Jowanna admitted, laughing. "But now we need to know what happened to you. Delia told Steven she shot you."

"True. She did that all right, but that's way ahead of the story." He squeezed her hand and they looked at each other as if they could never get enough of it. "A lot of crazy things began happening around here and, I'm sorry to say, I figured Kane would side with his only kin and tell Steven about our agreement to blow up the mine. That's when I sent for Jason…by the way, why didn't Jason come? I would have never sent for you. It was far too dangerous, the way I saw it."

"Ah, Dad, I'm sorry, but Jason died about ten years ago, in a boating accident. I don't know how your last letter got past Mother, but it did, and I decided to come in Jason's stead."

"I'm sorry to hear that. But looks like you did everything right. They must have intercepted your letter to me and figured I needed to go. I was on that ledge looking down, and someone pushed me from behind. When I fell, I played dead when I heard someone rushing down the mountainside. I felt a shot zing through my hat and it creased my poor old skull. I knew my arm had broken from the fall, but I hoped my legs were okay. I waited without breathing and heard footsteps running away. When I squinted through the blood and saw it was a female, I knew it had to be Delia. I laid there a long time before Apache Joe found me. I think Old Diablo was on my trail, too. I sensed he was nearby."

Mac took a deep breath and another sip of coffee while Kane and Jowanna waited.

"When Apache Joe came upon me, I'd nearly been done in, no water and the sun beating down something awful. I told him what happened, and that they wanted the mine, and Kane and I were going to blow it up so all the mining people wouldn't ruin this place. He thought that was a good idea, so I left with only my skivvies and stocking feet."

"My God, man, you could have died right there. Should have." Kane slapped him on the shoulder, Jowanna thought to hide some of his deeper emotions.

"I know. Joe wanted to let them think the puma had eaten me. So he took me to his hideout and crept down to the ranch or up to the cabin for food and water. I still didn't know if it was safe to come home, but I guess Apache Joe went on one of his journeys and forgot about me, so I had no choice. When I was just about here, I heard the mountain blow and knew it was good, then."

"Why don't I leave you two alone for a spell? I need to see to the horses, anyway." Without waiting for an answer, Kane left the kitchen and she heard the door close behind him.

"What are you going to do now?" Jowanna poured Mac another cup of coffee and pushed the tinned milk closer to him. She wanted to hug him over and over. His dark blue eyes belonged to her father, but the rest of him was so different after eighteen years that she didn't know what to think. He was weathered, like the desert had dried him from the inside out.

"I've had a lot of time to think, and I suspect I need to get back East and clear up some things that have been nagging at me all these years. Did you know that your grandfather swore I embezzled from him? I can't understand how your mother believed him, but she let me know I was the outsider and always would be."

"To give them credit, Jason and I never heard even a rumor about your supposed absconding with company money. I didn't know about the accusations until Steven and Kane told me. I'm sure if you go back that will all be settled, and your name will be fine."

"Will you come with me? I'll probably come back here after I've settled things, if that's all right with Kane. Your mother will probably be worried sick about you."

That idea had been giving Jowanna a guilty feeling lately. "I don't know, Dad." She liked saying 'Dad.' "I've grown to like living in the West. I can see how it called to you." She looked out the window at the mountains.

Mac cleared his throat. "I don't know how to go about having a fatherly talk with you after all the time that's gone by, but in good conscience I have to speak my mind."

*Oh, oh, what's this about?* She swallowed and turned back to look at him.

"It's easy to see something's up between you and Kane. Jowanna, I'd hate to see you hurt. Kane's a—well, he's a fine man, honorable and upstanding as they come, but he's a loner. I hope I'm not going to betray him, but we had a short conversation before you came down."

He rubbed the bandage on his arm as if it itched or was painful. Or he was stalling for time, trying to put his words together. Jowanna waited.

"He told me some of the changes he was going to make around the ranch when we exchanged the gold for money. They…they didn't involve anyone else, seems like. And he did mention you and tell me what a wonderfully independent daughter I had, and that he would hate to see you go but he knew you had to move on. I asked him right out, didn't he have any intentions toward you. He said flat out, no. It would be like pairing up a range-bred mustang to a pastured thoroughbred, and that never works. He was pretty steadfast about that notion."

She tried to keep the disappointment from showing on her face. It had been her idea to talk to Kane about their relationship, or whatever it was they had between them. This was 1948, after all, and people didn't have to marry just because they had sex, not anymore, but it seemed as if it needed some discussion. Mac must have noticed her look because he rose from his seat and bent over to kiss the top of her head.

"You're a beauty, besides being intelligent and feisty, and would make any man happy to be with you. So take heart and look for that special person. But I don't think it will be Kane. I'm just telling you the truth as I see it. I've been here almost eighteen years, as you know."

Jowanna reached to hold his hand against her cheek. "I'm sure you're right. It's fine with me. But I don't want to go back right now. I think I'll look around in Phoenix, see what comes up. I don't have any particular skills, but I'm sure I can find some way to earn a living."

He sat back down and regarded her with those dazzling blue eyes she remembered so well. "I've got to stay here for a week or two and gather my strength."

"I know. But I need to go as soon as I can. As soon as Kane can take me out to Albandigos. We'll keep in touch this time, so let me know when you get back here. And tell Mother…well, just tell her I'm okay and I'll call her when I get settled."

Mac stood up, leaning against the table to steady his legs. "If you don't mind, I'm going up to my room and lie down on a real bed and mattress for a change. Been looking forward to it." Jowanna came and hugged him and kissed his cheek. "Do you need help getting up the stairs?"

"Thanks, but no, I can haul these weary bones up

there by myself. When I've got my nap, Kane can look at my head and arm again."

When he climbed the stairs, she went out the door to the stables. Might as well get it over. He was obviously eager to get rid of her.

****

She found him in the stables, rubbing down Mirla with a soft brush. "I'm ready to go to Albandigos, whenever you can take me. I believe my father needs to stay put and recuperate before he leaves."

Kane shook back the hair from his forehead in that endearing way that Jowanna would always see in her memory. "This is his home, and he'll always be welcome here. I hope he comes back."

Jowanna's eyes threatened tears, and she looked away from Kane so he wouldn't see. *What about me? Don't you care?*

There was an awkward silence, and he walked to the stable door to look out at the desert, his broad back shutting her out. "The mountain looks so harmless in the early morning sun, doesn't it?"

She walked up to stand beside him. "It does," she agreed. He looked down at her and his eyes were troubled. She smiled a sad smile, to match the pain deep within his eyes. They looked at each other for a long moment, gray eyes melting into brown.

The thought of leaving was intolerable, but it must be faced.

"What will you do now?" she asked.

"Reckon I'll have to go into Phoenix. Report Steven missing. They'll suspect he and Delia ran off together, probably."

"That's what they were going to say about you and me."

No response from him.

"Does the idea of them wanting to be together bother you so much?"

His jaw muscles tightened. Then he relaxed and

continued to look at her.

They stood so close together, and she wanted to lean into him more than anything she'd ever wanted to do in her whole life.

"No, not that. It hurt most while I only suspected. Hurt to know I thought bad of Steven and maybe wrongly. I'd already given up on Delia. It was so clear what she thought of this place—and me."

"I'm so sorry about Steven. He did love you. It was just that Delia blinded him to everyone but her. She'd have left him too, eventually."

"I know. Oh, God, how I know. You're not having second thoughts about what we did —with the mine?"

For a moment she'd thought he was going to refer to their lovemaking in the cabin. "You hate the idea of having to trust someone again, don't you? No, I'm never going to have second thoughts."

He brushed away her question, refusing to be drawn into a deeper discussion.

She felt the wall he had erected between them, a shield of isolation he could hide behind.

"When I get the gold exchanged, wherever you are, you're entitled to part of it for what you went through here."

She shook her head, pushing back the tears. He was dismissing her as if she had been a stranger. "I don't want anything." *Only you.*

He stared into her face, his eyes dark and unfathomable. "I've never met anyone like you. Your mother won't recognize the lost little girl who first came here. I bet you can stand up to her now."

He was dismissing her to go back home to her mother.

She wouldn't. Not until she was independent and didn't have to stay. Jowanna couldn't even imagine yet how she would do it, but she had to strike out on her own. She had a little money left. Maybe she would stay in Phoenix, put down tentative roots. No, she couldn't be that close to him. She had to get farther away.

Steven had said the same thing about her mother not recognizing her. Now Kane's mentioning of her mother triggered thoughts she didn't want to grapple with yet.

"I'm sure my father had no intention of splitting up your ranch. He felt threatened and wanted someone here to validate your decision—to blow up the mine. I guess he thought Jason would be able to help him."

"Your brother couldn't have helped more than you have. You tackled the problem and persevered in spite of the odds stacked against you. I admire you for that," Kane said.

*I don't want your admiration, I want your love.*

She felt the tears swell her throat so that she couldn't have spoken aloud, though it seemed as if she had. She willed him to speak even a few encouraging words of tenderness, of need, and she would do the rest.

*Don't send me away. Please don't turn your back on me.*

Pride be damned, if he would only give her an opening, an indication to show he was attracted to her, she would tell him how she felt about him. How she had loved him since the beginning and would never love anyone else. Would that open him up?

He scuffed his boots against the door jamb, as if looking for a pile of desert dirt to kick. "I'm not much for saying thanks," he began reluctantly. He turned to her, catching her unaware, open. His eyes snared her gaze so that she could not look away if her life had depended upon it.

"Then don't. I don't need thanks." Her voice sounded cool and brittle and she cursed her sudden fear of rejection.

He took her arm and the warmth of his hard hand zinged from her shoulder down to her toes. She tried to hold steady and not tremble. "You're an unusual woman, Jowanna McFarland. You've got sand. You'd have made a good pioneer."

From him that was high accolade, and she felt it warm some of the icicles that had begun to chill her blood and enfold her heart. But she dared not allow that. She'd not leave herself open to any more hurt.

"I had help."

His dark brow raised quizzically.

"The Señora of the Superstitions." Jowanna faltered at his skeptical look that followed the stark announcement. She hadn't meant to open that can of worms, but something made her want it out in the open. The Señora should be recognized and a place found for her here at the ranch. It was obviously where she wanted to be.

"What?"

"Oh, don't look so fierce. I'm aware that you don't even like her name mentioned, but you owe her a lot. She helped, Kane. She really did save my life more than once. It was she who made Delia's perfume conspicuous when she was trying to warn me. I never put it together, though, until afterwards. Didn't you notice?"

He shrugged. "I suppose I was just used to smelling it. I reckon it was so much a part of Delia, I didn't notice it was still around when Delia was supposed to be gone. Maybe she used it herself, locked up there alone in that room."

"Hah!" Jowanna snorted. "She was too smart for that. At first I thought too that she might have just been tormenting you, but no, it was the Señora's way of helping me."

"I don't know..." Kane still looked skeptical.

"That's not the half of it. The Señora opened that little dormer window for me and closed it behind so they couldn't find me in my hiding place, and she prevented me from leaving at the wrong time. She warned me of the flashflood, but I didn't have sense enough to figure out what she was trying to tell me. She told me the boulder was coming down on me, and I rolled aside just in time."

He reached to take her tightly clenched fist in his big hand and opened the fingers, straightening out each one gently, as if avoiding the need to speak.

"Scratches all over your hand. Your nails are broken off."

"They'll heal," she said. *But I won't.*

"I've felt her presence, too," Kane finally admitted. "If there's such a thing as a good ghost, she's one. Still, I'd never get any workers to come here if they suspected her presence."

"Maybe she's gone now that the wickedness is finished."

"Maybe." He didn't look convinced.

She felt a loss when he released her hand, his eyes resting on her reflectively for a long moment.

"I've also looked out the window, as if through someone else's eyes—I've heard things. At first I thought it could have been my father's spirit left behind, but I think it was hers."

"What kind of things did you see and hear?" His voice sounded intent, as if he really wanted to know.

"I think I told you before, children playing in the courtyard. Sounds of men in the bunkhouse. Chickens and goats wandering about, things like that. If the Señora put those thoughts in my head, she must have wanted children so badly, she had to imagine them."

"I've heard things too, thought I was going balmy." Kane sounded relieved.

"Know what I'd do? I'd build a monument—a little shrine to the Señora and her lost husband and ask a priest to come and bless it. I think she needs validation so she can rest in peace—so she and her husband won't ever be forgotten. If she did take her own life, she needs forgiveness, absolution. After that, I imagine any workers would respect a dead person that lay in consecrated ground and not have to fear a ghost, then."

"You're right! Absolutely right!" His mouth curved in a slow smile for the first time in days, it seemed like. His eyes crinkled at the corners and his lips parted in such a way that it caused something inside of her middle to swell near to bursting.

Oh, Lord, how she loved him. Couldn't he feel it? He didn't want to, that was the only explanation. He would grow old and bitter, alone with his memories and regrets. And there was nothing she could do about it.

"Will you begin stocking the ranch with brood mares when things die down a little?" she asked.

"I reckon." His voice sounded hollow, unenthusiastic.

"You'll feel better about it when some time has passed," she consoled him.

"I hope so. Right now my dreams don't seem all that important. It's the Steven and Delia thing."

"Of course."

"When do you—when do you want to leave?"

His voice sounded husky, almost as if he struggled for control, but that was her imagination. Wishful thinking.

"Mother will be sending out the troops any day now, if I don't call soon. I'm not thinking of going back East, though, and my father is."

"What do you mean? What will you do?"

His questions sounded noncommittal, as if he were speaking to a distant acquaintance.

She couldn't take much of this last minute thinking and regretting. The sooner away the better. "I don't think I'm an Easterner anymore, actually. I'll figure something out. If you can take me out, I'll go ahead. My father and I won't lose touch anymore. We promised each other." She hated to leave her father after all these years apart, but he wanted to go to see her mother, and she didn't want to do that right now.

Kane shrugged. "Figured you'd be in a hurry to leave this place. I don't blame you."

****

After a teary goodbye with her father, and seeing that his wounds would heal in the weeks to come, Jowanna waved at him as Kane and she started on the bumpy trail out to the highway. They traveled a long way in silence, each lost in thought. There were so many things she wanted to say to him. But none of it would matter. He was mourning the loss of his beloved wife, and she could never hope to rival that memory. Even in death, Delia had won.

At Albandigos, he pulled up in front of the bus depot.

"I can stay with you until the bus leaves," he offered politely.

She shook her head. "No. I hate long goodbyes."

"Ah—take care of that suitcase. I put some money in the corner. You deserve a share, and that's all I had in cash. When I change some more, I'll send it to you. I know you and Mac will stay in touch now."

Jowanna shook her head, tears blinding her. Did he have any idea how much she didn't want to go home—to slide into her old existence? Gratitude mixed with despair at his reserved generosity. Of course she wanted to see her mother again, settle everything between them from an adult-to-adult perspective, but that would have to wait. When she arrived in Phoenix she would rent a room in a decent hotel and look for work. The money would give her a chance to do that.

"Thank you. That was very thoughtful. I accept."

"You had that coming and more. If it hadn't been for you..." He broke off, at a loss for words.

She reached up and, standing on her tiptoes, took off his hat, pulled his head down and kissed him full on the lips. The kiss lingered. She had to have something to remember the rest of her life, didn't she?

Their lips blended, he dropped the suitcases he was holding and put his arms around her in a tight embrace, lifting her up off the ground.

They finally broke away, breathless.

"Well, then. I guess that's goodbye," she managed, fighting off tears.

"*Vaya con Dios,*" he said.

*Don't let me go.* At first Jowanna thought she'd spoken out loud but when he turned to go, she knew she hadn't. She reached for her suitcase and pushed inside the door before the tears could find their way out of her eyes and down her cheeks.

Watching through the dingy, fly-specked window of the depot, she saw him jump into the pickup and drive away in a cloud of dust.

Jowanna let the tears fall then, her dry sobs finally yielding to the anguish of grief and loss. When she was empty of tears, she held her arms across her hurting chest as if to hold in the pain. She needed pain now. Needed it to keep away the terrible emptiness that would fill the rest of her days.

****

On the bus heading toward Phoenix, she watched the landscape flow by, and her thoughts flowed with it, back towards the ranch and towards Kane. Did she want the balance of her years left on earth to be empty? Could she possible wake up tomorrow knowing she would never see that dear face, look into those liquid brown eyes again?

She stood up and made her way to the front of the bus.

"I'm sorry, but you'll have to let me out here. I forgot something in Albandigos."

"But lady, we're miles out of town," the driver protested, pulling toward the side of the narrow pavement.

"It's okay. Please."

Grumbling under his breath while the few

passengers watched in open curiosity, he unlocked the side compartment and set her suitcases on the ground.

"It's a long ways back." He gave it one last try.

"I know. It *is* a long way back, but I've got to take the chance."

She watched the bus speed away, leaving a trail of dust behind as it lurched back onto the pavement. Her only plan was to hitch a ride back to Albandigos if a car ever came her way, and then get Old Charlie to take her back to the ranch. She had to make Kane see that they shouldn't be apart.

She picked up her luggage and turned toward the little town. Ahead of her, a vehicle came speeding through a cloud of dust. Kane's truck, coming her way at an alarming speed.

He stopped just beyond where she stood at the side of the road, leaping from the vehicle to grab and lift her up in the air in a bear hug, dancing around and around with her crushed in his arms.

They were laughing and crying and trying to talk at once. He solved that by claiming her lips with his and then kissing the tears from her eyes and cheeks tenderly.

"I guess you could put me down now," she whispered through her bursting happiness.

"What made you get off the bus?"

"What made you come back for me?"

They both laughed.

"Ah, sweet girl, I couldn't live without you. I wasn't sure if you felt the same, but I was determined to catch up with that bus and kidnap you, if I had to. Until I made you love me too."

She hugged him around his middle, feeling his heart beat in her ear. "You never have to doubt my feelings, Kane. I've loved you forever."

"I thought about my plans for the ranch, and it was all dust in my mouth. It meant nothing without you. You belong there. With me. No reason a mustang and a thoroughbred can't be together."

She felt her heart swell in her breast so that she couldn't have spoken if she'd wanted to. But she finally managed, "What about Steven and..." She couldn't say her name or let it intrude on her newfound happiness.

"I thought about it, and I have to forgive them. It's the only way to get on with our lives."

"Our lives. Maybe my father will come back some day and—and see his grandchildren." She blushed at her boldness and he laughed and picked her up to swing her around and kiss her again and again. She finally pushed away to look at him, unable to take her gaze away as if he might disappear, a figment of her imagination.

"Want to go into Phoenix? Get married there and have a proper honeymoon?"

"No, I don't want to go anywhere. We can make arrangements in Albandigos for our marriage papers, if you want."

"Good." Kane lifted her into the cab of the truck and closed the door, as if she might fly away from him. "Let's just go home."

She pulled his head toward her in the open window and kissed him thoroughly.

"Yes, let's go home."

## A word about the author...

Pinkie Paranya was born in Phoenix and now lives near Yuma, Arizona. She has authored 12 novels in different genres, which include romance, romantic suspense, early American historicals, cozy mysteries and paranormal thrillers as well as op-ed articles for newspapers and poetry. Currently she has had six books published. She enjoys gardening, pets, reading and of course writing. She has been a volunteer for CASA (Court Appointed Special Advocate) for children and was one of the founders of a local spay and neuter organization for companion pets.

Contact Pinkie at pkparanya@gmail.com
Visit Pinkie at http://www.pinkieparanya.com

Thank you for purchasing
this Wild Rose Press publication.
For other wonderful stories of romance,
please visit our on-line bookstore at
www.thewildrosepress.com

For questions or more information,
contact us at info@thewildrosepress.com

The Wild Rose Press
www.TheWildRosePress.com

## Other Vintage titles to enjoy...

SOURDOUGH RED by Pinkie Paranya: At the end of the Klondike gold rush, Jen and her younger brother search for her twin, lost and threatened in Alaskan wilderness.

DON'T CALL ME DARLIN' by Fleeta Cunningham: In Santa Rita, Texas, 1957, a librarian faces censorship and the exposure of a secret from her past. Will the County Judge she's dating protect or accuse her?

BLACK RAIN RISING by Fleeta Cunningham: Another in the Santa Rita series, with a country singer accused of murder, the courageous daughter of a radio station owner, and a little girl who needs an operation in order to live.

SHE'S ME by Mimi Barbour: A spoilt model pricks her finger on a rose thorn and is transported back to 1963 and into a chubby librarian's body. As "roomies" they learn a lot from each other and each finds the man of her dreams.

HE'S HER by Mimi Barbour: Same rosebush, different victims! And then there's the third of the series, WE'RE ONE by Mimi Barbour, with more to follow.

BAD BETTIE by Layne Blacque: In 1948 Los Angeles, a handsome cop's world is turned upside down when his squad raids a nightclub and he rescues the sultry blues singer.

SHATTERED DREAMS by Margaret Tanner: Three World War I soldiers leave a shattering legacy as they pass through Lauren's life. Which is killed? Which one's child does she carry? Which one does she marry?

A TRAIN THROUGH TIME by Bess McBride: On a sleek modern train heading to Seattle, Ellie awakens in the midst of a Victorian-era re-enactment. The leader of the group, handsome, green-eyed Robert Chamberlain, finally convinces her the date is 1901...